Decevito, Carey
Almost Forgotten / Carey Decevito—Paperback edition
ISBN-13: 9781988806020

Cover photography by Eric David Battershell
Cover design by Clarisse Tan, CT Cover Creations
Cover model: Zeke Samples

almost forgotten

THE BROKEN MEN CHRONICLES

book two

carey decevito

ACKNOWLEDGMENTS

I doubt that words will ever be enough to convey my never-ending appreciation and gratitude to the following people.

I would like to extend my thanks to Eric David Battershell, photographer extraordinaire. Without your amazing work, love of photography, not to mention your wonderful eye, work ethic, and dedication, I doubt I would have been able to find as great of a cast to create such wonderful covers for this entire series.

To Clarisse Tan, my cover designer. I'm looking forward to so many more cover collaborations with you. Your ambition, your humor, your enthusiasm are all so contagious. I'm so proud to have you on my team.

To Laurie and Marissa. You lovely ladies have been instrumental in making this series so much better than it originally was. Above the last-minute favors, the consults, the help in pushing my work, the editing, there's no way I could have put my best face forward.

And last but certainly not least, I owe a debt of gratitude to my readers. Without your support, I would be writing for the sake of my love of writing. I hope that you enjoy reading about Jake's journey as much as I did writing it.

CHAPTER 1

I eyed her from across Fairfax, an after-work institution for the upwardly mobile, knowing that in moments, I'd catch her attention. As suspected, while perusing the male population inside the establishment, her gaze froze on me.

I flashed my come hither smile. Some called it a panty remover; others have attested that it made their knees weak. Regardless of its effect, the women I set my sights on wound up vying for my attention in varying degrees. With a rosy tint to her cheeks, this particular one was quick to shift her glance.

I had no doubt that I looked good in my designer Armani, minus the claustrophobic tie I had worn earlier in the day.

As if she couldn't help herself, her eyes connected with mine, again.

Hook line and sinker.

Turning, I nodded to the bartender and indicated my desire for another drink by twirling the ice in my empty tumbler. It had been one hell of a week and I was in dire need of some down-time.

The sure things in my life since high school have been good money, an abundance of women, and great sex. For the most part, all three came easily enough.

I wasn't always like this, you know. As with anyone else

who leads a somewhat fulfilled yet semi-dysfunctional life, something happened to shape me into the man that I am today. Do I really want to rehash the details with you right now?

No.

Will I?

Stick around and you'll find out.

As predicted, the feisty-looking redhead donning a black mini dress headed in my direction. I tilted some of my premium scotch back and felt the burn as the liquor slid down my throat.

My cock took notice of the sway to her hips, the length of her slender legs, and the brief but sultry look she'd given me with those bright emerald eyes of hers. I followed her progress with a neutral expression, assessing every bit of the vixen that I could, giving nothing of her effects away.

I wonder if she's a natural redhead.

She came to a stop beside me, shifting so she faced the bar, but not before giving me another quick once-over and a shy smile.

Boy did I love a wonderful combination of coy and assertive in a woman. And this one pulled it off with perfection.

Noticing the twinkle in her eyes, I knew she held secrets that begged to be discovered under that shy façade of hers. As she licked her red lips, I knew that I could know all of those secrets if I played my cards right. In fact, I was so certain that she would be the cap to the end of my miserable week that I was already playing out how she would look with that sinful mouth of hers wrapped around my cock while I fucked her face.

I swallowed the last of my scotch and turned to her. "Out alone?"

She waited to catch the bartender's attention and huffed when he once again passed by her for a duo of men at the other end of the bar. "More like ditched. Can't a girl get a drink around here?" She didn't seem too disturbed about being left to her own devices, however. "Friend bailed out to spend the night with their boyfriend."

"Hmm." I trailed my fingers across the top of her hand which lay on the bar. Goose-bumps spread over her forearm. Swallowing hard, her eyes met mine in brief shock before they cast themselves downward to watch the progress of my digits. "That's a shame, honey. A beautiful woman like you shouldn't be left alone. I guess I have her to thank for gaining your company."

She lifted her head and I saw her cheeks pinken. "It's him."

"Excuse me?"

"My friend." Her lips quirked up. "He ditched me for his boyfriend."

My jaw dropped at the unexpected announcement and her husky laugh at my reaction told me I hadn't recovered fast enough from the shock. Her laugh was something else though, as I felt the twitch in my crotch for the second time in under fifteen minutes.

Giving up on her drink request, she turned to face me, looked down again at my playing fingers on her hand before gazing up at me and biting that plump bottom lip of hers.

The wheels were turning in that pretty head of hers. When that sexy grin spread across her face, there was no doubt in my mind on how my evening was going to end. I had her right where I wanted her.

"Can I get you a drink?" I asked, my fingers continuing their trail up her forearm.

"I'd like that."

CHAPTER 2

The night was young and *Red* hadn't shown any sign of leaving my side at any time, what with her constant touching, flirting, and brief brushes of her lips as she whispered words to set me on fire by my ear.

She was quite the looker, if you're into the whole artificial cleavage, makeup, nip-tuck kind of look she presented. Don't get me wrong, she was cute, hot to be honest. She was just too damn perfect which made her perfect for one night of hot, intense fucking and nothing else. She'd fit in with all the others before her—the 'love them and leave them' kind.

You may think me shallow but I'm a guy…with needs. After a week like I've had, where I've watched families torn apart by domestic violence, adultery, unemployment, and death, I dare you to be sitting in my shoes.

My release from a hectic week is in the form of women and booze, as you might have gathered. Not enough to be deemed a functional drunkard, simply enough to let go of the stresses of the week and unwind. Call it a celebratory release of sorts. The occasional cigar helps, but I reserve that for when the boys and I get together. Which hasn't been often as of late, seeing as they've all tied themselves down for the most part. But that's not for me. Not since… Well, never mind that!

Red broke me away from my dark thoughts of matrimony and all things alike when she said, "What do you say we get out of here?"

My smile held all the promises of an exhausting and blissful night ahead for both of us. "I say you couldn't have had a better idea."

A lingering look at those legs of hers as she preceded me out the door and I found it difficult to believe that we'd make it to my place before I ended up with those slender stilts wrapped around me.

After hailing a cab, thanks to too much alcohol, I pulled her to me for a deeper taste of those glossy lips of hers. She tasted of the wine she had been drinking, with a subtlety of chocolate.

Delicious.

But not as good as... No! I stuffed those thoughts out of my mind. Or at least, I tried to.

Fifteen years have gone by and still, no one measured up to *her*. No matter how I try to stop it, my mind always compared my numerous conquests to the one woman who ran from me: Danica Withers.

It was because of Danica that I was who I was. No, not the family law practitioner—the Casanova. I was young. A fool. My naïveté caused a lapse in judgement at the not-so-ripe age of eighteen.

It's true what they say about love being blind.

If only I hadn't figured it all out the hard way, maybe things would be different now.

I fell head over heels in love with Danica, but after giving her everything, she left me with a note. Some letter that didn't explain much of anything, yet to this day, like a masochist, I carried the fucking thing everywhere. It was in my wallet, serving a reminder whenever I doubted my current state of affairs where relationships were concerned.

Danica left me bearing nothing but a shattered soul, not to mention a hell of a lot of resentment, and complete disregard for all things that entailed commitment to the fairer sex.

By the time I'd pulled myself together, I had sworn off love. I remember getting the typical platitudes about how I'd realize that I did want love when the right one came along. All of them viable comments I had laughed and brushed off.

No. Love wasn't for me. I was better off without the complexities of commitment.

And it's been that way since Danica's departure.

Sort of.

It worked for me, and I live by the old adage of not fixing things if they weren't broken.

I wish I could say that my fifteen years of phobia towards commitment had erased all sense of yearning, but despite being ninety-five percent womanizer, there was that five percent of the dreamer that haunted my thoughts on the occasional night. It was apparent, the minute I started comparing *Red* to Danica, that tonight was one of those nights.

What the fuck is up with you, man? Get your balls back into the game and send this one off with a smile that'll last her through 'til next week.

And so, my womanizing conscience won out. It always did. But I was growing tired of having to fight with myself.

By the time we reached my house, I had no idea as to the extent of my state of undress, being so wrapped up into my flavor of the night. My shirt lay unbuttoned and un-tucked at the front.

I paid the driver and rushed us to my front door, tripping over my pants, which were undone and sliding down my legs. I smirked at the giggling woman before leading her through the threshold ahead of me. Kicking the door shut, I dropped my pants and pinned her to the solid oak.

"I can't wait," I said against her smiling lips and moved to nip her jaw.

She hissed and arched her body into mine. "Then don't. Nice place you've got here."

I hushed her with a rough possession of her mouth before saying, "The only thing I want to hear from you right now is you screaming my name, or better yet, moaning your appreciation while you suck my cock." I nipped the skin below her ear and was greeted with a moan.

Those legs had been heaven, wrapped around me as I had pumped into her heat. However, her best feature had been her mouth. Those swollen high-glossed red lips surrounding my cock as she blew me to orgasm by the front door had been amazing. So amazing that I took her twice in my bed before I sent her home.

No woman ever spent the night.

It was a rule.

They may have made it into my bed, but they never stayed there long enough to fade from bliss to sleep. I always extricated myself from the situation before hope could develop.

I know I'm a bastard, but none of my women are lied to. I'm not into trickery. They always know what they are getting into from the very beginning. It's not my fault some develop the notion of something greater being possible while in the throes of passion. Some just got it in their heads that they could help me somehow—change me.

It's fair to say that, over the years, I've been called every unflattering name in the book. But it has to be said that I've also been propositioned for additional no-strings-attached soirées.

Jotted numbers and business cards were a frequent occurrence, but I never kept them. Oh sure, I've slept with the same woman more than once since Danica's departure, but it was out of convenience on both our parts, when the night presented little to no opportunity. Aside from that, I was a one-time-thank-you-ma'am kind of guy. No more. No less. The faster I fucked them, the quicker they were out the door and out of my life. The less time to form attachments, the smoother things went.

It was safe.

It was enjoyable—on both counts, I'll say.

It was my utopia.

B y the time I returned from my shower, I heard the front door latch close and I knew *Red* was gone.

I let my towel drop and reached into my dresser for my underwear, noticing the business card she'd left for me on the edge of the piece of furniture.

I shook my head. *Predictable.*

Dressed, I grabbed the tiny piece of paper and headed downstairs to the den.

I poured myself a drink of scotch from my reserves in the cabinet, dropped the card where all the others have ended up in the past: the shredder.

I let out a sigh and sipped the liquor. Savoring the elixir and its smooth burn as it slid down my throat, my earlier dark thoughts consuming me once again.

The upcoming weekend was going to be a long one. Why had I agreed to it again? Oh yeah, because despite my commitment issues with women, I was loyal and reliable when it came down to my friends. They meant everything to me, especially Paxton.

In the morning, I retrieved my car from the Fairfax's parking lot and headed out to Paxton's house, which had been transformed into wedding central for the day.

The man and I have been best friends for as long as I can remember. After the debacle that was his first marriage, I still couldn't believe that Pax had put faith in love again, and was even more shocked to find out that he had himself a new woman. One, I can say, that was the complete opposite from his ex-wife. Alissa was sweet, and a hot little number too.

I had laughed at his excitement when he'd told me about her. The guy had stars in his eyes and it was comical how consumed with her he had become.

Over the last few months, while helping them plan their nuptials, I had grown to think of her as a little sister. I could see what the man saw in her. And those eyes of hers, they were only meant for him and no one else. The man needn't worry about her wandering. She was loyal.

Truth is, I'm a little envious he's found someone to be happy with.

To have a woman look at me the way she does him. I sighed and got out of my parked car. *That kind of thinking will get you into trouble, and you know it.* I shook my wanting thoughts out of my head as I took my keys out of the ignition.

I'm thirty-four and I have a whole life of bachelorhood in front of me. I was fine with that—for the most part… I think.

Here's a fact for you. I did try a relationship after Danica—after graduating from law school. It didn't work out. I got bored, couldn't stand being tied down. The woman I was with claimed that I didn't want to put in the effort a relationship needed. Maybe she was right. Then again, thoughts of Danica had haunted me left, right, and center with that particular woman. And so, I broke it off.

It was then that I realized that the bar had been set high without my knowledge. The hilarity of it all was that grown women couldn't compete with an eighteen-year-old girl, or more like the mere memory of her.

I've never seen a man so calm like Paxton had been earlier today. Had I known that a man could be that mellow on his wedding day, I would have told him to run for the hills when he had paced the room, nervous and frantic on the day he had wed Julie. It was a testament that he and his first wife had been doomed to fail, but this time, with Alissa…

Is it possible that two people could come together that easily and make it last?

My parents had done it.

Plenty others had as well.

I knew from past experience, but my job had also influenced my skepticism. Truth is, I lacked the will to take that leap too.

Go ahead, call me a coward. I doubt that I'd try and prove you wrong.

I had watched as the two recited their vows, as if they were the only ones in their backyard, despite the seventy-five or so guests present. There was something about observing the two of them that struck a chord. I wasn't quite sure, but I shook it off as quick as it hit me, rubbing the ache in my chest while I stood behind Pax, smiling like the dutiful best man that I was.

Why the multiple bouts of enviousness? I don't know. But I sure as hell didn't like these tumultuous emotions that roiled through me.

They danced their first dance as husband and wife. My thoughts turned to the hurdles they'd overcome in their short time together, the most recent being her miscarriage, no more than three weeks ago.

Fuck did that phone call hurt when Paxton got a hold of me. Seeing him broken at the hands of Julie, his ex, had been one thing, but my best buddy being torn apart because the life of his unborn child had been forfeited, was another.

Hadn't Jasper's cancer scare been enough? In that moment, I had questioned a lot about life and its fairness.

I admired Paxton for the fortitude he showed his fiancée. She had blamed herself for their loss. And I had been the one to stand at the room's doorway, keeping everyone else out, all the while witnessing every little account.

Her tears.

Her screams.

Her words of failure.

My heart broke with Alissa's heart-wrenching cries, so much so that I had gotten misty-eyed myself. Hell, it was impossible not to grieve for those two.

Paxton hadn't wanted to hear any of it, though. He did the best he could at the time. He was hurting too. It had been their child, a symbol of a fresh beginning coming to a halt far too soon.

He'd held Alissa to his chest, refusing to let her go, kissing, cuddling, as he lay beside her on the far-too-narrow hospital bed.

At one point, when one of her crying jags had subsided to a hushed whimpering, I had watched as he tilted her face up to his. She fought to avert her gaze from him, but he refused to let her hide from him.

"How can you even look at me after this?" She struggled to keep her emotions in check. "I'm unfit. I failed. Why would you marry someone who–?"

"Stop it, just stop it!" The boom to his voice had made her jump in his arms. "I love you, Alissa, you hear me… *you*! It's not your fault, none of it is your fault, sweetheart." He kissed her forehead. "You heard the doctor. There was no way of knowing this would happen. You did nothing wrong. It doesn't mean we can't try again."

"But I wanted *that* baby." She sobbed into his chest.

The remaining pieces of my heart had shattered as I heard Paxton say, "Me too."

It's safe to say that the memory of that day, the strength that two people could share together, would always stay with me.

CHAPTER 4

At first, I didn't notice the woman that waltzed up to me, too enthralled with the newlyweds and memories both recent and past, not to mention that feeling of envy that had consumed me for what felt like the millionth time today.

"Nice speech," she said and smiled down at me. "Is this seat taken?"

I smiled at her in my typical charming way. "Help yourself, honey. Friend of the bride or groom?"

"Bride." She watched the happy couple, and got comfortable in the seat next to mine. "To be honest, I was shocked to find out that she'd met someone. When she called to tell me that she was getting married, I thought she had lost her mind."

I laughed. "I know what you mean."

"Considering some of the idiots she's dated in the past, I'm floored she took the chance at all."

I nodded. "He's a great guy, he'll treat her right."

"She got lucky," the woman said. "It's why I don't bother with relationships."

I chuckled. "Amen to that." I held out my hand. "I'm Jake, by the way."

She grasped it in hers and smirked. "I know."

"And you are?"

"Yours… for the night," she said and gained my full attention in the process.

"Well…" I eyed her from top to bottom. "I think I might have to take you up on that offer…?" I hung on my words so she could introduce herself.

"Mia."

"Beautiful name for a beautiful woman." I got up and pulled her with me so she stood. "Would you like to dance, Mia?"

"What kind? I'd prefer horizontal, myself." She winked.

Christ! I laughed. "All in good time, honey. There's no rush."

A few drinks and a couple of hours later, we stumbled into her hotel room, she being tipsy, and me making sure she didn't trip and fall, thanks to those heels of hers.

Mia wasn't wasting time. She peeled away at her clothing on her way to the bed and was left in nothing but her red lace thong as I followed, removing as much as I could of my attire on my way.

I took in the sights. "Woman, you're a wet dream come true."

"Shut up and fuck me, Jake."

Who was I to argue with her?

Tackling her to the bed, I kissed her hard and hovered above her body, my shirt discarded to the floor, my belt loosened.

I trailed my lips downward and nipped her jaw as she leaned back onto her elbows with a sensual hiss. Her eyes closed and her head tilted toward the mattress, opening her neck for my possession.

By the time I reached her navel and circled her belly button with my tongue, she flipped me over and began to divest me of my tuxedo pants. My briefs followed at the same time.

"Not your first rodeo, huh?"

"Hardly." She grabbed the condom from my fingers, tearing into the packaging with her teeth and sheathing me.

"Have I mentioned that I love a woman who knows what she wants?"

"I kind of figured." She gave me a wry grin.

When the condom was on, I let her straddle my waist and position me at her entrance, but that was as far as she got.

My hands held her hips in place, preventing her from plunging down atop me. With one swift upward thrust, I pushed hard into her, pulling her down onto me. Her breath caught, and she fell forward onto her hands to brace herself. The guttural moan she emitted was enough to drive me wild with lustful need, so I flipped us so I was above her.

"Fuck, yeah!" I said into her neck and stayed still.

"Fuck me, Jake," she said as if the wait for movement was painful. "Fuck me, hard!"

Sex was always great, not to mention the release at the end, explosive, but my favorite part was the variety of noises and sounds that I could get a woman to make in the throes of passion. I couldn't care less that they screamed my name. It was the other expletives they managed: the moans, groans, grunts, whimpers, and the looks on their faces, the way their eyes changed as I plunged deep into their hot, wet pussies, taking what I needed from them as they took from me. Watching them lose control was one hell of an aphrodisiac, and I was never satisfied unless I knew she was. I strived for the most intense climax and for the most-part, I succeeded at my task. Not one complaint as of yet, aside from perhaps wanting more and being denied.

I got up to leave Mia after a three hour session between the sheets.

"No need to rush, stud."

By habit alone, I knew I needed to get the hell out of

Dodge. "I have an early morning tomorrow. I wish I could stay but I can't."

"It's Sunday, what's so important on Sundays?"

"Work," I fibbed, pulled my pants up, shoved my arms in my shirt sleeves, bent over and kissed her forehead. "Thanks for tonight."

I was quick to grab my socks, shoes, and tuxedo jacket and get out as she yelled, "Anytime." The door closed behind me with a loud click.

The only thing worse than having a woman spend the night was spending the night with a woman in her bed.

An old couple walked out of the elevator, heading for their room, as I tried to stuff my shirt down my pants and make myself look presentable. The man shook his head, smirking at me, while his wife looked appalled at my state of undress.

With my shoes on, I slung my jacket over my shoulder and high-tailed it home.

By the time my head hit the satin pillow, I was unable to stop pondering the day's events.

Paxton and Alissa looked happy, so much so that it was almost sickening. How my best friend and his new wife made it look so worthwhile and easy, I would never know. And I knew that it hadn't been a cake-walk for either of them.

In the midst of thinking and taking in my large home, I became aware of a void I could no longer ignore.

I felt lonely.

Being alone in my large home had never bothered me before, so why did it seem to all of a sudden?

Sundays have always been my day to relax. Women were never part of the agenda. It's always been me, myself, and I, and sometimes the guys, if their women were willing to part ways with them for an afternoon or evening of football, or if their jobs didn't interfere.

Today was one of those days where I was on my own. I was glad. After two back-to-back nights of frolicking about, I needed to get my head back in the game.

I didn't like that I was relying on the attention of women more often. What was worse was that with the frequency of women came an increase in thoughts about Danica and my loneliness.

Like an oozing sore, the pestilent thoughts I had fallen asleep to came back upon waking.

I headed out for a run to clear my head, seeing as next to sex, it was my cure-all. Waving to a few housewives on my block as I passed, I set the pace that would lead me into a good hour's worth of cardio.

I slowed from a jog to a walk and rounded the corner to the coffee shop by my home when my hour was up. A caffeine boost was needed next.

As always, the barista served me with a smile and a lack of flirtatious subtlety when she skimmed the tips of my fingers with hers while passing my cup of Java.

I headed out with a quick nod and made a beeline toward my posh abode. I had managed to clear my head some, but the minute I slowed my pace, the thoughts I had managed to ward off during my run were there waiting for me to deal with all over again.

As I got to my front door, I forced those thoughts away. I had better things to do, like a full day of football, rest, and relaxation. Too bad that went to hell in a hand basket by ten o'clock that night.

With my buddy Brent's call, last night, I walked into my office on Monday morning with a sense of unease. Suffering with breast cancer, his wife had taken a turn for the worse, and I'd been tasked to take over one of his cases.

Being ill-prepared by not having ample time to study the case didn't sit well with me. I knew that it was a big one because Brent had said so. If handled right, this case could put me up for partnership with the firm.

Seated in the conference room, early and waiting on the other party to arrive, I figured I'd pull out Brent's case notes and skim through them to make sure I knew as much as possible about what I was dealing with.

Bent over, fishing away in my briefcase for my notepad, I was greeted by a set of endless legs, tucked away in a navy pin-striped skirt.

As your typical virile man, my hormones took over and my eyes scanned from her four inch heels, up those bare stilts that disappeared beneath the aforementioned skirt. It hugged a tight ass with hips that swayed as the woman walked toward the other end of the conference room table.

I felt a twitch down below.

Down boy.

It wasn't until I stood and looked over that I found myself

looking into bright blue eyes that held me captive with their familiarity.

Tight-lipped, she said, "Mr. Landen." Her expression was replaced by one of confusion. "I was under the impression that we were meeting with Mr. Brent Townsend?"

What the fuck? "Yes. Well…" Her counsel looked between her and me with curiosity. "Mr. Townsend has asked that I handle his caseload seeing as he's been pulled away for a personal emergency, Miss…"

"Actually, Mr. Landen, it's Mrs. Spalding, for now. Shall we get down to business?"

It was safe to say that I felt like a complete idiot during our meeting. Combine my lack of preparedness with the old memories of our past and I can guarantee you my focus was far from sound. This case had just gotten more complicated.

By the time our hour was up, I couldn't high-tail it out of there fast enough. Making a beeline for my office, I told my assistant to hold my calls and turn away any visitors.

She's back. Damn.

Wasn't there a rule that protected people from having to deal with personal and business mixing together? I guess not. Then again, it's not like Brent or my employer were aware of my personal history.

Fate sure knew how to be mean.

I sat at my desk, intent to work on this afternoon's paperwork needed for other clients, but I wasn't able to make much sense of anything.

Giving up on regaining my focus, I let out a loud breath, ran my fingers through my hair and made a decision.

I pushed the button. "Sally?"

"Yes, sir?" I heard back from the intercom.

"I'm taking the afternoon off. Clear my schedule for the rest of the day. I'll be working from home."

"What about your twelve thirty, sir? We've already re-scheduled him once."

"Call Stan and apologize. He'll understand. Reschedule and make a reservation at that new bistro that's just opened down the street. I have it under good authority that Stan has a penchant for great French food."

"Right, sir."

"Thank you, Sally."

Stuffing the work I needed to tackle in my briefcase, I left the office, hoping for something—anything—that would divert my mind from its current thoughts. If only I could get myself out of handling Brent's case, but I knew it was too late since we were due in court Wednesday.

I was stuck.

And I was far from happy about it.

＜e CHAPTER 6 ⁊＞

Not only was Fairfax one of my haunts to unwind after a long week, but it was also my joint of choice when I didn't feel like being home and cooking dinner for myself.

In case you're wondering, I'm not the typical bachelor that relies on takeout for sustenance. Thanks to my mother, I can more than hold my own in a kitchen.

I picked up my beer and swallowed a generous amount.

Danica Withers was back in town and looking better than ever. I found myself unsettled at that fact.

So this Bruce Spalding guy is her husband.

I hadn't a clue that she had married. Then again, I couldn't have known considering the day she left, I swore to forget everything about her. The prospect had seemed easy enough at the time. The reality… Well, it's safe to say that she still consumes my thoughts every so often.

Someone approached the booth I was sitting in, waiting for my meal to arrive. When I looked up, there stood none other than Danica Withers with those bright blue eyes of hers.

Damn, she hadn't changed much in fifteen years. Now that I had an extra moment, I took more notice. Her body had filled out in all the right places. Her tits were larger and displayed nicely in a silk camisole, covered by an open blazer and those hips that attached to those fantastic legs had gotten wider. The entire package showed that she was built just right for a night of bliss.

I found myself thinking back to the night we lost our virginity to each other, and my mouth began to water.

She cleared her throat and my attention was diverted to the unwanted guest who now sat across from me.

"Jacob, it's been a long time."

My heart raced. *Oh, this isn't good, not good at all.* Skipping all reminiscent talk, I cut straight to the point. "What is it, Nica?" I asked, realizing that I used the nickname I had given her back in high school.

I cursed my slip of the tongue when I saw her bright smile. It was a smile that had rendered me to my knees a little more than once or twice; the one where I would have done anything for that girl—once.

But not anymore.

I forced the memories of pain to replay in my mind so I remembered why I couldn't go there with her or anyone else.

"I haven't heard that nickname in ages," she said with that sweet melodic voice of hers. "It's really good to see you, Jacob." She attempted to cover the top of my hand with hers, but I yanked it away as if she would burn me the moment she made contact. She hesitated but continued. "How've you been?"

What's she up to? "Isn't there somewhere else you should be?"

She looked surprised at my flat tone, but it didn't seem to deter her. "In case you haven't noticed, it's a little busy in here."

"And?"

"*And* I saw you when I came in to get some dinner to bring back with me so I figured that–"

I didn't let her finish. "So you figured that you'd come

over, pop a squat and shoot the shit with your soon-to-be ex-husband's lawyer?"

"I was going to say an old friend, but…" She averted her eyes.

I knew I hit a nerve. She looked sad, but old bitterness had come seeping through, and I couldn't help myself.

"But what? We're not friends, Danica." I twisted the proverbial knife in a little deeper. "Sure, there was a time when I carried a torch for you, but don't think that after the way you left me, that friendship would be on the table."

Call me bitter, call me cynical. I'll be the first to admit that I was both. Okay… maybe a bit more on the bitterness spectrum but can you blame me? The woman shattered me when she left without a proper explanation.

"I see," she whispered. "I'll leave you alone, then." She made to get up, but my body had other ideas.

I latched onto her wrist before she could get away. I could feel her pulse racing as my thumb rubbed the junction between her arm and hand.

"Why?"

"*Why* what?" She seemed to be fighting some emotion I couldn't quite make out.

"No phone call? No email? Nothing but some vague Dear John letter."

"I couldn't." But she never elaborated. I studied her face, my hand loosening its grip. "Goodbye, Jacob. I'll see you in court on Wednesday."

Pulling her wrist out of my grip, she walked away. She made a quick stop at the bar where the waiter grabbed a slew of bags and handed them over to her. After she paid the man, she handled the bags and left without a backward glance.

"Here you go," I heard, knocking me out of my daze. I looked up to find Ben, the owner, and a good friend of mine.

"Thanks, man." I reached for one of the fries. I no longer had much of an appetite.

"You saw her, huh?" I gave him a small nod in response. "Still hung up on her?"

"Hell no!" I said louder than intended. The patrons sitting at the nearest table turned their attention toward us. Ben thought it comical, as he gave me a single pat on the back and took a seat on the edge of the bench across from me. I didn't miss his sympathetic look.

"Sure doesn't sound like it. It didn't look like it either. You know that her move here is permanent, right?"

I stared at Ben and wondered aloud, "How much do you know about her?"

"A lot. Mike, her brother, and I are still tight. Their Dad hasn't been doing well. He's been sick with cancer, but I think I heard something about him being in remission now." I nodded to that piece of information. "He left the company to be managed by that idiot husband of hers. There was talk about him selling his shares to the guy or something like that. I don't know. Anyway, I think he thought he was doing the company some good, but it backfired. Turns out that Dani's hubby was embezzling."

Fuck me! "Let me guess, now that they're getting divorced, he wants her part of the company as part of the settlement because he's so broke that he needs to sell the damn thing in order to regain his losses?"

Ben nodded. "That's what Mike thinks. How'd you know?"

I felt rage surfacing. I spoke to Spalding this afternoon. Wanting to know more about his background, it was clear that the man had omitted some crucial pieces of information; information that would make a difference in court and a judge's ruling.

"Because I represent the son of a bitch."

CHAPTER 7

After my run-in with Danica and talk with Ben, I headed home. Finding myself at my desk, I searched for whatever it was that I could find on Bruce Spalding. It was time that I educated myself further on my own client. Seems like Mr. Spalding was keeping a few skeletons in his closet.

It was as I suspected.

The man's track record started off clean as a whistle. A very bright and clever entrepreneur, self-made millionaire with his business trades. It was no wonder he was good at what he did.

Up until eleven months ago, that is. That's when things began to look shady.

I was sifting through his many quarterly financial reports and noticed that things fell into a progressive decline as time went on—and fast. In an eight month timeframe, he'd sold off three-quarters of his umbrella companies and it looked like he was attempting to liquidate the remainder. What was odd was that he was also acquiring other companies at the same time.

Where Withers International was concerned, things were trickier for Spalding, as Danica, her brother, and her father owned a third each of the company.

I smirked. Maybe daddy was smart after all.

I also found a trail of paperwork detailing the transfer of Danica's father's portion to Spalding. It had yet to be signed and notarized, but the document did exist. My guess was that Withers put everything to a halt the minute he found out that his son-in-law wasn't being up front with him.

The more I looked into the man's business dealings, the more I saw that The Spalding Corporation, Bruce's parent company, was doing more than fine.

I guess that's where the embezzled cash went.

With no choice but to remain as Spalding's representative, I made a decision. And I can tell you right now that he wasn't going to like me very much by the time things were said and done.

I knew I was great at what I did, and I knew that I could win this case for him. As much as I would have loved to be made a partner, I also knew I wasn't comfortable with acquiring that title over some crooked deal.

If I lacked a moral compass, I could have gone through with it, and come up on top, but I knew what would happen to Withers International if I won. Withers' company would cease to exist all because of some selfish and irresponsible schmuck like his soon-to-be-ex-son-in-law.

There had been a time when I thought nothing but greatness about Danica's father. The man came from a solid background of entrepreneurs and was driven for success. He was a hard man to deal with, but it served him well over the years, turning his tiny home-based company into a multi-billion dollar international conglomerate that dealt in public relations.

Despite his blatant dislike of me hanging around his daughter, not to mention his disdain for my social status, I had admired the man. To be honest, I doubted he wanted any boy to infringe upon his daughter's higher education. What father did?

With a loud huff, I ran my hands through my black hair and got up. I took a look at the clock and was baffled at how much time had passed between the beginning of my research and my coming to a suitable decision. It was nearly midnight.

CHAPTER 8

The next day, I woke up earlier than usual, confused and horny as fuck. Groaning, I rolled out of bed, to end up in a cold shower in an attempt to relieve myself.

I hadn't slept much the night before, tortured by thoughts of Danica and that pin-striped pencil skirt of hers. My night was haunted with images of her over my desk, her legs wrapped around my waist as I buried myself deep inside her heat.

I used those images and that of her mouth taking my length as I thrust into her with abandon to get myself off. Once done, I shaved my stubble, did something presentable with my hair, and dressed. Cursing my bloodshot eyes as the only proof of my lack of sleep, I headed to work.

"Come in," I called out to the person who'd knocked on my office door. Typing up an email reply to Brent who was checking in with the case and filling me in about his wife's prognosis, I held up an index in pause to whoever entered.

"Sir," Sally said.

"One moment." I rolled my cursor over to the send button, clicked, and lifted my eyes to her. "Yes?"

"Mr. Lowell is here to see you."

I smiled. "Send him in." She nodded and made to leave. "And Sally?" She turned to face me. "You know to just send that man in without checking with me first."

"You looked so preoccupied earlier that I didn't want to take a chance that you might not be up to visitors."

"I'm fine. Thank you, Sally." It felt odd to have a woman who was old enough to be my mother, calling me *sir*. "I've got to fix that." I mumbled to myself when the woman disappeared.

"Talking to yourself like that, it's not healthy." Paxton shut the door behind himself.

"Aren't you supposed to be off somewhere with your new bride or something?"

"Postponed our trip for a few months. Allie's got something big going on at work and she can't get away." His face grew serious. "Funny thing happened earlier today when I took Jasper to the mall, though."

I knew what was coming next.

"**S**eriously, am I the only one who's been out of the loop about her being back?" I asked with exasperation after Paxton told me about his run-in with Danica. "Is this why you're here, to check up on me?"

Paxton looked at me, his mouth opening and closing much like that of a fish out of water. "Well…"

"You want to know the truth?" Of course the man nodded. "Fine. I'm handling her husband's affairs in their divorce. Did you know she was married? I can't believe—"

"She looks good."

"Are you blind? The woman's only gotten better over the years." My words came to an abrupt stop as a self-satisfied smirk spread on my best friend's face. I crossed my arms over my chest. "What are you getting at?"

"Ben was right. You're still hung up on her."

I groaned. Word sure got around fast. "That ship sailed away a long time ago, pal."

I knew I was in denial. Why couldn't I just accept that Ben and Paxton were right and be honest with myself?

Because you don't want to be open to that again.

"Do you have any clue as to what kind of shit I had to put up with after she left? Oh, that's right, you do. You were the messenger boy. By the way, thanks for that."

At this point, I was up on my feet, wearing a hole in the carpet at the front of my desk.

Paxton's amused expression grew, and I could tell that the man was trying his best to stifle a bout of laughter. "Wow! After fifteen years, she still has your balls in a vice." His boisterous laugh broke loose and bounced off the walls of my office. I stopped dead in my tracks, fuming at his words. After a short while, his face went taut. "Seriously, you have to figure this thing out between you two. It's been so long. Get some closure. Fuck her brains out. Talk to her. Tell her what happened, the truth, after she left. Christ, just do something! I'm tired of seeing you in this funk. It's time you moved on, man, and you playing around isn't you."

My earlier conversation with Paxton played over and over in my head as the day went on.

The man was right. I had to do something to get Danica Withers out of my head for good. Maybe now that she was in town there would be a way of closing that proverbial door to our past? Could I have that kind of heartfelt conversation with the woman who'd brought nothing but grief after she'd left me?

My machismo kicked in with a, *Hell no!* I knew that this predicament was going to be a tough one to move on from, even if I thought I had long-ago buried it. I hated the fact I hadn't moved on from those old wounds. I'd disguised my hurt with lust, liquor and ladies. Proof was in the fact that I compared every suitor to her and they all came up lacking, thus preventing me from erasing her from my mind.

For all intents and purposes, Nica was no longer. and Danica Withers was a new woman. One I no longer knew—a mere stranger. Something about that thought process told me that I was wrong in my assessment and that she was every bit the same girl I knew back in high school. The hurt look in her eyes at Fairfax had been telling enough.

Still, she managed to move on and you didn't. What does that say about her? Maybe her father had been right all those years ago; maybe I hadn't been enough for her.

CHAPTER 9

Wednesday, oh bloody Wednesday. With much dread, it came before I knew it.

I was due in court in an hour and nothing seemed to be going right.

Withers gave me a disgusted look as he and I crossed paths in the courthouse hallway, most likely at my representing the man that was attempting to take his daughter's share of his company. I was disgusted with myself for representing Bruce Spalding, but I wasn't about to let him see what I had up my sleeve.

I was about to dupe my own client. And if anyone knew that I was about to sway the courts by behaving mediocre at best with my counselling abilities, I'd have to say that I'd be out of a job real quick and that no one from here to Timbuktu would ever take me on as partner or any form of legal counsel for as long as I lived. I was about to throw away the biggest case that could make my career and for what? A woman I had fallen in love with when I was eighteen? No. It was because of principle.

Believe that if you think that's what'll help you feel all warm and fuzzy when you're sleeping in a box in the alley behind Fairfax this time next year. You'll be lucky to still have a job after this stunt.

Maybe I had let this case get the better of me, but I knew I had to do it. No matter how I had once felt for Danica, or how I feel now, which I can't begin to hypothesise about at the moment, it did boil down to principle.

"All rise," the bailiff called out.

I rose to my feet, my client beside me, wearing a smug expression as if he had already won the case.

I smirked, wondering how long it would take before he lost that self-assured composure of his.

Cases were presented, battles were waged, and the war was fought. I may have "forgotten" a few key questions in my cross-examination, but my ultimate goal had been attained. Once or twice the judge had given me an inquisitive look, the jury seemed convinced, and Spalding seemed to have been knocked down a peg or two. The man was fuming with fury.

Watching Danica jump up at the judge's final ruling with glee put a smile on my face that was hard to conceal.

Spalding should have been ecstatic not to be incarcerated for his embezzling stunt. Forfeiting his claim on Danica's shares of Withers International would ensure that criminal charges wouldn't be laid. I got mixed feelings about this agreement. It seemed that Withers looked weary with the ruling, while Danica was overjoyed.

In my opinion, the settlement was far more generous than what I would have advised for had I been Danica's lawyer. I guess that was the difference between their counsel and me. Regardless of this, the information of the outcome of this case would be out for public consumption within the day, and Spalding's reputation would be tarnished just the same.

With a loud curse, Spalding was the first of anyone to

stomp out of the room, followed by his media relations man-
ager, both, I might add, without a business-like handshake.
The local media hounds awaited them as they exited the solid oak double doors to the courtroom, and the din of cameras
and their flashes could be heard.

I remained seated, not willing to be part of the press fren-
zy outside. I was never one for the glitz and glamour of the
high-profile assignments.

I packed up my papers, stowed them away in my briefcase and when I turned, I saw Danica hug an adolescent boy,
followed by her father. She peered at me over her father's
shoulder and I nodded, conceding my defeat.

I took another look at the boy that was still wrapped up
between the two Withers' and walked out of the room using
the side door, thrilled by the way I had pulled the wool over
everyone, yet wondering what that fleeting look of panic in
Danica's eyes had been all about.

CHAPTER 10

Friday came all too soon and instead of partaking in my regular frivolities, I opted to stay home. It had been a rough week, but somehow spending time milling about people hell-bent on a good time and dashing advances just didn't seem like my proverbial cup of tea.

Upon my return to the office on Wednesday, I had received a call from Brent to give me hell for, and I quote, "dumping my case in the shitter". My bosses had been none too pleased with my less-than-stellar performance too.

My excuse for being off my A-game must have been convincing enough. I told them that their client had a curveball of information, and that due to the last minute change of litigator, I couldn't have represented him with the best of my ability.

I can also tell you that I was now further away from becoming partner than the day I started working for the firm.

As the week went on, I found that I didn't give a damn about my lackluster stature with the firm. What seemed like a career-long goal no longer seemed as important to me. With each passing day this week, I wasn't sure that I wanted to work for people who were willing to bat for criminals and who enjoyed playing the system. It wasn't why I'd become a lawyer in the first place, and I was quick to realize that I had grown resentful of the fact I held no control on choosing who I represented.

The weight of the Spalding versus Withers case pressed down on me, and I knew I had some important decision-making to do about my employment. I wasn't quite sure what the outcome of this latest revelation of mine would yield, but I knew that it was time for a change.

The doorbell rang.

Looking for a distraction, I went to answer. I didn't expect to see who stood there. A kid. One that looked all too familiar somehow.

"Can I help you?"

"The lady across the street told me that you could help me out. My mom's car broke down and she'll kill me if she finds out I took it out without my license."

My gaze grew suspicious and I crossed my arms over my chest. "How old are you?"

He averted his guilty gaze from mine. "Fifteen." I pondered his answer and the fact that he was familiar, yet I still couldn't place him. "So, are you going to help me or what?"

I shook my daze off. "Uh, yeah, sure. Where's your car?"

Up the street was a brand new BMW sedan, ill-parked against the curb, with a flat.

I nodded my approval as I parked behind the vehicle. "Nice car."

"Thanks." He walked toward the trunk. "The spare is in here, but I don't know how to do this kind of stuff."

I proceeded to get the tire iron, the spare, and the hitch from the trunk and got to work.

He leaned onto the car and watched me in silence.

"I know you, you know," he started after a moment.

"You're that lawyer that blew his case against my mom."

I stopped all movement and looked up at him. That's when it clicked. He was the teenager from the courtroom that Danica and her father had hugged.

"What do you mean?"

He smirked. "Come on, man. I might be a kid to you, but I'm not blind or stupid. You blew that case on purpose."

"Seriously, kid…" Had I been that obvious? "You have no clue what you're talking about."

He rolled his eyes. "Sure I don't." He crossed his arms over his chest. "I watch Law and Order, CSI and all those shows, you know."

I chuckled at this self-assured teenager's words. He reminded me much of myself at his age—always looking to be right.

"That shit ain't real," I said. "Half of what you see on TV never goes down that way in real life. Trust me, I know."

I finished with the tire and put the flat in the trunk along with the tools I used to do the job. "Now, you're going to jump in my car and I'm going to give you a ride home. If your mother knew I let you drive underage, not to mention, without a license, she'd have my balls."

"And judging by the piss-poor way you defended Bruce, you'd lose hands down, hot-shot."

My head snapped in his direction with shock. The moment my consternation faded, my head tilted back and I laughed. Who knew a mere teenager could be so entertaining.

"Where to?" I asked as he hopped into my car and buckled up.

"It's a few blocks down and four blocks over, by the park." I knew that area well since it was on one of my regular jogging routes.

The drive was spent in silence until I couldn't

take the whirlwind of thoughts sloshing around in my head.

"So Danica's your mom, huh?" I asked. "What's your name anyway? I'm Jake Landen."

"I know who you are, remember?" The kid snickered. "Jordan, Jordan Withers."

He extended his right hand to take mine after I parked in the driveway of a beautiful two-story brick home.

"Your—"

A stark raving mad Danica stomped out the front door, waiting on the front porch with her hands fisted on her hips. "Jordan Jacob Withers, get your soon-to-be grounded ass in this house now!"

Jordan winced. "I think I better go. Thanks for the ride."

"No problem, kid." I nudged his shoulder. "I'll see if I can make her go easier on you."

He opened the car door and proceeded to get out. He peered down into my car and smirked. "Thanks, but I think we both know who'll win this one, hot shot." His expression sobered, and when his mother called to him again, he shut the door with a look of dread dominating his face.

I watched as a skittish Jordan hurried past his mother into the house and couldn't help but notice that the apple hadn't fallen that far from the tree. She was very much like her father whether she was willing to admit it or not.

Definitely hotter.

I kept watching her and then her eyes narrowed on me. She stomped her way toward my car. *Fuck!* With a cleansing sigh, I turned the ignition off and exited.

"Jacob?" She looked at me with worry, every bit of anger and annoyance leaving her features. "How... Well, uh... Small world."

"Your car is up the street from my place. Seems like he wanted to take a joyride, but he ended up with a flat. It's fixed enough for you to take it in and get everything checked. I can have it back to you just as soon as I get back to my place."

"I can't believe he did that. What was he thinking?" She shook her head in disbelief. "Thanks for not letting him drive back. I don't know what I would have done if something happened to him. He's my life."

"It's fine, no bother at all, really. He seems like a really good kid." I turned and proceeded to open my car door to get in.

"Jacob?" Her voice was so soft that I almost missed it. I looked over at her with a questioning look in my eyes. "Do you think you could wait a minute? It would be easier all around if you just dropped me off at my car and I drove it back. I'll just let Jordan know where I'm headed off to first."

"Sure thing, Mrs.–"

She cut me off with laughter in her eyes. "It's Ms. now and Withers, not Spalding."

"Duly noted, Ms. Withers."

Her nose scrunched up. "Please don't ever call me that."

"Fine, Nica." I slipped using that nickname of hers for the second time this week.

Old habits died hard.

With the smile that graced her face, my lips couldn't help spreading into a smirk, and reality hit like a punch to the solar plexus.

God, I missed that smile.

CHAPTER 11

Reasons as to why I felt nervous with Danica sitting next to me in my car evaded me. Come to think of it, she had been the one girl that could make me feel nervous or unbalanced. There had always been something about her—a challenge perhaps? She sure as hell always managed to keep me on my toes.

"So…" I broke the awkward silence. "I hear that you're back for good?"

Yeah," she said almost at a whisper.

The lull in conversation overcame us again.

I pulled over and parked next to the curb behind her car. For the longest time, she sat there, staring out the windshield.

I noticed that she looked tired. I was right in my initial assessment of her. She hadn't changed. She still wore her emotions on the surface. Although hardened by what life had thrown at her, her body language said more than words could ever say, and what it said was that she wasn't quite ready to leave the confines of my vehicle for some reason.

I turned my head and stared out the window, wondering if I should say something. Her floating out into space grated on my nerves, increasing the edginess I felt.

"Jacob?"

"Huh?"

"Thank you." She smiled but it didn't reach her eyes.

"You're welcome."

She pulled her car keys out of her purse and made to get out. With hesitation, she exited and then bent down to peer inside at me. "I appreciate what you did for Jordan today." I nodded. "Take care of yourself."

With that, she shut the door, crossed over toward the front of her car. I watched as she paused to look back at me from her open driver's side door. She gave me a quick wave and got in. When her car coasted forward, I pulled a U-turn and headed home.

What was it about that woman that had me thinking of her so much in the last week?

Stuck in my thoughts, I headed to the den, poured myself a drink and settled in the living room. I turned the stereo on and was thankful that the radio was set to an alternative station. For tonight's mood, it was perfect.

I figured it was high time to figure how to get Danica out from under my skin. We were bound to be bumping into each other, what with some of our social circles intersecting. And let's face it, the city wasn't all that large and we lived near each other.

I set my empty glass down, surprised that I had guzzled the dark amber liquid and failed to notice the burn when it went down.

When my head hit the sheets that night, I vowed to forget the resentment, the hostility, and most of all, the anger. It might just be time to start fresh. Why couldn't I? What was the point in me being bitter anyway? We were just kids back then, right? Maybe, in time, my cynicism would disappear too.

CHAPTER 12

Sweat covered my bare chest. The sheets were tangled around my waist.

Groaning, I managed to catch my breath. *What the fuck?*

It was that damn dream again. This time, it was more vivid and had grown even more explicit.

I looked down to find myself pitching a tent in my boxers.

Rubbing myself to relieve some of the tension, I tried to roll over, ignore my semi-painful erection, and fall asleep again. The memory of the feel of her lips over my heated skin, her fingernails digging into my shoulders and those legs of hers tightening like vices around my hips was etched into my imagination.

I lifted my head, my bedside clock reading five-thirty. I settled onto my back and covered my eyes with the back of my forearm.

Something's got to give.

Disentangling myself from my bed linens, I shifted my legs off the mattress, got up, and headed for my closet, stretching the tension out of the rest of my body.

My *cure-all,* which had always been reserved for weekends, had become somewhat of a daily ritual due to my early risings over the past week.

Slipping on my shorts, I was relieved to see that the throbbing in my dick had calmed. I covered my chest with a form-fitting black t-shirt and opted for a baseball cap. Grabbing my iPod, I marched downstairs to get my shoes.

The frequency of my early morning runs was starting to grow on me. It was better than hitting the gym before or after work on weekdays. I loved the feel of the road underfoot. I felt free. Maybe that's why my runs always worked in clearing my mind whenever I felt consumed with certain overwhelming thoughts. As of late, those thoughts surrounded a certain raven-haired, blue-eyed devil in angel's clothing.

I cranked the tunes to drown out my musings, set foot to pavement, and let my feet be my guide.

Early mornings were quiet. I didn't have to worry about neighbors or too much traffic from pedestrians or cars.

I set my pace to an energetic jog at first, and by the time I neared the park, I upped my tempo to a full out run. Turning onto the gravel trail that took me into the woods, I didn't notice the oncoming person until it was too late.

Bodies crashed together and I fought for balance as my hands reached for shoulders to prevent the other party from falling over. Grip tight, stance stable, I froze at who stood in front of me.

"I'm sorry," I heard, but my eyes were fused to the person who still had yet to look up and see who it was that she'd bumped into. "Talk about a brick wall." She rubbed her nose. My surprise gave way to chuckles, and that's when her head snapped up and her eyes widened. "Jacob?"

Her nose scrunched up and she jumped back from me, my hands falling to my sides. I reached for my ear-buds as my mind scrambled about, trying to figure out what to say next. The fact that she'd backed away from me as if I was the most repulsive thing to her hadn't gone unnoticed.

Her actions rubbed me the wrong way and Mr. Rude came out to play. "Watch where you're going."

"I'm not the only one at fault!"

"I'm sorry." I avoided her gaze, regretting the tone I had taken with her. The woman had my emotions twisted like a pretzel. "Are you okay?"

"I'm fine."

"Good." I decided on sticking to a more dry and unaffected front. "Enjoy your run." I proceeded to pop my earbuds back in and turned to move past her.

"Wait." She grabbed my arm.

I turned and looked down at her hand, and then back up to her face. My brow rose in question. "Well, what?"

Her gaze went to her hand on my arm and I felt her thumb rubbing small circles. I pulled it out of her grip. Her warmth wreaked havoc on my senses. Her nearness always had. I needed distance. Lots and lots of distance right now, what with that dream of mine being so fresh and all.

"I'm sorry for being so short," she said. "Lots on my mind, you know?" She crossed her arms at her chest, thrusting those glorious breasts of hers up, which accentuated the look of that tight sports tank she was wearing.

"No, I don't know. But I understand."

She nodded.

When she didn't say anything else, I made to continue on with my run.

"Listen," she began, and sighed, "would you like to have coffee some time?" She looked beside herself with nervousness. "To talk?"

Now she wants to talk? I was about to say no when I heard the exact opposite escape my lips. "Sure." *What the hell?* But before I could think of some excuse to negate my agreement, she smiled. And just like fifteen years ago, I found myself wanting to bend over backwards to be on the receiving end of that smile of hers again. *The witch.*

"Good." Her smile widened. "I really want to know what you've been up to since I left."

"I doubt you'd find any of it interesting."

"Your eyes should be brown instead of green with the

bullshit that just came out of your mouth." Her lips quirked up again. "Word has it that you've captured the hearts of many." She was teasing, but the lack of humor in her eyes denoted that she wasn't unaffected from what she'd heard about me since her absence. *Interesting.*

A dry chuckle escaped. "Well, that's to be debated."

"Sure." She offered a dry laugh. "It amazes me that you're not married."

"Checking up on me?"

"No." I couldn't help the slight disappointment that lined the pit of my stomach with her quick answer. "I would have asked, but Pax told me."

I crossed my arms over my chest. Could she tell I felt defensive? "What'd he tell you?" For the life of me, I couldn't figure out why I felt ashamed of how I'd been living my life up until now, or why I cared what she thought of the man I'd become.

"Nothing much, aside from the fact that you were the same old Jacob Landen I knew through school." I breathed a little easier. I wondered what she'd say when she found out the truth. "I should let you get on with your run." I nodded. "So, coffee, soon?"

"Sure."

"Okay." She smiled, and this time the light danced in her eyes.

And just as quick as she'd plowed into me, she high-tailed her fine spandex-covered ass in the opposite direction I was heading. Hips that swung from side to side, and those curves of hers were so smooth and generous, they should have been illegal.

"What the fuck were you thinking?" I asked myself. The rustling of the warm morning breeze could be heard up in the treetops, as if whispering a response that I couldn't decipher.

All I knew was that I was in trouble.

CHAPTER 13

I found myself at Rex's that night, another one of my haunts, scoping out the scene. I had gone home after my run, showered, and moved about my regular Saturday habits. After a day of errands and a few office fires to snuff out, it was time for a bit of fun.

Just as I turned from getting my drink from the bar, my favorite blonde walked in. She looked around and when her eyes found me, she smiled that sexy smile that reminded me of what those lips were capable of.

Brandy was what you would call a 'fuck buddy', if you want the short and crass version of it. She always popped into my life when I needed a distraction most, and tonight, I sure as hell was at the top of the list where distractive needs were concerned.

"Why, hello there, handsome." She came to a stop beside me. I kissed her cheek while she slid a nail down my bare forearm. "It's been a while."

"It has." I smiled at her. "You alone?" She nodded. "Let me get you a drink?"

We'd been catching up with one another for about an hour when something caught my attention. In the back corner sat a trio of women in animated conversation, giggling on occasion. It was one of those giggles that caught my ear. I would recognize it anywhere, even after all of these years.

As if sensing that I was watching her, Danica's eyes connected with mine, and she lifted her drink, toasting me with a lazy smile.

"Who is she?" Brandy asked.

"Who?"

"That woman over there who you seem to be stuck on?" she said in a *duh* tone.

I watched as the three ladies seemed to be having a good time. "Just someone." I turned to Brandy.

"Right." She moved closer. "You want to get out of here?" She rubbed her palms on my chest in an up and down motion.

No, I answered in my head. Enjoying the view in that far corner, I wasn't quite willing to part with it just yet. Also, the idea of leading Brandy on for the night felt wrong too. A second later, Danica caught my eye and waved me over.

"Excuse me for a minute." I kissed Brandy's cheek. "I'll be right back."

"Sure, stud." She laughed. "Take your time." I watched as she walked away and headed for the end of the bar where two men had been eyeing her since her arrival.

That's what I loved about no attachment sex.

There was no jealousy.

It was carnal, a fulfilling of sexual needs.

Turning to the barman, I got him to get the ladies at Danica's table each a drink and headed in her direction.

"Hi!" Danica got up, a little more cheerful than I had seen her since her return. Judging by the way she was leaning on the table, it was safe to presume she was tipsy. "Girls, you know Jacob Landen, right?"

I made to correct her. "It's Jake." Aside from my parents,

she had been the only one I allowed to call me by my birth name.

The two women turned to face me, and I recognized one as Alissa, Paxton's wife, and the other, the one with the glare, as Danica's best friend from high school.

"Hi Jake." Alissa got up and hugged me and I returned her hug with a kiss on the cheek.

"How you doing, sweetheart?" I asked. "Enjoying marital bliss?"

She giggled. "Couldn't ask for more."

When I pulled away, Nicole hadn't moved or said anything in greeting. Allie looked at me with an arched brow and my gaze went to Nicole.

"What, no hugs, no handshakes?"

"Bite me!"

"No thanks," I chortled. "I'm full."

The chorus of *Nikki* and *Jake* from both Danica and Alissa were simultaneous. We had been scolded like two five-year-olds and suffice to say, we were behaving like them too.

"What the hell is wrong with you, Nikki?" Danica asked and my eyes flew to the woman from my past.

"What's wrong with *me*?" Nicole answered.

"Yes, what's your problem?" Danica reiterated.

"He's my problem." My head snapped in Nicole's direction, who wore a sour expression, pointing a manicured index in my direction. "This man-whore is my problem. Every weekend he's out, sleeping around, getting his jollies off on some unsuspecting woman."

My heart sank into my gut.

"What?" Danica turned and looked at me. Ashamed was one way of describing how I felt, but humiliated seemed more appropriate. "Well…"

I snorted. I may not owe Nicole anything, but I sure as hell wasn't keeping my mouth shut. "Unsuspecting? Right." I looked at all three women, Alissa wearing a look that resembled sympathy, Danica looking taken aback from her best friend's news, but her eyes denoted curiosity, and Nicole, well, the woman's look of repulsion was quite evident, along with her pleased expression for spilling the beans. "Excuse me."

I turned to leave and made my way to the washrooms with Alissa calling out for me to come back. I chose to ignore her. I needed to take a leak, but in reality, I was looking for the nearest exit.

I was halfway to the restrooms when I heard her. "Jacob?"

"I'll be right back, Nica," I said over my shoulder without looking at her. I shook my head at the train-wreck my night had become and walked through the men's washroom door.

If there was a way to ensure Danica's loss of interest in having anything to do with me, her knowledge of my proclivities was one way of achieving it. The burning question in my mind at that moment was why did the thought of never seeing or speaking to her again, or the fact that I might even repulse her, sting so much?

CHAPTER 14

I surmised that it would be best for all parties involved if I left the bar altogether when I vacated the restroom. I dabbed the water away from my face with a paper serviette and made for the door. Refusing to look in Danica's table's direction, I stepped out.

An arm grabbed onto my wrist from behind and pulled me back before I could exit the hallway and make my way for the door.

Everything happened so fast.

Pushed against a wall, mere seconds later, I had a pair of lips fused to mine, tasting of margarita and sweet sugar. By instinct alone, my eyes shut to enjoy the flavor and heady closeness of the woman's proximity.

It didn't last long.

Snapping back to reality, I pushed on the warm body that pressed against mine and found myself peering into eyes I never thought would ever be that close to me again. "What are you doing?" Dumbfounded, my confusion gave way to me feeling incensed.

She smirked, displaying that dimple in her left cheek I had forgotten about. "What's it look like?"

My gut twisted. "I can't do this. Not here, not now, not with you like this. No." I shook my head. "Just, no." A look at the hurt in her eyes almost had me caving right then and there. My thumb and forefinger pinched the bridge of my nose as I bowed my head, which pressed my forehead to hers. Closing my eyes, I took a deep breath and hoped to be graced with a bit more mental clarity which never came. "I've got to get out of here." My eyes opened. I watched as she took a step back, her hands sliding down my chest as I peeled my back off the wall. Cupping the sides of her neck, I tilted her head forward and kissed the top of it. "Goodbye, Nica. Have a nice night." I offered her a solemn smile.

My feet in motion, I moved away, feeling used. Did she think that because I had my fair share of women that I'd be willing to give it up to her or anyone else so easily? That was a huge resounding 'no'.

I made it to the door when Brandy stopped me with a hand on my bicep.

I forced a smile and shook my head. "Not tonight, honey." My voice sounded bleak.

She nodded in understanding and her eyes sliced toward Danica's table. "I saw that. Are you okay?"

"I'm fine." I kissed her cheek. "Catch you later?"

"Sure, stud." She winked, released my arm, and I left the premises.

Sitting in the driver's seat of my car, I was trying to validate what possessed Danica to kiss me after knowing about my proclivities.

The more I thought about her kiss, the more my groin tightened, serving to feed my frustrations—both physical and psychological. One thing was clear; the kisses from my dreams didn't hold a candle to the real thing, drunken or not, not to mention the ones from my past that I'd committed to memory.

"Fuck!" I hit the steering wheel of my car before turning

the key over in the ignition and peeling out of the parking lot.

Trouble was rearing its ugly head, there was no doubt now.

Getting over Danica Withers was a task that I now feared I would never accomplish. Damn, that hurt a man's ego when said man was used to accomplishing everything he'd ever set his mind to.

If Paxton asked me now, I was ready to admit it to his face. I'd never gotten over Danica. How could I? I never got the answers I needed back then, and I wasn't any closer to getting them at the moment either.

But it wasn't just that.

All these years, I was convinced that I detested her, but I didn't. I couldn't. My heart beat a little faster when she was around, my libido kicked into overdrive, and my brain halted all thoughts when she laughed.

Fuck!

Maybe that coffee date wasn't such a bad idea after all. It would be a chance to set the record straight. Maybe once the air was cleared I could get on with my life.

I slammed the door to my car and headed up the walkway to my front door.

I was more confused now than I'd ever been. Danica said she wanted to be friends, but then pulled that stunt at the bar. The thought of considering her as a mere acquaintance left a hollow feeling in my chest, which I tried to ignore. I couldn't imagine being around her, but I also couldn't imagine not having her around, either.

Pouring myself a drink of whiskey, I carried my glass and bottle with me to the living room and sat on the couch. I took a sip and sighed at the burn. Letting my head drop forward, I leaned onto my knees.

What a clusterfuck!
Oh yeah, I was definitely in over my head.

CHAPTER 15

I jumped up startled, grabbing onto the couch's armrest to regain my balance after the doorbell rang. Drinking had drowned some of my confusion, so I had continued to drink.

I must have passed out.

Not bothering to look at the time, knowing it was late, I headed to the door to see who it was, hell-bent on cursing out the one that had brought me out of the erotic dream I had been in the middle of.

Forgetting about my lack of shirt and the erection I was sporting, I opened the front door. I stumbled back and held tight to the knob to keep from falling over when I took in my visitor.

I rubbed at my eyes, looked up at the ceiling, and sighed. Some higher power sure as hell had a mean sense of humor.

"What is it with you?" I left the door open, turned and headed back to the living room, shuffling my feet. "You're back in town for a week and now you're everywhere!"

"Jacob?"

I let out a frustrated breath. "It's Jake. What do you want, Danica?" I turned to face her.

She closed the front door and proceeded to walk to me. Okay, maybe more like prowled.

"You." She pushed me onto the couch. "I want you, Jacob."

She took advantage of my shock and straddled my thighs.

"It's Jake–" I tried again, but her lips made contact with mine in a fierce and hungry kiss.

My hands made their way to the tops of her knees and traveled up her bare thighs, her skirt having ridden up. Her skin was soft and warm.

I couldn't help it. I kissed her back, feeling my way to that luscious ass of hers, and squeezed. She jumped in surprise which brought her even closer to my hardened cock. I groaned in her mouth as my tongue slipped out to taste her. She opened when I feathered its tip over her bottom lip, licking the seam.

Her hands were in my hair, pulling me into her while her nails scraped my scalp. The taste, combined with the feel of her, had me intoxicated. My earlier alcohol consumption didn't help either.

When my hands reached for her shirt, she pulled back to let me hike it over her head, her eyes half-lidded and glazed with lust. I took my time, letting my fingertips travel down her shoulders and back up again. She was beautiful. More than when we were in high school.

Her generous breasts, tucked away behind very thin black lace looked ripe for the taking. She bit down on her bottom lip when I grazed a globe with the back of my fingers, the nipple pebbling. By the time I did the same to the other one, she let out a soft whimper.

I fisted her hair in one hand. "Beautiful," I said before my other hand went behind her to undo the clasp of her bra.

I pulled her head down for another drink at what I will testify until my dying day, as being the best lips I have ever tasted. She moaned loud, her hands reaching down between us to work the button from its eyelet on my pants.

My zip now lowered, her hand snuck in and the feel of warm taught flesh meeting her soft touch did me in. Whatever resolve I could muster to stop the insanity that was my life, in that moment, left me altogether. I was fucked—quite literally and figuratively speaking. Okay, not yet, but I was well on my way to the former.

She got up and held out her hand to me. "I take it your room is up there?" She motioned in the stairwell's direction, and all I could do was nod, my mouth having gone dry.

I took her hand and let her lead me up the stairs. The view from behind was fantastic and it took me everything I had not to pick her up and rush her to my bed.

When we got to the landing, she paused and looked at me for directions. I pulled her to the left, through the double doors, dropped her hand, leaving her where she stood, as I moved closer to the bed.

She started for me, her bare tits hypnotizing as they jiggled while I watched her undo the zip to her skirt, wiggling as she sent it to the floor. She kicked the garment to the side and approached me. High heels and black lace; everything else should be illegal to be worn by this woman. My parched mouth now watered at the prospect of a thorough tasting which caused me to lick my lips.

"Looks like you approve." She sported a lascivious grin.

Coming to a stop in front of me, her hands reached for my hips, urging my slacks downward.

She knelt down, her hands rubbing up my thighs until one went to the back to cup an ass cheek through my underwear, and the other began to tease my throbbing dick. I arched my head back to soak in the feel of her hands on me.

Caught up in the moment, I was brought back when I felt the hard tugging of material down my legs. I looked down, my dick bobbed its approval, and after noticing, she looked up into my eyes and winked, that long forgotten dimple making another appearance.

Who are you? I asked with my eyes.

Our first time with each other had been fantastic, albeit clumsy. The woman that knelt before me now was something from another world. She was the same, yet she was different: confident, cunning, and more experienced without a doubt. She knew what it took to take a man to the edge and make him want to drop off into the abyss.

Her mouth opened and just as I thought she was going to say something, she gripped my shaft and licked the head.

I growled at the sight.

Sliding her mouth around and down my length, she moaned, sending delicious tremors through my body. My vision filled with spots.

"Fuck!" My legs quaked and one of my hands tangled into her hair.

I might get it on a regular basis, which means that my stamina was something to boast about, but this vixen of a woman already managed to bring me to the brink of exploding before I got her out of her underwear. I was suffering a complete and utter loss of control, which never happens.

Before I could put a stop to her ministrations, I felt her pull back and then plunge me deeper than before into her heated mouth. The tip of my cock hit the back of her throat and while she massaged my balls, she made to swallow me whole, her muscles milking me. My entire body tensed, my balls tightened with a release I no longer was sure I wanted to postpone.

She sucked on the down stroke and tightened her lips, humming on the up. There was no way I was going to stop her. Tonight was going to be a long night of playing. It was too late to turn back now. I would gift myself this night.

I gave her fair warning about my impending eruption, but she was relentless in her pursuit. She kept up her pace and when I blew, she surprised me, swallowing every last drop.

My cock dropped from her mouth with a popping sound. She collected the drop of fluid that had seeped through the side of her mouth and licked it off her finger.

"Holy hell, woman." My erection was still ever present.

Humming a giggle, she kissed up my stomach and got to her feet.

I needed her closer, so I pulled on her forearms until our bodies were pressed together, standing at the foot of my bed. She looked at me with a self-assured smirk, pleased with her handiwork.

"I take it you liked it about as much as I did?" she asked.

I had no complaint. I growled right before smashing my mouth to hers, tasting myself. It hadn't happened often that a woman swallowed for me, but this time had beaten all others combined—times ten!

My hands picked Danica up by her ass, demanding that she hold on by wrapping her arms and legs around me. I turned us around and laid her down over the sheets without once breaking our aggressive kiss. Her back arched off the cool feel of the satin as I slid us up the mattress, toward the pillows.

I pulled back, kneeling between her legs and looking down at her crotch. "It's time to lose those." I eyed her feet. "But you're keeping the shoes." I ripped the lace with my bare hands.

"Oh God, that's hot! I always wondered how it would feel to have a man do that."

I chortled before getting back to business.

My hands rubbed up her outer thighs, coming to a stop on the tops of them as I eyed her womanhood. The sheen of the juices on her pink lips begged me to taste her. I pushed her knees up and further apart. My thumbs rubbed the crease where her thighs met her torso, toward her pussy, and began spreading her lips to get an unobstructed glimpse.

I lowered my head.

"Oh!" She sucked in a loud breath as my mouth kissed her bare pubic bone. The sight of her hairless was enticing. She hadn't been hairless our first time together, and I hadn't acquired that preference until later years, but the woman that lay beneath me now covered every single preference of mine as if she knew my list.

I blew on the dew at her entrance and felt her hips lift off the mattress. With one hand, I pressed her into the sheets.

Lying on my stomach, I traced around her clit with the tip of my index finger. She gasped.

"You're much more vocal than I remember."

"I'm a lot more than that, Mr. Landen. Maybe I'll show you some time."

A growl made its way into my throat.

I had to have her now! Just for tonight. I didn't care about sleep. I could sleep tomorrow, or better yet, when I was dead.

I sucked her bud into my mouth with enough force to get a yelp from her, but I knew she liked it, what with the loud moan and a buck of her hips that followed. She tasted like heaven, better than I remembered.

"Oh! Oh God, Jacob!" She moaned louder and louder. I felt the tremors start deep with my fingers. My mouth was on her clit and I had two digits up inside, tapping and rubbing away on her sweet spot. Her legs began to quiver. "Fuck! Fuck me!" I couldn't help but smirk at her profanity.

Definitely not the same Danica. Then again, I wasn't the same Jake either.

At the peak of her climax, she grabbed my hair and pulled me up to her face for much needed kisses. I loved the mix of pain and pleasure her grasp inflicted.

I pulled away from her hungry kiss. Her face was flushed. It was, by far, the most sated face I had ever looked upon, and like a bad habit, I wanted to see her eyes glaze over when I took her to even greater heights again and again.

Reaching over to my bedside table, I opened the drawer and grabbed a condom. Danica pulled it out of my hand and looked at me. "Can I?" I nodded.

After she rolled it on, I took her hands and positioned them above her head. "Keep them there." I wanted to build her up until she begged me to take her.

Reaching down below, I tweaked her hypersensitive bud with my thumb. I savored one breast, moving on to its twin, watching as their peaks hardened. I grew more aggressive with each suck, lick and nibble, moving between both mounds of flesh.

"So responsive," I said against the underside of one breast.

Something became evident tonight. Danica enjoyed a little bit of pain with her pleasure. The thought that she was more of a match for me in the bedroom than I ever thought scared me, but not enough to stop what was happening.

After giving her breasts enough attention, I moved south. I pulled my hand away from her heat, feeling that she was on the verge again. My hands trailed to her stomach. I noticed the very faint stretch marks on it.

"Don't look at them," she said when my fingers began to trace one.

I looked up to see she had turned her head, avoiding eye contact.

My voice grew stern. "Hey!" Her head snapped back and her eyes connected with mine as I crawled up to hover over her. I offered her a tender smile. "I like them. I think they're sexy as all hell."

She looked perplexed. "You do?"

I nodded. "Very." She searched my eyes, trying to see if I was lying. "Let me show you."

One minute, it was sweet and gentle as I teased her slit with the tip of my dick, and the next, I plowed into her hard, making her scream, "Oh God, yes!" Her core gripped me like a vice and her back arched off the bed.

"I think someone likes it rough," I said in a singsong tone into her ear, rooted to the hilt and unmoving.

"Don't stop!" she scolded. "Fuck me hard, Jacob. I need you so bad."

I looked down into her pleading eyes and smirked. "You don't have to tell me twice." I pulled back so my tip remained inside her before thrusting until I had her filled again. I felt her clench my cock harder this time around. *Oh fuck, yeah!*

Our bodies lay spent and glistening with sweat. It had been the best damned sex I ever had. The minute I regained my breath and my wits however, the regret was waiting for me, as I'd predicted before losing my head.

What had I done?

Why was I so weak when it came to her?

Why was she here of all places?

What did she want?

Where were we…? The screech of a record being scratched sounded in my head. We? There wasn't a 'we'. There wouldn't be an 'us'. Without a word, I got up, left Danica in my bed, and headed for the bathroom.

Distance. I needed distance.

CHAPTER 16

After a shower and a whole lot of thinking, I returned to my bedroom, my emotions still reeling. I was on a downward tailspin to crashing and burning.

I must be a glutton for punishment.

In my bed, Danica slept, the sheets around her torso, covering her gorgeous assets, her hair strewn across the king-sized pillow and her lashes brushing her cheeks.

What was I going to do? A woman never spent the night. I never spent the night with a woman. Not since Danica.

Had it been any other woman, I would have woken her up and called her a cab home, but I couldn't bring myself to do that to her.

I was quick to realize that there were a lot of things I couldn't bring myself to do, or prevent from doing, around the bewitching woman, and that was the crux of it all, wasn't it?

Instead, I slid onto my side of the bed, covered up and lay soldier straight on my back. I shut my eyes and prayed that sleep would take me.

And it did.

I woke up in the early hours of the morning to find myself wrapped around Danica's back. The comfort and warmth of our position made me want to savor it longer and I dozed off.

When I roused next, signs of Danica were nowhere to be found. Well, not in my bedroom anyway.

I got up and went in search of the coffee I could smell.

My head hurt from the drink, but it seemed like it would have hurt more had I not had an animalistic frolic last night to burn off most of the alcohol in my system.

When I got to the kitchen, a pot of coffee was brewed fresh and a note lay on the counter beside the percolator.

Jacob,

I'm sorry I couldn't be here when you woke.
I had to get back home. Last night was... Well,
you were fantastic.

Nica

I smiled at the note, but I couldn't deny the sinking feeling in the pit of my stomach that her absence caused.

Questions began to run amok in my head. What did she want from me now that I had fucked her seven ways to Sunday? Was it a one-time thing? God knows that leaving it at that would be the smart thing to do. Did she want more? Did I want more?

I groaned. An intense run would be useful, but with the pounding in my skull, there would be none of that for me today. I settled on a day filled with a whole lot of sulking, nursing my self-induced pain, and a whole lot of nothing.

Pouring myself a cup of coffee, I headed straight for the couch, plopped myself down on it, and surfed the channels for something to watch. I settled on an old black and white western that I'd watched one too many times.

A few hours later, I heard the front door open and close,

startling me out of a doze. Not many people helped themselves to entering my house, and I knew just who it was when I saw two feet come to a stop beside me.

I rolled onto my back and Paxton hovered above me.

He shook his head, sporting a smirk and louder than necessary, he said, "Looks like someone had one hell of a night!"

"Tone it down, will you?" I sat myself up and realized I was still in my boxers when the couch throw fell to the floor.

"Jesus, put some clothes on!"

"Just give me a minute, all right?"

"Coffee?"

"It's a few hours old, but help yourself to brewing another pot." I made my way toward the stairs.

It wasn't until I slid my t-shirt over my head that I realized that Danica's letter still rested beside the percolator. What were the chances that Paxton would miss it?

None. I sighed.

As I walked downstairs, I prepared myself for a scolding or some kind of wisecrack.

"What's this?" I heard as my feet hit the landing at the bottom of the staircase.

A mistake.

I ran a hand down my face as Pax held the note in his hand, waving it like a flag as he took a sip from what appeared to be a fresh cup of steaming coffee.

"Nothing," I mumbled and headed to fetch myself another cuppa.

"*Nothing?* Really, Jake?" he asked with incredulity. "Sure looks like someone indulged in another someone last night and she spent the night. I thought you had a rule against that, no?"

"Pax, just leave it, all right?" I was far from thankful of his reminder that the one person I allowed to spend the night had disappeared on me the first chance she got. She'd left me again.

"Alissa told me that you two had a run-in at Rex's last night, but she didn't mention that—"

I cut him off. "It's not like that."

"Then what's it like? Danica left the girls before they were willing to call it quits, saying that she had to get home. This," he waved the page for emphasis, "tells me she never got there."

I blew a long drawn-out puff of air, annoyed that my best friend was putting the blame on me. "I didn't make her do anything if that's what you're getting at. She did it all on her own."

"Then explain to me why my best friend, who's been hung up on this woman since we were kids, who's told me time and again that nothing would ever happen if she popped into his life…" His voice trailed off. "Just tell me why you'd do this to yourself? I mean, I love Danica as a sister, but come on! She wrecked you the first time around. Aren't you a little terrified that she'll destroy you this time?"

"Because it was only once!" My words jarred the pounding in my head. "It was just sex. Fuck, man, I didn't proposition her. I left the bar and came home to end up drinking until I passed out. She showed up here with plans of her own."

"Whoa! What?"

I dropped my ass in a chair at the kitchen dinette. Paxton took a seat across from me and I started from the beginning.

I mentioned how I felt embarrassed about her finding out about my exploits via a hostile Nicole. It seemed like my abundance of experience had appealed to her so much that in her drunken haze, she had sought me out.

"What do I do?" I asked, as I sat leaning forward, my elbows on the tabletop with my face resting in my hands.

"What do you want?" Paxton asked.

"I don't know." What *did* I want? That was the million dollar question, wasn't it?

Danica, I heard myself thinking. So much for thinking that one night of passion would help erase the urge to be wrapped around her and buried into the heat of that luscious body of hers.

"Dude, you're really fucked," Paxton said.

"I know, man, I know."

He sighed. "Here's what I think."

"Do I really want to hear it?"

"Probably not, but you're going to hear it anyway."

Here goes.

When all was said and done, Paxton had stuck around for some football and overdue guy-time.

I wasn't pleased with my best friend's suggestion from earlier, and thus his words hadn't done much for my already grumpy mood, but I couldn't disagree with him. Despite my urge to have her again, I knew it wasn't healthy, and until I knew where the both of us stood, I couldn't allow anything physical between us to happen again.

After my mentioning it, Paxton had thought that the coffee date was a good idea. Talking was a definite must, but he also stressed that all he wanted was to see me happy again, no matter what it took.

Being stubborn, I argued that I was happy. The man shook his head and told me that I had tricked myself into thinking that I was. As always, Pax was better than looking in the mirror to see things for what they were.

After last night, I knew for a fact that I wanted Danica in my life, no matter what. She was a beautiful person, inside and out. Selfless, loving, and passionate about everything she undertook, of every relationship she garnered, which is why I had been so hurt fifteen years ago.

It hadn't been like her to just up and leave, or to make a

decision that involved us without running it by me. Before we dated, we were the best of friends. Even then, she felt the need to consult with me and Paxton prior to making her mind up about anything.

I needed to find out. I needed to know what happened all those years ago. And when I knew, then I could decide what my next move would be.

I got to bed early, knowing that I had one hell of a week ahead of me. Soul searching with regards to Danica had led to me forgetting about what I intended to do about my job.

One thing was for sure, though; starting tomorrow, things would change. It was time that I grabbed on to my life and shaped it into something I was happier with. I never realized how out of control things had gotten, and my love life was one of a few things affected.

I may have been living the dream, one I had come up with after Danica's desertion, but that dream had evolved into a nightmare and it was high-time for me to act and put a stop to it.

Maybe it's time for me to go off on my own.

Darkness came, and so did my erotic visions of a certain beauty who had wreaked havoc on all of my senses less than twenty-four hours before.

CHAPTER 17

I had a day of hell to contend with.

First up was my lunch meeting with Stan. His forgiveness was instantaneous as he sunk his teeth in the foie gras he ordered for himself. I indulged in a coq au vin, which I'd heard was one of their specialities. The reviews were right, it was delicious.

"As much as this has been pleasant," Stan began, "I wanted to talk to you about my contract with Blake, Davenport, Smith & Michaels."

"What of it? You know you're not going to get a better price than with us, Stan."

"It's not that." He took a sip of water. "After hearing of your firm's involvement with The Spalding Corporation, I'm not sure that my company and your firm are a good fit."

My fork stopped mid-way to my mouth. "What are you saying?"

"I've made my successes based on honesty and hard work." He wiped at his mouth with his napkin, then set it down. "It's nothing against you, Jake, but I've started to look for new representation."

Just like that, I was losing my biggest client.

It was in that moment that I made a life-altering decision. It may have been a tad impulsive, but something niggled at me that this was the time for me to take my shot.

"Stan, hear me out." And I went on and presented my case as if I was in front of the toughest judge in the county.

I spent the last three quarters of an hour in Blake's office by the time Robert realized that he couldn't change my mind.

I was leaving, opening my own practice.

"Jake, you know that with Shouldice & Sons closing up shop last month that their clients are shopping. Seeing as their clientele was referred to us, it would be a good time for you to redeem yourself," Robert said.

"Are you trying to sell me on the partnership again, Bob?" I asked.

"You know we can't give you that right now what with the Spalding fiasco," Bob said. "But once everything blows over, it's an idea worth entertaining again, provided you get your head back in the game."

I wanted to tell the man to take his partnership and shove it up his ass. He could offer it to some other poor sucker without a soul. I couldn't be bought. Maybe five years ago, but not now.

"I'm sorry Bob, but I'm not changing my mind." I presented the man with my hand. "It's been a pleasure, Bob... Blake. I appreciate you guys making this place feel like home for as long as you did, but I know I'm making the right move."

"If you're ever looking for–"

I laughed. "I'm a lawyer, Blake. I think I can handle things."

"Best of luck to you," he said.

I smiled, nodded my head, turned, and took my final walk to my office.

I grabbed my box of belongings and empty briefcase. I had packed up as soon as I'd arrived this morning.

I took one last look around and walked away, pausing at

Sally's desk to give her a hug and a kiss on the cheek with promises to stay in touch.

"If you ever need anything, Mr. Landen, give me a call." She gave me a motherly squeeze.

"Will do, and the same goes for you." I smiled. "And I think it's time you called me Jake. Mr. Landen is my father, and I'm too young to feel so damn old."

She giggled and I saw her eyes gloss over with unshed tears. "All right, Jake. You take care of yourself, you hear?"

I nodded. "Yes, ma'am."

I received a few well wishes and pats on the back with promises to get together for beers from former colleagues on my way to the elevator. After stopping in to wave to Brent, who was on the phone at the time, I left the dream I had for so long in my life's rearview mirror and looked on toward my future.

I thought that I would feel bereft, remorseful and hesitant with my decision, but I couldn't use any of those sentiments to describe the emotions I felt as I drove away. I was excited, scared, and most of all, empowered with what I had accomplished.

No one saw my latest decision coming, and it felt good because I knew that my mind hadn't been influenced by anyone else but me. I was taking a huge risk, but with Stan as my only client, I knew that it would be enough for now. His business at BDS&M could have kept me in my current lifestyle alone. Even with the massive fee reductions we discussed toward the end of our lunch meeting today, I would have no problem maintaining the same livelihood. And if money ever got tight, my caseload was so light that I wouldn't have a problem handling a few additional clients.

First thing was first, however, I had documents to draft up and finalize tonight for Stan's approval and signature come tomorrow morning.

When I got home, someone waited for me on the front step.

I got out of the car, took my box of belongings, set my briefcase on top of it and proceeded to the door.

"Please tell me that you haven't gone and driven your mother's car and it's in a ditch somewhere." I looked around for any trace of Danica's vehicle.

Jordan snorted, his foul mood apparent. And still, I felt like nothing could bring me down. "Funny." The word came out dry. "What's up with the box? Did you get fired? I can't blame them you know. With the way you threw that case, you would have been gone sooner if it were me."

A grin spread across my face. "I quit, but thanks for your professional opinion."

"An unemployed lawyer and that's a good thing?"

"For me it is." I unlocked the front door. "And I'm not unemployed. I'm just a little dry on clients at the moment, but the one I have is more than enough to survive on." I dropped my box and briefcase on the floor inside the door and came back out to sit on the step beside him. "So, why are you here? Should I be worried about the car?"

"Shut up about the damn car already!"

"Hey kid, I hope you don't talk to your mom like that?"

He smirked. "Nope, just you." Talk about mood swings.

I gave him a playful punch to the shoulder. "What's up?"

How was I supposed to know that coaxing something out of a hormonal teenage boy over pizza was going to land me in a two-hour conversation about girls, school, sports, girls again, which led us to a girls and sports combination? Was I ever that bad at his age?

Prior to that, Jordan confessed that he'd gotten into a spat with Danica and ran off. Still grounded for the stunt he pulled with her car a week ago, he hadn't cared for the re-percussions. I remembered similar moments in my teenage years. Times where I felt misunderstood by my parents.

"I just wanted someone to talk to. She didn't understand." He looked away. "I would have talked to Granddad, but he left for Austin this morning. The only person that came to mind was you, so I came here."

I didn't know if I should feel honored or offended for being his last resort. I chose honored. "So what's the deal?"

"There's this girl…"

I tilted my head back and laughed. "This is all over a girl? You're fifteen!"

"Almost sixteen!"

"Fine, you're almost sixteen. Still too young if you ask me." I knew that to be bullshit considering I had been his age when I knew, without a doubt, that I wanted his mother as more than a friend.

"Okay, Dad!" He rolled his eyes but that was more than enough to shock me into muteness.

Seconds trickled by as I studied the boy that was a spitting image of his mother. He had her cheek dimple, her black hair, but his eyes, they were a clear emerald green.

I heard the snap of fingers in front of my face and jumped back. "What the fuck man?"

He laughed. "Do you always talk like that around kids?"

"It's nothing you haven't heard at your age, so what's it matter?"

He shrugged his shoulders. "I don't know."

"What about this girl? Why does your mom have her panties in a twist about your interest in her?"

"Dude, don't talk about my mom's panties!" He screwed up his face in disgust.

I grinned, shaking my head. "I'll ask again. *What about this girl?*"

"It's not so much the girl, but what I said after Mom said I couldn't go to her birthday party on Friday."

"And that was?"

"That if my dad was around, that he would let me go." He bit his bottom lip. "But I never meant any of it. I was just mad. Everyone's going to be there and…" He looked at me with such worry and regret, and then bowed his head.

His father isn't around? Something constricted around my heart for both the boy in front of me and his mother.

"Have you ever met your father?"

"No."

"Has your mom ever talked about him?"

"Nope."

Before I could lead the conversation further, I heard the screeching of tires and I knew someone was in my driveway. Seconds later, the slamming of a car door followed, and Jordan's gaze filled with panic over the pizza box.

Danica. "I don't think I can do anything for you this time, kid."

Instead of the doorbell, I heard fists banging on my door and words that weren't audible, thanks to the barrier.

"Stay here and let me talk her down a bit."

"What makes you think you can?" he asked. "I mean, you just said that you can't do anything for me."

"I don't think she knows that you're here. If I don't get her to calm down, this'll all be over before it starts. Think grounded for a month, forget your current weeks' worth. From what I saw last week, she's just like her father."

"How do you know all this?"

"Long story. I'll tell you some time. Right now, let me deal with her." I pointed over my shoulder with my thumb, toward the front door.

⚬ **CHAPTER 18** ⚬

I opened the door and saw a frantic Danica standing there.

"Is he here?" she asked, sniffling. "Is Jordan here? I thought he had gone to his room and when I went to check, he was gone. I don't know what to do. I–"

Crap! What do I say? If I said *yes*, then she'd fly off the handle and march his ass back home and give me shit in the process for hiding him out and not bothering to turn his ass around or bring him home. If I said *no*, then I'd be lying and I don't lie.

In a soft tone, I chose to bite the bullet. "Yes."

She didn't react the way I thought she would, which had me worried. I expected a slap, a few hits, something painful, or maybe yelling. Instead, she collapsed to the concrete step before I had a chance to get to her.

I bent over, picked her up off the ground, and brought her to the living room where I sat her on my lap on the couch, holding her the way I used to when, very much like her and her son, she had had an argument with her father.

"Shh." I tried to soothe her.

Most of her erratic mumblings were indiscernible through her sobs, but I managed to make out bits about Jordan's awful words and something about her calling him an ungrateful bastard son before she broke down again.

I turned to see us being watched by Jordan and I waved him over, knowing that it wasn't my place to make things right.

"Mom?" I felt out of place, but I couldn't seem to extricate myself from the situation, seeing as Danica held onto me with a death grip. "I'm sorry I ran off. I didn't mean what I said. Mom?" She wasn't responding. "Mommy?" His softened voice seemed to have done the trick.

Danica pulled away enough for Jordan to kneel in front of her. She cupped his face in her hands and aside from using my lap as a seat, it was as if I didn't exist.

"Baby, I'm sorry too. I didn't mean it. I was just mad and hurt." She pulled him toward her and they hugged, me leaning my body away so I didn't get nailed by stray arms. She breathed a loud sigh. "Thank God you're okay." Her tears had run dry. "I know that this move is hard on you, baby, but–"

"Mom?" She pulled back so she could see his face. "Can you get off of Jake, it's kind of weird."

She giggled. And just like always, my heart sped up at the sweet sound. Her eyes, now apologetic, I nodded. "I'll give you two a minute." When she got off of me, I couldn't get my ass out of the room fast enough.

I headed for the kitchen and grabbed a beer from the fridge. Popping the cap, I took a nice, long pull from it. The last fifteen minutes had been filled with so much raw emotion that I didn't know what to think. My mind was reeling. I didn't get how someone could have been with her and then left. With a son no less! What the hell had happened to her after she left? Whatever it was, it wasn't all that long after I found myself alone.

I was saddened by her situation, and enraged against the good-for-nothing idiot who had left her to fend for herself. From what I'd seen since her return, Danica was a great mother. And Jordan, he was pretty damn fantastic too. The kid kept me on my toes, and he had a rather amazing ability to read people. That father of his had no clue what he was missing out on.

Looking out into the backyard through my patio door, I didn't notice Danica's approach.

"Thank you," she said. "I– He told me that you two talked. I appreciate you being there for him."

I shrugged my shoulders like it was no big deal. "It's fine."

"It's not." I turned to face her, brows furrowed. "He should be able to come to me with anything. Instead, when he did, I snapped and he ran." She sighed and rubbed her temples. "Why am I telling you any of this?" She turned away from me, but didn't make a move to leave. "After fifteen years, you'd think it would get easier."

I wasn't quite sure what she meant by that, but I figured she was speaking about childrearing.

"Don't worry about it," I said, but I was once again distracted by the kid's age. *Fifteen.* Shaking those thoughts from my mind, I continued, "From where I'm standing, you're doing a great job."

She turned to face me again and offered a solemn smile. "I'd like to think that it would be easier if he had a father." Her face scrunched up in disgust, but I also saw resentment—and was that guilt? "I've already tried that route and failed with Bruce. It's just me and him. I guess that's what it's all cracked up to be, huh?"

"I guess." I didn't really agree with her. "Can I ask you something?" She nodded her response. "Who's the father? He told me that he'd never met him, that he doesn't know anything about him. I get the sense that–"

"I-I…" she stuttered.

She's hiding something.

Before she could answer or I could push, Jordan walked into the room. "Mom?"

A look of relief washed over her face. "Yes?"

"Can we go home now?"

"Sure." She turned toward me and shrugged her shoulders. "I guess it'll have to wait for another time." She walked up to me, palmed my face with both hands. Lifting onto the tips of her toes, she kissed my cheek, remaining close for a moment before pulling away. Whispering, she said, "Again, thank you."

Jordan was smirking at me as if he knew a secret I didn't. "Any time." I eyed the kid. "And you, try and stay out of trouble with your mother for more than a week at a time. But if you need me, you know where I am."

"Yeah, unemployed."

"I have a client."

"You got fired?" Danica asked.

"I quit, there's a difference."

"So you're pulling a *Jerry McGuire* and starting your own practice?" She smiled and I returned it with one of my own.

She remembered. It felt like ages ago since we'd talked about that.

"Show me the money," I quoted the infamous line from the movie. We both laughed.

"Dorks." Danica and I turned to face Jordan, who stood all too pleased with himself.

"Mind your manners, mister!" she said.

I laughed and her gaze came back to freeze on mine. Silence ensued.

"Mom, if you want to stay, I can walk home you know."

"I'm coming, I'm coming!" I smiled at the two of them. "I better go." She looked to her son. "We need to have a little talk, and then I'm sure someone has homework to do."

The guilty look spread over his face. "Busted!" I gave him a soft punch to his shoulder.

Arms crossed over his chest, he said, "I could bring you

up on charges for child abuse, you know." Laughter danced in his eyes.

"You and what lawyer?" I wrapped my arm around his neck and pulled him along toward the front door.

"I don't know, how about the one that whooped your ass last week?" he suggested. "Oh, wait, that won't work. You threw the case, remember?"

Danica turned to me. "What?"

"Yeah, Mom, he did. I told you he did, remember?"

"That's enough, kid," I warned.

"No," Danica said. "Did you?"

I shrugged my shoulders. It was easier to look at her son than her. "Perhaps." Jordan stood behind his mother, his arms crossed at his chest, his shoulders bouncing with silent laughter.

"Come on, Mom." He opened the door and pushed her outside.

As Danica walked to the car, I grabbed Jordan's arm to stop him and whispered, "You shouldn't have told her."

"I like watching you squirm, hot shot." He grinned. "Catch you later?"

"Drop in whenever, kid."

"Cool."

CHAPTER 19

I was up until two in the morning, drafting up papers and contracts to include all the clauses that Stan and I had discussed over our lunch.

Intent on revising my document with a fresh perspective, I woke at six o'clock. Pleased with everything, I rushed around to get ready only to realize I had a single thing to do today: get my contract signed. For the first time in years, I came to a conclusion. I was looking forward to a day's work.

Dressed in my usual shirt, suit, and tie, and convinced that everything would be according to Stan's liking, I printed off two copies of the contracts, stowed them in my briefcase, and made my way out the door.

I walked through Standhope Incorporated's glass doors and smiled at the receptionist. "I'm here to meet with Stan."

"Is he expecting you?"

"He is. I'm Jake Landen."

"Please have a seat and I'll let him know you've arrived."

Standhope Incorporated was one of the largest construction firms in the area. Founded on donations and government grants alone, they were well-known and respected in the community for building and setting up low-income family housing.

Two years ago, Stan's wife, Hope, a former teacher, started an education fund that drew in more philanthropic benefactors and yielded even more money for their linked causes. Suffice to say that Jacksonville's shady neighborhoods were taking shape, improvements being made and its residents were more than happy to see them happen.

The education program survived on monies generated by an annual ball which Hope organized, and let me assure you, those tickets didn't come cheap. The leftover funds from the ball, as well as those that trickled in throughout the year, paid for Standhope's employee salaries as well as the building, rehabbing, and restoring of the buildings they owned.

The domicile component to the foundation had been established over a decade ago. When Stan discovered he couldn't run both Standhope and his construction company, he sold half of his business, hired a President for it, and stayed on with the foundation, bringing along some of his most trusted contractors with him.

"These people need the help more than me having to build some millionaire a mansion or some new office building," he'd once told me.

I was further humbled the day I found out that beyond the salaries, his functioning office costs, as well as the building his office was in, had come from his pocket.

No wonder the man had issues with my former employer's stand on ethics.

"Jake!" Stan's voice reverberated against the lobby walls.

I stood up to greet the man who seemed to have an added bounce to his step this morning. "Good to see you, Stan." I shook his hand.

The signing went off without a hitch. Pleased with the reduced fees, the various clauses we had discussed, as well as the additional allocations, he put his pen down and shook my hand.

"In a year's time, you'll be able to build that new learning center in that neighborhood you just took on," I said. Yes, the amount that he had paid my former bosses had been that substantial.

"I like your way of thinking, Jake, and I'm sure Hope will love you all the more for it." He smiled. "Listen, if you're interested, I know of a few organizations that may be able to benefit from your help. I'm not sure if you're willing to do pro-bono, but I know Anna is in dire need of someone."

"Pro-bono is something that's held an appeal to me. Lord knows litigation fees aren't slight. But I need to get my legs back under me first, Stan." Something about the way Stan mentioned Anna made me say, "I have to ask, what makes you mention Anna out of everyone else?"

Stan began to relay Anna's story.

Proof was in the pudding, as they say. I felt validated and thus satisfied that I had branched off on my own. Money wasn't an issue, and it appeared that I might be gaining clientele soon enough.

Parking my car, I got out and stared at the five-thousand square foot monstrosity that stood before me and shook my head. I had no business buying something so large. Hell, I had no family, I was single. Most of the rooms lay empty and if not, they seldom saw a human presence.

I bought the place for my love of architecture, but also because I was compensating for the lack of things I had while growing up. We weren't poor, we just tipped the scales from middle to lower class. It's why I needed a scholarship to go off to college and make it through law school.

The day I signed that letter of offer with Blake, Davenport, Smith & Michaels, I jumped at the bigger and finer things in life. I had made it in this crazy game of life, and the first thing I did after buying a car was pay off my parents' mortgage and put a sizeable down payment on my first home.

I headed toward my front door, listening to a message from Brent, asking me how my first day of unemployment had gone. I laughed. It seems he hadn't received the memo about Standhope leaving BDS&M and me bagging their business.

Brent and I have been friends since college, being part of the same graduating class. It was a surprise when he walked through the firm's doors, a few months after I had been hired.

Since then, Brent and I made a point to hang out from time to time. Whenever it was, you could tell that his heart wasn't in it much, but to please Beth, his ailing wife, he gave in. She would crack jokes that he was driving her nuts by hovering over her when he wasn't at work. He didn't think it was funny, all too aware of his limited time with his wife.

It was a sad story and one I cared not to ever witness first hand. To watch as his vibrant, energetic and beautiful woman sped her way through declining health, as cancer ate away at her, was heartbreaking. Brent loved her with all of his being.

I dreaded the day the news came of her imminent death, where friends and family would have to jump in and help him pick up the pieces. Brent and Beth's situation was a constant reminder of how short life can be.

CHAPTER 20

The rest of the week flew by, and my phone rang a few times with potential clients. Stan sure worked fast at getting the word out. Of the handful of potential clients, I had turned most of them away, with the exception of Anna.

Thanks to Stan, I already knew most of her story, and upon our first meeting, I had decided that I was going to help her out. With the hand of misfortune life had dealt to the woman, it was time for her luck to turn around.

At first glance, she appeared as if she came from a humble background, what with the over-worn pant-suit, the purse with the broken strap, and her exhausted expression. That is, until she opened her mouth. From that action, it was clear that she was well-educated, proper, and proud. The haggard appearance was due to being overworked with refusal to fail. It was familiar. I had seen it on my parents' faces a time or two, the closer I got to graduating and heading off to college, prior to my being granted my scholarship.

Much like my admiration for Stan, Anna awed me with the passion she demonstrated and the emotion her words held as she told me about the small charity for orphaned and homeless children she was trying to revive. She had under a year to turn things around, or it would cease to exist.

I could tell that she held little faith in litigators. I couldn't blame her. Her former legal counsel had swindled most of the money she had in the foundation's account and she was now using her personal funds to make things happen, funds that were dwindling at a rapid pace.

As I listened to her story, a new plan of action with regards to helping Anna was taking shape. There was more I could do for her than handling the legal aspect of her business. With her approval, I told her that I'd run with my idea and touch base as soon as I had an answer for her. Her drawn face brightened and all evidence of exhaustion and worry dissipated prior to her departure.

With Anna gone and a warm feeling building inside, I picked up the phone and called Withers International's local offices. A woman sounding more like a high school student answered.

"I'm looking for Ms. Danica Withers, please."

"May I let her know who's calling?" I gave her my name. "Please hold." I sat in my office chair, waiting with impatience before the young woman came back. "Mr. Landen?"

"Yes?"

"Sorry for the wait. Ms. Withers said that she could really use that coffee right now."

I laughed. "Tell her that I'll be there in half an hour."

As I hung up, my mind began to wander. I was so excited to help Anna that I forgot what meeting with Danica could entail aside from my pitch for help. Would she want to talk more than business? My stomach churned with anxiety.

Gathering my wits, I made the decision to keep this visit short and sweet. There'd be other times to rehash the past and discuss what happened between us a week ago, including Monday's unfinished conversation about Jordan's father.

Since when had life grown so complicated?

Heading for my car, I got in and sped off towards the center of town.

CHAPTER 21

I walked through Withers International's doors and stopped at the reception desk. "Mr. Landen, here to meet with Ms. Withers."

She got up. "Ms. Withers has instructed me to bring you to her office. You can wait there." She led me to a rather large suite with mahogany furniture and finishes. "She's just finishing up with a client and will be right with you. Can I get you anything while you wait?"

"That won't be necessary, thank you."

She exited the room and shut the door behind her.

I took my time looking around. On the massive desk that dominated the room, there were a few photos of her and her father, an older one of her parents, and one of her and Jordan.

I stopped to pick up the frame that contained mother and son, and smiled at the two silly faces looking back. It looked like a recent photograph. I leaned on the edge of her desk, admiring the pose. They looked happy, but I could tell that there was something missing in Danica's eyes. To anyone, they wouldn't have seen it. To someone who knew her, she looked tired—haunted—like the spark that used to be there had gone out and had never returned.

"It's my favorite of the two of us." I jumped at the sound

of her voice, looked up and handed the frame into her out-stretched hand. Smiling down at it, she said, "I replaced the old one with this just this morning. It was taken the day we won against you in court."

I nodded in understanding.

She set the frame down and I caught the spicy-sweet scent of her perfume. She smelled good enough to eat.

And just like that, scenes from my dreams began to re-play in my mind, combining with the fresh memory of the feel of her body against mine from our most recent tryst.

If you thought that my erotic dreams had faded after that night, you're wrong. If anything, they had grown more vivid and intense. With more time on my hands this week, I was now taking lengthier runs and my hot water bill was going to be next to nothing.

Caught up in my head, I didn't realize how close she was until I felt the flat of her hands on my chest. I blinked and found myself looking down into her bright blue eyes.

"It's good to see you again, Jacob." She stretched up and kissed my cheek. As good as it felt to have her close enough to hold her, I needed to back away before my main reason for being there turned into a personal campaign.

I cleared my now parched throat. "It's good to see you too." I grabbed her hands, removed them from my chest, and let them drop to her sides before moving from between her and her desk.

She turned to face me and leaned back on the edge of the intimidating piece of furniture. Her arms were crossed at her chest and she looked as if she waited for me to say some-thing.

"I'm assuming that this isn't a social visit, so let's deal with business before we go for coffee, shall we?" Her busi-nesslike tone sent sparks of lust straight to my groin. I've always loved a woman in charge and last weekend, she had more than delivered on that.

"Right."

Things couldn't have gone better. Jumping at the chance to run PR for an organization that might not live to see the next year, but that she believed in, Danica was determined to look after Anna's needs herself. Despite my mention of reduced fees, Danica argued that the services would be free because it was time for WI to get with the times and broaden their philanthropic commitments and outreach.

If anyone could turn things around for Anna, I knew Danica could. The fact that Anna wouldn't have to spend a dime on the services was a plus.

In the seat across from mine, excitement gleamed in her eyes. "Let me work out a plan to present to her. I know that we can turn this thing around and recoup the money she's lost." She perked up in her seat and clapped her hands together. "I think we should celebrate!"

I leaned back in my seat and smiled at her enthusiasm. "Remind me to hire you if I ever run for Congress."

"You?" She leaned forward and slapped my thigh playfully. "You'd be the poster boy for indiscretions."

"That was mean." I feigned insult. Despite her joking manner, her words stung.

"I'm sorry." Her hand came to rest on my knee and never left. I looked down at it, feeling the heat which spread to my groin. This situation had trouble written all over it.

Before anything could happen, I got up and headed to her office door. I turned to look at her and she seemed disappointed, not to mention, caught up in her own thoughts. "You coming?" Her head snapped up to look at me. "I thought you said you wanted to celebrate?"

She sighed. "About that. Uh, can I take a rain-check?"

She was flaking on me. For a moment, I was relieved because it meant that I wasn't singled out in feeling the tension between us, but I was also annoyed that she was trying to back out.

Well, I wasn't having any of it.

I stalked up to her and stopped when we stood toe-to-toe.

"Jacob…"

"It's just a drink, sweetheart." I grinned. "We'll save coffee for another time."

"All right."

CHAPTER 22

Opting for Fairfax, we found a table secluded from the coming-and-going of patrons. It wasn't busy as of yet, seeing as it was mid-afternoon, but that would all change the moment work let out for the masses.

"I love it here." Danica sighed and looked around. "I was happy to hear that Ben went through with opening this place despite everything he's been through." I watched the emotions cross her face. I knew that Ben and Danica knew each other well, what with her brother, Mike, and him being close friends and all.

A year older than the both of us, Ben and I had gotten closer over the years. I wouldn't go as far as to say that we were the best of friends, but we were more than mere acquaintances and hung out on a regular basis when he managed to get away from Fairfax.

Ben lost his wife and newborn daughter two years ago, in a fatal car collision. I never heard the specific details about the night, only that he'd been driving while Candace was unbuckled, tending to their daughter—then everything changed for him.

According to various newspapers and word of mouth, Ben's wife was thrown from the windshield the instant the vehicle made impact with a deep culvert after hitting a patch of black ice. She was impaled by a tree limb.

Their daughter later died in hospital from being shaken while the vehicle flipped over on its descent. The newborn's cranium had suffered a partial detachment from her spine. They never knew until they moved her. Even with securing her beforehand, everything went to hell.

"Jacob?" I felt her hand on mine.

"Huh?" I shook the morbid thoughts out of my mind and looked at Danica sitting across the table from me. "I'm sorry, did you say something?"

"Is everything okay?"

"Yeah, just thinking." I forced a smile. "I love it here too. I try and stop in when it's slow so Ben can take a break. I don't think the man stops much except for when it's time to close up."

"You're right." I jumped as Ben came to stand at our table. "What can I get you two?"

"I'll have a glass of white wine." She looked from Ben to me. "I'll be back. The little girls' room is calling."

Ben sat down and I felt his eyes on me as I watched her walk away. "I didn't expect to see you two out together."

I might have been too quick to say, "There's nothing going on."

"Uh-huh." He wore a knowing grin. "You know you two were perfect together, right?"

My brow arched. "Why do you say that? If we were, she wouldn't have left. You know, it's not that she left really, it's the way she did. I could have dealt with phone calls and letters. It wouldn't have gone down the way it did."

"Did you ever stop to think that there were reasons why she never kept in touch?" His expression had gone serious, almost haunted. He knew something. "Listen, all I can say is what Mike's told me over the years because we're like brothers. Danica's like a sister to me. With that said, it's her story to tell, so I'm not going to go into details with you. Just know that she didn't want to leave and she did want to keep in touch. She just couldn't." Ben got up and stood in front of me. My gaze was stuck to the table. "Mull that over before you decide anything. Whiskey, straight?"

"Yeah. You better bring two and a Bud Light chaser."

"You got it."

I wasn't quite sure what to do with the information Ben had given me.

I caught sight of Danica walking toward me and smiled. As she arrived, so did Ben with our drinks.

"Here you go, folks. Would you like to see a menu?"

"That wouldn't be a bad idea." Danica looked my way before shrugging her shoulders and I nodded. "I'm not in the mood to cook tonight."

"Two menus, coming right up."

What with the way that she took a few large gulps of her wine before setting it down, I would have said that Danica was nervous.

I laughed. "Pace yourself, honey. I'm sure Ben's got more back there for you."

She smirked. "We are celebrating aren't we?"

"But there's no need to get drunk because of it." I downed the first of my whiskeys, ignoring my own words.

She harrumphed. "Says the man who's drinking straight liquor." I laughed. "So when are you planning on letting Anna know?"

"Tomorrow."

"Can I be there? I'd like to meet her."

"I was planning on calling her." Quick to notice her look of disappointment, I added, "But we could go see her instead." The smile that beamed told me that I had said the right thing.

"Hey, what are you doing for dinner tonight?" she asked.

My chuckle lacked the humor it needed. "Same thing I do every night, eat alone."

"Not tonight, you're not. We'll order our food, I'll get something for Jordan, and then we can head over to mine if you're up for it."

I hesitated. "I don't know." Was it a good idea? Jordan is going to be there, it's not like you'll be alone—and you kind of miss her kid.

"Come on." Her eyes were hopeful. "Jordan's been asking about you all week. He wants to know how we know each other."

My heart thumped out of my chest. "What did you tell him?"

"That we attended school together as kids." Then she smiled that mischievous smile of hers. "That you were the high school sweetheart that got away." As soon as she said this, she looked away with a blush.

"You didn't!" I laughed.

"I did." Her blush deepened and she kept on talking. "I didn't know what to say! I mean, one minute he's bragging on and on about how cool you are and how he doesn't feel like a kid around you, and the next, I'm spilling my guts about our past and then–" Her words froze and her features darkened.

"What is it?" I made a grab for her hand.

"Nothing." She shook her head. "It's nothing. It's all in the past and I'm here in the now… with a great friend. And I'm fine."

"Fine?" I wasn't going there with her *friend* comment. Not yet.

She nodded. "Yep, fine."

"Seems to me that you're doing more than fine, Nica." She blinked and slid her hand from mine. "You're running a multi-billion dollar company with your brother and father. You're a single mother who's raised a rather too-smart-for-his-own-good son. You're beautiful and successful. And despite the years and whatever's happened between then and now, you're still the same sweet, giving person that you've always been." *Where'd that come from?* My words were honest, but why had I felt so compelled to let her know what I saw, what I thought? *You know you've never been able to stand to see her looking down or doubting herself.*

She gave me a shy smile. "That's sweet of you."

CHAPTER 23

We received our food and headed out. I followed her car over to her place. On the drive over, I found myself overwhelmed with nerves about the evening ahead.

I tried to convince myself that it was just dinner with friends, as she'd said earlier, but the memories from last weekend kept replaying in my mind. Needless to say, I stuffed those erotic images in the recesses of my mind and trekked on. I could be her friend, right?

I stood behind her as she let us in. She called out to Jordan.

"Living room!" he said.

My feet were glued to the entrance floor as she headed into what I figured was the aforementioned room's direction.

When she realized I hadn't followed, she turned around and laughed. "What are you waiting for?" I felt my face heat up, removed my shoes and walked toward her.

"Hey, Mom." Jordan gave me a puzzled look. "Hot shot, what are you doing here?"

"I invited him over for dinner." She lifted the bags she still carried. "I picked us up some food from Fairfax."

"Oh." Why did he seem bummed out? "I was hoping that—"

"What is it?" she asked.

"Well, Trevor asked if we could hang out at his place to-night." His eyes met mine and went back to his mother. "Can I?"

"That Trevor Callaghan kid?" He nodded. "Are his parents going to be there?" Another nod. "I would have liked to have met them before you stayed over."

"Callaghan, as in Marty and Clara Callaghan?" I asked. Jordan looked at me, hesitated and then nodded. I laughed. "No need, Nica, you know them from school."

Seconds trickled by and Danica's eyes widened. "No way! Marty and Clara got together?" I nodded. "I always knew they'd be perfect!" She was cute, sounding all school-girl-ish.

"Mom!" Jordan called her attention back to the present. "So, can I?"

"Yes," she said. "As long as it's okay with Trevor's parents."

"Thanks, Mom."

"Give them a call and make sure to let me know what time I need to drop you off for."

"No need. Trevor said he wanted to pick up a couple of games and some movies. I'll get him to pick me up."

I watched as Danica pondered this and then nodded. The kid sure knew how to play the game. I could see why Danica worried about him.

Throughout dinner, I was subjected to what I would call the Jordan Inquisition. He asked about how high school had been for me, what sports I played, what subjects I detested most, the girls I dated, *and* Danica, all in that particular order. Suffice to say that the conversation was easy enough until we arrived at the topic of his mother and me.

"Mom said that you were the one that got away?"

"More like the other way around, don't you agree, Nica?" I looked at her as I mumbled over a mouthful of food.

I was uncomfortable talking about our past. We were about to rehash pain from our youth with her son in the room. I would have preferred to discuss things with her alone first, worried that her observant son would became aware of how deep my feelings for his mother once ran.

"Why do you call her that?" he asked.

"What, you mean, *Nica*?" He nodded and my eyes met his mother's. She gave me a sad smile. "It's a nickname I gave her a long time ago."

"She doesn't like it," Jordan said.

"Jordan!" Her head snapped to her son.

"What? You don't!"

"You don't?" I asked.

"It's not that, it's that I don't like hearing it from anyone else but…" Her voice dropped along with her eyes.

Jordan's gaze swayed between us. "But I thought… When Bruce–" His words halted when his mother's gaze turned to ice. "Oh! Okay, I get it, now. It's a thing between the two of you."

"Exactly," Danica snapped. "Now can we leave it?"

"How'd you guys get together anyway?" Jordan continued.

"We were friends. For the longest time, it was her, Paxton and me," I said.

"Paxton's the man you met at the mall the other day," Danica added.

Jordan nodded. "So you were all friends, and then what?"

"Why the sudden interest?" If he wasn't going to answer his mother having asked the same question, maybe I'd have better luck.

"Because I want to know more about you. Mom never talks about the people she left here when Granddad took her away."

Took her away? That was an interesting choice of words from a kid his age.

"Jordan, that's enough!" Her words were terse.

"No, Mom! You never talk about that time in your life. I want to know!"

She slammed her hand on the table and stood up. "No! It's too hard to deal with, dammit!" When I looked at her, her gaze was lowered and averted from me.

"Nica, it's…" I said.

She tilted her head toward me but never lifted it enough for our eyes to meet and turned to exit the room. "I'm sorry, Jacob. Just give me a minute, okay?"

It was safe to say that dinner was pretty much over.

"What did I say?" Jordan asked.

"I think there's stuff that your mom doesn't want to talk about, and you're being a jerk right now by prying."

"Excuse me?"

"Well, you like it when I tell you like it is, you've said so yourself, so I am. Here's what you need to learn, kid," I started. "When a woman tells you that she doesn't want to talk about it, it's not code to push for more details. For a perceptive person, I would have thought that you would have figured that one out by now since it's just you and her."

He sighed and lowered his head. "I know something happened back then. Something big." When he looked up at me, I saw a storm of emotions there. None of it looked good. "I thought that if I pushed, that she'd finally tell me." He sighed. "I caught her and Granddad talking a few months ago. They mentioned me a few times so I went to find them in the living room and see what was going on. Their faces were so serious. They looked like they'd been arguing about me." He bit his bottom lip.

"What makes you say that?"

"When I walked into the room, Mom looked like she was about to cry, like just now. Granddad looked like he was about to explode, and they both stopped talking."

"I see." He seemed like he was right on the money, but Danica or her old man would have to be the ones to answer that one.

The doorbell rang, ending our heart-to-heart. Fifteen minutes had passed since her departure and Danica had yet to return to the dining room. I had a feeling that she was avoiding me more than her son.

"That's me." Jordan got up. "It was nice." He shrugged his shoulders.

"Make sure you kiss your mom goodbye before you go."

He laughed. "What are you, my father?"

"Nope, but aside from your grandfather and uncle, I'm all you've got, so suck it up, buttercup. You know I'm right… about your mother I mean. She could use a little love right now, and an apology wouldn't hurt either."

He seemed to think about what I said. "I know." Holding out a closed fist, I did the same, and he bumped it before meeting my eyes. "And for what it's worth, you're right about everything you just said. I'm glad you're around. You're cool. Later, hot shot." He walked off.

Dumbfounded at his admission, I said, "Later, kid."

CHAPTER 24

I waited until I heard the front door shut, signaling that Jordan had left before getting up from the dining room table and gathering our food containers.

Entering the kitchen, I caught sight of a very ponderous looking Danica who hadn't even noticed my presence.

She sat at the round dinette table with a glass of wine and the bottle in front of her. The scene reminded me of last Friday, except my poison of choice had been the aged whiskey that had been gifted to me by a client last Christmas.

"You know you'll pay for that tomorrow, right?" She jumped. "I'm sorry." I set the takeout containers on the island counter-top and leaned my hip on its side.

"I'm the one who's sorry." She sipped her drink. "This is not how I planned for the evening to go."

Curiosity got the better of me. "So how did you plan on spending your evening?" My feet took me to stand beside her. I grabbed the bottle of wine, topped her up and she nodded toward the cabinet so I could help myself to a goblet of my own.

Pouring myself a generous glass, I joined her, where she had yet to reply to my question. I sat down and sized her up. Her gaze was trained on her drink, her fingers rolling it around by the glass' stem. "Now tell me. What did you plan for tonight?"

She snorted. "Aside from not chugging this bottle?" Her chin jutted out toward it. I nodded. "I sure as hell didn't expect my son to push me that far down memory lane."

"It wasn't so bad with us, was it?"

She lifted her gaze to my eyes. "No, it wasn't." She smiled and I smiled back. "I'll always cherish those times. Hey! Do you remember...?"

And that's how one bottle became two, and before I knew it, we were laughing like a couple of hyenas drunk on their last meal.

There was no way that I would be driving home tonight.

It was like the old times, before she left, before we had dated, reliving old memories about the two school jocks and the tutoring cheerleader—our fabulous trio.

By now, we'd moved from the dinette to the living room couch. She had turned the TV on to some action flick but it didn't matter. We talked and drank through the whole thing.

When it ended, I looked at my watch and made to leave.

She grabbed my wrist to stop me. "Stay." I looked down as she remained seated.

"I shouldn't."

What I didn't say was that I wanted to. I hadn't had this much fun in a while. I didn't want the night to end. But like all good things, they had to, didn't they?

"Please?"

Damn. Could she look lonelier? "I can't." My voice lacked conviction.

"You can." She got up and faced me, toe-to-toe. We were close. I could smell the sweetness of the wine we had been drinking on her breath, mingling with her perfume and the subtle scent that was her own.

"I really should go." I lifted my hand and tucked a loose

strand of her hair behind her ear. She didn't argue with me that time despite her obvious look of disappointment.

I moved in to kiss her cheek and paused, soaking the feel of her smooth porcelain skin against my lips. She tilted her head so as to let my day's regrowth scrape against her cheek as I pulled back. When the sides of our faces parted, she leaned up and caught my lips with hers for a quick kiss that lasted much longer than it should have.

Her hands came to my chest while mine held the sides of her face.

Something was happening with me, and I wasn't quite sure what it was yet, or if I'd be capable or willing to stop it.

Where our kisses from last weekend were hard, demanding, and animalistic, this one was deep, slow, and passionate.

After returning her kiss with my own, I leaned my forehead against hers and kept my eyes closed. When they opened, I groaned at the sight of her hooded eyes.

"Stay." I felt the tug at the bottom of my shirt.

"I can't." I looked down to see that she'd unbuttoned the entire thing while we had been kissing. "This can't—"

"We're two adults. We know what we're doing." Her hands were on my pants but I stopped her progress. "What?" She backed a few feet and reached for her blouse buttons. "Don't you want me, Jacob?"

Shit. I swallowed hard. "You have no idea."

"Then take me," she said, walking backward toward the stairwell. She paused at the first tread and shrugged off her blouse.

My hormones were clouding my judgement. I knew that giving in to her wasn't smart. At least, not until I knew what happened all those years ago. I needed to know how she felt back then, where she stood now. But most of all, I needed to know how I felt, what I wanted, because it was clear to me in this moment that I no longer wanted the same things I did last year, last month, or even last week.

I felt her hands on my chest. "Where'd you just go?"

Looking down, she was in nothing but her bra and underwear.

I groaned and my hands reached and pulled her into me hard by her hips. Instead of answering her question, I attacked her mouth with mine, delving deep, and drinking in her taste.

The only one I've ever craved. The only one that ever satisfied me; but also, the only one that would make me regret too.

Backing her up toward the stairwell, I yanked my lips from hers, turned her around to face the stairs and smacked her ass. "Get up there before I change my mind."

— CHAPTER 25 —

Pushing her down onto the bed, I made haste of my clothes, baring myself to her. The smile on her lips told me that she liked what she saw. The bite of her bottom lip told me that she desired me. And the lick of that bitten lip was my undoing.

God this woman drives me crazy!

Rushing the bed, I reached for her. I stripped her of her bra and underwear and took a swift plunge into her depths. She arched into me, emitting a loud moan. My frantic thrusts were met with her own as we came together in the most intimate way two people could when crazed by liquor and raging hormones.

"Damn you're tight," I said against the skin of her neck.

"You feel so good." She bit my shoulder, her fingernails digging into my back. "So big." Her tongue licked up the side of my neck.

I growled when I felt her clench me with her heat. Something felt different from the last time, but I couldn't pinpoint what as my lustful haze held me prisoner.

I kept thrusting until I heard her blissful cries of release resonating off her bedroom walls. I pulled my face from her neck and took in the sight before me as her climax rolled on.

That face, full of passion, lust, hunger, amazement; hell, I could go on listing what I saw flash through her carnal expression. It was raw, it was beautiful. She was beautiful.

As her tremors ebbed, I picked up the pace again, my lips fused to hers. I wanted to make her explode like that again—make it more intense if I could.

"Oh, Jacob!" she cried into my mouth, her pussy began to spasm again. It wasn't long now, and I was thankful because I could feel my own need to explode become more demanding with each thrust.

"God, I love it when you say my name like that." I nibbled her jaw.

In an instant, she had us flipped over and was riding me without breaking us apart.

I grabbed her hips and helped her pump up and down my shaft. I could feel the head of my cock hitting new depths, to the point that she was bottoming out. If it bothered her, she showed no sign.

Her head arched back, her speed grew frantic. Reaching behind her, I felt her hand massage my balls and within seconds, I was crying out her name while she cried out mine on her second climax.

Momentum slowed with our eyes connected until I pulled her down on top of me and rolled her under me. "Jesus, woman." I couldn't seem to catch my breath.

She began to laugh one of those hearty laughs that could make everything right in the world. "That good, huh?" She brought my head down to hers and kissed me nice and slow.

I nuzzled her cheek. "Mmm… You have no idea. You're amazing."

She hid her face in my chest. "I think I could get addicted to you. You're too much fun." She kissed my chest and I pulled away to see her face.

I arched my brow. "Fun?"

"Yeah." She smiled up at me, but I looked to the left of her face, at her pillow, my body having gone rigid, and not in a good way.

As with the last time we were together, that familiar pang of regret was back.

It must have showed on my face because she cupped my cheeks in her hands and turned my gaze back to her. "What's wrong?"

"Nothing." I shook my head and rolled off of her to sit on the edge of the bed with my back to her. She rushed to her knees and covered herself with her bed sheets. *How could I have been so stupid?* I let my head drop into my hands and closed my eyes.

"Jacob?"

I ignored her, glimpsed down and saw why everything had felt so different. No condom. *Shit!*

I grabbed my underwear, pulled them on before reaching for my jeans, anger sinking in, more at myself than her, but she deserved some of it too.

"Jacob?" I kept ignoring her. "Would you please talk to me? What the hell is going on? Jac—"

I swung around to face her. "What do you want from me?" My eyes narrowed. "We've had our fun, now I'm heading home." She stared at me without saying anything. "What, two orgasms wasn't enough? Sorry, honey, but I'm not a machine!"

"Jacob?" Her voice quivered. "I thought that this was what you wanted." I didn't answer as I turned my back to her again and put my shirt on. "Wasn't it?"

"Sure. Yeah, it's what I wanted," I said with sarcasm. I eyed her over my shoulder as I did up the last button.

"Then what's the matter?"

Walking back toward the bed, I exploded. "*You* making your mind up about what I want is *what's the matter*. Did you think that I'd have fucked you again tonight if I was playing around?" I could feel my blood boiling and I didn't like the sensation. "Never mind. Don't answer that. It doesn't matter anyway. The past is in the past. It's better off that way," I said, trying to calm myself down. I kissed the top of her head. "Don't bother getting up. I'll see myself out."

"Wait! We're still on for tomorrow with Anna, right?"

"Yeah. Fine," I said, dejected. "Bye, Danica."

I left her place, sat in my car, and realized I shouldn't be driving. I hit the steering wheel, letting my frustration out.

Leaving the comfort of my car and locking it, I proceeded home, on foot.

I didn't know who I should be mad at more; Danica, for thinking so little of me, or myself, for thinking that this charade was just that, a charade, and that it wasn't turning into something more. Tonight, I allowed a small chink in my player armor to remain open and I'd been played.

Half an hour later, I was home and no less pissed off since I realized that we hadn't talked about our lack of protection. How could I have been so stupid? *You've been asking yourself that same question a lot lately.*

As I settled in bed, I heard my cellphone go off beside my head. Grabbing it, I wondered who it could be. *Unknown number.* It was a text. I opened it.

I'm sorry. Nica

I found myself hitting the call button instead of texting back. It rang once before she picked up. "Hello?" She sounded on the down and out.

"I'm sorry too," I paused. "Um, we didn't use protection."

I heard the whoosh of her breath leave her lips. "I know. It's okay. I've been on the pill since Jordan was born and I'm clean."

It was my turn to let out a loud breath. "Me too."

"I'll see you tomorrow?"

"Yeah, tomorrow. Goodnight."
"Goodnight, Jacob."

CHAPTER 26

The next day, Danica and I visited Anna to give her the good news. It had been awkward at first, but our excitement with helping Anna aided curbing the discomfort.

When I dropped Danica off at home, she invited me in, but I declined under the guise that I had other plans. She didn't seem convinced, but she didn't push either.

Throughout the first half of the week, I poured myself into what little work I had. I finalized the remainder government forms I needed to fill out and submit to ensure that my business was legitimate. I opened a business account at the bank. I even went to the point of contacting Stan to see if he and Hope needed any last minute help with the ball which was in a week's time.

I had RSVP'd for two, but it's what I'd always done over the years. If I brought someone along, I did, and if I went solo, then so be it.

I hadn't heard from Danica at all since Saturday morning and our meeting with Anna. The worst part about it was that the more I tried not to think about her, the more she consumed my thoughts.

By late afternoon on Thursday, I was playing with the

idea of getting in touch with the woman. This whole unsolved issues thing had me riding thin on patience, not to mention sleep.

"Jake," I heard being called from my front door.

"Out back." Paxton came out onto the patio. "Beer's in the fridge."

Paxton sat on the outdoor sofa beside me, popping the cap off his bottle. For a minute, he sat there without a word and in the next, he burst out laughing.

My head snapped in his direction and my eyes narrowed. What the hell was so damn funny?

"When are you going to admit to yourself that you still love her?"

"Fuck off." I brushed off his comment. "Why are you here?"

He sobered. "Danica asked me to come by."

"She what?"

"Call her, Jake. I'm not getting in the middle of this more than I already am." He took a sip from his beer. "You two need to talk, and as far away from a bed as possible by the sounds of things." I looked up at him, wide eyed. "Oh, I know it happened again."

"She told you." My voice was flat.

He shook his head. "She didn't have to. It was written all over her face when I mentioned you."

"Ben said something happened to her and that's why her father moved them away. You wouldn't know anything about it, would you?"

"No." He bowed his head, and it was as if he was reliving the day she had left, the day he had to bear the bad news to me. "You really need to talk to her."

"I'm not sure if there's anything to talk about now." I looked over at him. "She's changed, Pax."

"Of course she's changed! Did you think that she wouldn't? Fuck, man, open your eyes, even you've changed! We've all changed! It's what life does to you," the man said.

"You know you're stuck. Without talking things over with her, you won't be able to move on. And neither can she."

"I get that."

"I don't think that you do. Let me ask you something." I could tell he was searching to word his question just right. "Why do you think it is that you haven't moved on? You can't tell me that you haven't had a decent lay from any of those women you've been with. I've seen a lot of them. They were smart, beautiful, and successful. And some even tried to get you to settle down. One even managed it for a short time if I remember right. Why is it that every time a new woman comes along, you can't commit?"

I growled. Fury boiled over and the words were out of my mouth before I could even process them. "Because I still love her, dammit!"

"There you have it." He got up, set his half-empty beer down, and rubbed his hands together to signify that his work there was done. "I'm going home, but before I go, here's a word of advice–"

My teeth clenched. "And what would that be?"

"Stop being mad at her and take a good look in the mirror. You're just as at fault this time around as she is. And another thing…" My eyes narrowed on him again. "Tell her how you feel."

"I can't."

"Why not? You did it fifteen years ago. If an eighteen-year-old can do it, so can a grown-ass man."

True. But what happened on Friday night had left my ego flat. "Because she doesn't feel the same way."

"How do you know, have you asked her?"

"No." I sighed. "I just do all right?"

"Fine, but a woman like Danica won't be around forever, Jake. She's single again, it'll only be a matter of time until she's not." I nodded in agreement. "By the way, Alissa and I are having a barbecue on Saturday. The wife says for you to be there. I wouldn't–"

"Tell her I accept."

"Think on what I said. You might be surprised to know how she feels."

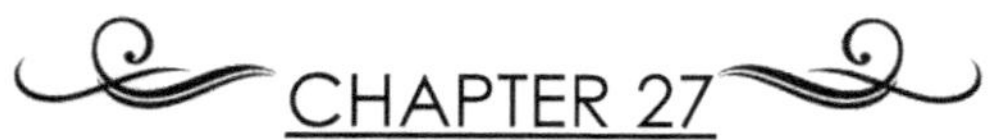

CHAPTER 27

I lost count of how many times I dialled her number and hung up before the call could be connected.

Analyzing what Paxton told me to do, I wasn't sure if I could. My best friend tended to be right more often than not. That fact alone freaked the hell out of me because that meant I had to have a serious heart-to-heart with Danica.

On a similar note, I thought about what Ben had told me. If what he said was true, and she hadn't wanted to leave fifteen years ago, why had she? She had a month before graduation. She was eighteen, a legal adult, she could have stayed. *But she didn't.* What happened to make her go?

Jordan flashed through my mind. The kid mentioned that his Granddad had taken his mother away from Jacksonville.

Jordan.

He was fifteen, bordering sixteen.

I did the math in my head and it couldn't have been any clearer. *She got pregnant.* All of a sudden, some of the pieces fell together.

Wrapped in those thoughts, I didn't realize I had hit the call button and that the call had been connected. "Hello?" I heard from my lowered hand and brought the phone to my ear. "Jacob?"

I cleared my throat. "Yeah, it's me."

"Is everything okay?"

"No, not really." Well, it was the truth after all. I wasn't going to tell her that I was on the verge of freaking out, so I expelled a long breath. "We need to talk."

"Okay. When?"

Now. "When's good?"

"How about now? Jordan's at soccer practice, and then he's got a school project to work on with Trevor. He'll be at least another hour or so."

"Just come over. I'll be out back," I said.

"I'll see you in a few." She ended the call and then I realized that I wasn't at all prepared for any of what was about to take place. I rubbed a hand down my face.

When Danica came in, she came straight to the back. I sat on the chair and not the sofa on purpose—securing physical distance was of utmost importance for me right now. I needed to be able to think, and I couldn't do that if she was too close.

"Hi." She offered a small smile.

"Hey." I gave her my best, which was a tight-lipped grimace of sorts. "Can I get you something to drink?"

"I'll have one of those." She pointed to my bottle of water.

After my call to her, I dumped the last of my one beer and switched over to bottled water. Since alcohol consumption had been part of the equation the last two times we were alone together, I wanted to make sure that our precursor to temptation was out of the way. I needed a clear head.

Getting up, I went to fetch her water. "Thank you."

"You're welcome." I took my seat.

"Listen–"

My hand went up. "I have one question for you, and I need you to be straight with me." She nodded. "Why did you leave?"

She looked as if I'd hit her in the gut with a two-by-four. Her face lost its color. With a hint of green, she looked as if she was going to be ill. *What the hell?* Something horrible had to have happened. In that moment, my suffering didn't quite matter.

Even if you're her kid's father, and she's held that information from you all these years? Anger was quick to replace the sympathy I felt toward her, but I wasn't going to give into it just yet. That would be jumping to conclusions, and I wasn't keen on making things worse. I needed answers and staying level-headed would be the way I would get them.

Danica cleared her throat and opened her mouth as if about to say something and then closed it.

She tried again. "That night…" she began and I knew that she was referring to the night where we had first been together. "It was the most amazing night ever. With you, I always felt safe, loved. You made me feel cherished. When I told you I loved you, it was real. I didn't lie. I need you to know that."

The emotion on her face lightened the anger I felt, but not by much. "Then, what happened?"

She swallowed hard. "Please let me speak. It's hard enough to say without having you ask more questions. I promise I'll answer all of them, after… if I manage to get this out."

I nodded.

"When you dropped me off, Dad and I got into a huge fight about me coming home past curfew. You remember how he was back then?" I nodded again. The man had been all about regimenting his kids. "After our fight, I snuck out of the house for some air. I ended up at the park." Her gaze was intent on her fingers twisting around on her lap. She took a deep breath. "Something went wrong.

"A guy walked by and sat beside me on the bench I was sitting on. I thought it weird because there was a free bench beside mine. He gave me the creeps so I got up to leave and headed home. I didn't know he was following me until my feet hit the pavement and I heard his footsteps." She closed her eyes, licked her lips. "They sounded rushed and then I realized that he was getting closer. I got scared.

"I ran. I ran so fast, Jacob, but he caught me." Her eyes snapped open but I could tell that even though she faced me, she wasn't seeing me; she was seeing the past. "He threw me to the ground, pushed up my skirt. H-he ripped my under-wear off and… and…" Her voice broke and my stomach turned. "He raped me, Jacob. When he was done, he crawled off of me and ran off, as if I had been a blow-up toy and he'd had his fill."

My anger had climbed and evolved to pure rage but it was no longer directed toward her. I clenched my fists on my lap and held my silence.

"It hurt to get up. I ached everywhere. I managed to make it back home and collapsed onto the floor when I got through the front door. Mike was there and yelled for Dad to come. They took me straight to the hospital." She looked down and wiped at her silent tears. "The guy didn't wear a condom." My heart sunk into the bottom of my gut.

"That night, Daddy made the decision to move us all. He was already in the process of opening the office in Austin and he didn't want me here where I could relive the horrors of that night. The next day, we all flew out there and he hired a moving company to pack the rest of our stuff and ship it to us.

"Despite what happened, I didn't want to go, but Daddy dismissed what I wanted, like always. He was convinced that I was too distraught to make up my own mind.

"A month afterwards, I begged him to let me come back. When he asked me why, I told him that I was in love with you, that I wanted to come back to you." Her smile con-tained so much sadness. "You should have seen him fly off the handle with that revelation." Her laugh was humorless.

"He said that if you loved me, that you'd find a way to contact me. But how could you when you didn't know where I was? Sure, you could have talked to Nikki, but I had cut her out by then too.

"When that never happened, Dad pacified me with a promise that I could take a week during the summer holidays and go find you myself. I believed him.

"A week later, I found out I was pregnant." Her hand clutched her stomach and she sniffled. "They gave me the morning after pill, the night of the rape, but it didn't work. I was on birth control too." I nodded. I knew that. "My OB told me that the morning after pill isn't as effective as most think, and since I hadn't been on the pill long enough, that that's how it happened."

"Jordan?" I whispered. She nodded. "So J-Jordan's his?" It had to be. She wouldn't have kept this from me if he weren't.

"I don't know." My eyes widened. "They never caught the guy."

My head pounded as if someone had taken a sledgehammer to it. I wanted to say something but I couldn't.

"We made love without a condom that same night, Jacob. He might be yours, but he might be his." She spat the last bit as if it left a sour taste in her mouth. "I never said anything because I was ashamed. I still am, but I can't run from it anymore.

"First, I blamed myself for being stupid to have left the house so late at night. Second, I felt as if I had asked for it because that's what he kept telling me while he was…" She shook her head as if forcing the memory out of her mind. "Third, when I couldn't provide the answers I knew you'd want right away, I waited until the answers came. They never did.

"I blamed Dad for convincing me to stay in Austin. I blamed myself for doing what my father had told me to do like the dutiful and obedient daughter. We still argue about it to this day." This brought back mine and Jordan's conversation about him walking in on his mother and grandfather.

"Jacob, my life changed that day and most of it, not for the better. I wouldn't trade Jordan for the world. He's my son, no matter who his father is. It took me a long time to accept that genetics didn't make up a person's character.

"Back then, I thought that you'd want nothing to do with him or me if we found out that he wasn't yours. It was shallow of me and I was a coward and I'll forever regret taking that decision out of your hands. It was easier to disappear than to come back and deal with everything, especially when I was dealing with therapy, a child, and school." I groaned. "We were so young. My life became complicated, but it wasn't ruined. I made a lot of stupid decisions back then. Staying away from you both was and wasn't one of them."

I wanted to ask her how she figured that, but she wasn't done talking.

"My parents supported me. Mike helped too. I stayed because my dad threatened to cut me off if I left. All I wanted was to finish college and come back to you. But you had college too, and law school on top of that.

"You worked so hard to get that scholarship and I couldn't just show up with a kid, five years later, after I'd graduated, and expect you to accept things, juggle us both, your school, and a side job, when he might not be yours. You deserved better."

Taking a cleansing breath. "There. I said it. That's why I left. It wasn't because I wanted to. I didn't call or write because I'd lose my parents' support. I couldn't risk it. If it were just me, I would have left and come back to you, but I had Jordan to worry about. I know I was stupid with the way I handled things, but it's done now. I can apologize until I'm blue in the face, but I doubt it would ever be enough."

CHAPTER 28

Dumbfounded, I sat with my elbows on my knees and my face in my hands. "So you're saying…" Okay, so realizing one thing in my mind and then wording it was a little difficult at the moment. "Fuck." I took a deep breath and looked at her. "I might be Jordan's father?"

She nodded.

I knew I should be furious with her, maybe even yell and kick her out of my house. But I couldn't. I didn't even want to. I can tell you that I would have loved to beat on the son of a bitch that took everything away from both of us years ago, sparing a few swings for her old man. I knew the man knew how to get his way, but I never once thought he'd manipulate his own daughter, knowing she'd do anything for his approval.

Overwhelmed, I wasn't sure if I should say or do anything until I had some time to digest Danica's revelations. There were plenty enough to give the entire neighborhood block indigestion.

Without my thinking it, I shot to my feet and began pacing the deck-boards. I paused and looked at her. She watched me, but didn't dare say a word. I shook my head and resumed my pacing. The second time I halted, I huffed out a large breath and looked up at the sky.

For the life of me, I couldn't control my erratic thoughts. I couldn't get them organized enough to process things, so I continued with the pacing. Her hand on my bicep stalled me.

I turned to face her and was met with a tearful Danica, wrapping her arms around my torso.

My arms lay limp at my sides. My body wasn't functioning with my head, and my emotions seemed to have left me altogether. Talk about bad timing.

"I'm sorry, Jacob." She broke the silence. "I'm so sorry."

Her apologetic chant continued until something bloomed inside of me. I wasn't sure what the emotion was yet, but it did cause my arms to wrap around her.

At first, she stiffened in my arms and then her arms tightened their hold. I couldn't help but return the gesture, my cheek resting on top of her head. Her chant continued at a whisper, and I don't think that she realized that she was still doing it.

I pulled away enough to use a hand and tilt her chin up so I could see her face. Her eyes were closed tight and tears streamed down her cheeks at an unstoppable rate.

"Shh…" I urged her to stop and cradled her head back to my chest. She seemed to calm down with the small reassurance.

When I deemed her calm enough, I took a step back and held on to her shoulders at arm's length.

"Jacob…"

I let my hands fall away from her. "I need to think." I avoided eye contact. "I understand why you left and I really can't blame you for staying away for some of that time, but…"

"You're wondering why I didn't come back sooner?" I nodded and turned my back on her. "By the time I was done with school, Jordan was six and in school himself. I know it's a poor excuse, saying that I didn't want to take him away from his friends, his teachers, his family, but it's the truth, even though that's what I've done by moving back here.

"I had also just started to work. I did try looking around, but no one wanted me, despite knowing who my father is." Why was she bitter? "Dad was the one to give me my job at Withers International and believe me, I worked to get to where I am today. If anything, I had to prove myself more than every Tom, Dick, and Harry in that place. I stayed in Austin because it was where my job was, and Dad refused to let me relocate here, and let's face it, I loved what I did. I felt like I owed my dad for giving me a shot when no one else did." Somehow, this part of her explanation rubbed me the wrong way.

"You could have called! I'm listed!" *I would have done anything.* But I was glad I kept those words to myself.

"Would you have listened?" I knew that my probable answer would have been a negative. "I could have called, but despite my therapy, I still suffer from the same fears, embarrassment, and guilt from before. That doesn't go away, Jacob. I had no clue as to what you'd been up to. I didn't know if you were married, or if you had your own family. I could have asked Paxton, but that would have invited more questions for me, and I figured that if anyone back home deserved to know anything firsthand, it should be you." Her voice dropped to a whisper. "Since I wasn't ready to spill the beans, I tried to move on."

"And Bruce?"

"I met him when my father hired him as a consultant. They got along great and so he set us up on a date of sorts. It was a company workshop weekend. Before I knew it, we were together, and a year later we were married.

"After you, I knew that I'd never find better. Jordan was eight. He needed more than Dad and Mike as male figures in his life. In the off chance you had a life of your own and because I was too damn scared, I settled.

"I never loved Bruce like a woman should love a husband. He never tried to stand up and be a father figure to Jordan. Honestly, I don't think he wanted kids, which made me wonder if he was with me for my business." She snorted. "He proved that suspicion by trying to steal my father's company out from under our noses. He would have succeeded too, had news of his embezzling hadn't gotten out. Had Dad signed those contracts, transferring everything from him to my ex, we would have nothing. Thank God that didn't happen, and we won our case." Our eyes locked. "Is it true?"

"Is what true?"

"When Jordan said that you threw your case so we'd win, you said *perhaps*." She waited but I didn't answer. "So, is it?"

"I did what I knew was right. I knew how hard your father worked to build that company. As much as he and I never got along, it wasn't right to see what a man built be taken away by a crook. I was a last-minute substitute lawyer, and I couldn't refuse the case, so I dug around, found things about Spalding's business practices, and figured out a way to make him hurt. Just because your dad was stupid in hiring him doesn't mean that you and Mike should suffer."

She made to approach me with sincere gratitude in her teary eyes, but I held my hand up to stop her. "Don't."

"Thank you," she said and looked away. "You have no idea how much it means to me."

"I would do it all over again."

"Even after what I've just told you?"

"Your father's the one who left you with no choice. He's the one who's used you all of these years. I–"

Danica's cellphone rang. "I've got to get this. It's Jordan." I nodded and let her answer. Within seconds, she hung up. "I've got to go." But she didn't make to leave. "Jacob?" I looked up at her. "Are we going to be okay?"

"I don't know." I was being honest. Our eyes met and she nodded. I wanted to say more, to tell her that everything would work itself out, but I couldn't. I couldn't promise her that. Everything just seemed too bleak right now.

She broke our connection first, turned away, and walked

toward the inside of the house. I watched as she paused by the patio door, keeping her back to me. "I'm really sorry, Jacob."

"Me too," I whispered.

CHAPTER 29

I lasted the total of an hour in the confines of my gigantic home. I couldn't even stand the patio, claustrophobia setting in even in the great outdoors. I rushed out the door, locked up and headed somewhere where I knew I could clear my head.

I drove the forty-five minutes into the countryside and came to a stop by the massive barn. I marched to the house, let myself in, and found Paxton, Jasper, and Alissa in the kitchen.

"Jake?" Alissa looked puzzled, but her expression went straight to worry when my eyes met hers.

"Hey." I kissed her cheek then ruffled the tyke's hair. "Jasper. Allie, can I steal your husband for a bit?"

"Everything okay?" With a brief shake of my head, she reached and squeezed my hand and said, "Just go, I won't wait up."

I left their kitchen and headed outside, my best friend on my tail. Making my way straight to the back of the barn, I opened the back doors and located the four-wheeler. The keys were missing.

"You might need these." Paxton dangled them on his finger and pocketed them instead of handing them over. "Talk, then you can ride."

I let out a long drawn out breath and ran my fingers through my hair. "Where do I start?"

"From the beginning, where else?" He could be such a smartass at times.

I chuckled without much humor. "Wise ass." The man waited with his arms crossed over his chest, leaning on the old, beat-up tractor behind him. "Danica's leaving had nothing to do with me, that much is for sure," I said. "I have a serious bone to pick with her father, though. If I ever see the man again and that fucking bastard... I can't believe–" I stopped myself. My eyes stung, but I held the tears back, tapping into my rage instead of my grief, and growled. "She was raped, Pax."

The walls surrounding us vibrated with Paxton's single word. "What?"

"And Jordan..." I continued. "Oh God, Pax." My legs gave out on me and my ass landed on the edge of the ATV's seat.

"What happened to Jordan, Jake?" I had to set his mind at ease from the worry I saw on his face.

"Nothing." I met his eyes. "N-nothing's happened to Jordan. It's just–" Panic hit me tenfold, and my breathing became labored. It felt like the world was closing in on me, snuffing the air from my lungs. I saw dark spots on my peripheral, ringing started in my ears.

Paxton grabbed my shoulders and shook me. "Hey, man, breathe!" I didn't. He tried again and when I didn't cooperate, the son of a bitch punched me in the jaw. My head snapped up to look at him in shock. He backed away, knowing that there might be retribution. "I'm sorry, dude. I had to do something to get you to snap out of it."

There was no urge to retaliate. Instead, I caught my breath, massaging my jaw. "He might be mine, Pax."

"I must have heard wrong. Did you just say–?"

My eyes locked with his. "Jordan might be mine," I repeated. "What the fuck am I going to do?"

"What do you mean by 'might'?" Before I could answer, I saw the realization spread onto his face. "She doesn't know?"

I shook my head. "They never caught the bastard." I kicked a clump of dust at my feet. "Now, how in the hell do I deal with a fifteen-year-old when I haven't been able to deal with his mother?"

He sighed. "I can't answer that, but what I can say is get a damn paternity test, and get yourselves some answers." He was right. "Wow, a kid!"

"I know."

"A fifteen-year-old!"

"A smart one at that." I smiled at the memory of our bantering episodes.

"Dude, you could be a dad." It was clear the man was in shock.

"I know!"

"That's scary."

"Hmm…" My mind began to wander on what I should do next.

"But it's fucking fantastic!"

"Huh?"

"Well, yeah. I mean… Oh, never mind what I mean." He clapped the side of my arm. "So what's your plan?"

I snorted. "What plan?" I began to list things on my fingers for him. "Pax, I just found out that the girl I loved in high school left me by force after being raped. She has a kid that may, or may not, be mine. She was coerced to stay out of touch with me because her father thought I wasn't good enough for her, despite the fact that she'd told him that she loved me at the time. He told her he'd cut her off if she left, so in order to save her education and support her son, she stayed." I got up to pace as I gave the man the entire story and finished with a frustrated growl.

Paxton broke the silence first. "Okay, I get it now. I don't think there's a plan for this one." He ran his hand over his face. "And I thought Allie and I were complicated with the hell we went through."

Cue the sarcasm. "Yeah, a real pickle."

"You said earlier today that you love her. Has any of that changed with what she told you?"

I had to think about that one for a minute.

Had it?

I replayed key moments of the day, of the past, of what's transpired between us since her return. Despite her reasons, she had done it all for love. In a twisted way, she kept everything from me in order to ensure I got the schooling, the life, the success she thought I deserved. Someone who knew Danica through and through would understand. And I knew Danica—down to the very tiny atom that was her. In that moment, I realized I understood it all. It didn't mean that I was happy about her choices. Christ, I was put through hell with no answers for fifteen years! But I still understood.

"The truth?" I paused to see if I'd missed anything in my mind. "No, nothing's changed." I let out a pregnant breath. "But everything else has."

"If you could do anything right now, what would it be?"

"Right now?" Pax nodded and his smirk transformed into a knowing grin. "Right now, I'd like to wipe that smug look off your face. Fuck!" I ran both hands through my hair and fisted it with a tug.

Paxton howled a laugh and I let my hands fall to my sides. "I hate to say it, but, I told you so!" he said in a sing-song tone.

I punched his arm. "Yeah, yeah… so, we going for a ride or you going to pussy out on me and head on back to that wife of yours?"

"I'll take my wife." He gave me a wicked grin as he rubbed his arm. "At least she kisses me after she punches me."

"Good point." I shook my head with a light chuckle.

"Nope, good woman," he said as we walked out of the

barn, closed the doors and headed toward my car. "Are you sure you're all right? The wife gave me a free pass. We can go get you drunk, get you–"

"I'm fine. I mean, I'm still blown away by everything, but…"

"It's pretty amazing isn't it?" he asked. "The feeling you get when you get a bit of clarity?"

"Yeah."

"I can't say I blame you." He patted me on the shoulder. "Hit me up if you need an ear, or a drive home."

"Thanks man, but I think the drinking will be done in the comfort of my own home. No car service will be needed."

"You're welcome. And this bomb of yours doesn't get you off for Saturday, by the way."

I laughed. "Wouldn't dare piss that woman of yours off."

Seated in my car with Paxton having disappeared inside his house, I realized that a weight had been lifted. I still had a lot of thinking to do, but figuring out what to do next didn't seem as daunting of a task when it came to Danica and me.

As I drove home, a plan began to take shape.

CHAPTER 30

Friday morning, I was greeted with a guest I wasn't quite ready to deal with, but I wasn't going to put my foul mood, due to lack of sleep and troubled thoughts, on him.

"Jordan?"

"I need your help." He walked past me and entered the house like a man on a mission.

"Why is it that every time you show up on my doorstep, you need my help?" Funny how his sudden need had erased my gloomy demeanor, making me feel better, and then it struck me. "Wait a minute, shouldn't you be in school?"

"Um…"

"Jordan!"

"But it's important, I swear!"

"What's so important that you had to ditch? You know your mo–"

"It's Mom's birthday today." He said this as if I should have known all along. "Normally I have Granddad to help me out, but it's just me and Mom now. I need to get her a gift."

"So you need a ride."

He shrugged his shoulders as if it were no big deal. "Yeah, if you're up for it." His eyes told me that my answer meant the world to him, despite his feigned nonchalance.

"Let me get dressed." I smiled at his brightening features.

After all that I'd learned yesterday, I found myself taking a moment to study him. There was no doubt that he looked a lot like his mother, but looking at him closer, his black hair could have been mine, his square jaw, mine, his height and build, well, that could be a toss-up since the men on Danica's side of the family towered at six feet, plus. His eyes were like mirror images of color, the same clear green as mine. *Or maybe you're just trying to see things for more than what they are.*

The more I thought about things, the more I found myself hoping that Jordan would turn out to be mine. At least there'd be a way for him to understand and know that his father had always wanted him instead of settling with the knowledge of him being a product of a brutal crime. Don't get me wrong, as much as these thoughts comforted me, I was scared shitless. What did I know about raising kids? I was an only child!

Hours later, we had nothing but a suitable card for Danica.

"You're just like your mother, except you don't know what you're looking for." I laughed. He looked at me confused from across the food court table. "When we were kids, she asked me to go with her and find a gift for her mom." His goofy grin came out. "She made me go to every shop with her until she found the perfect thing. A few weeks later, against my better judgement, I agreed to go with her for your Uncle Mike's birthday gift. Took her longer that time around."

"Really?"

I could tell he enjoyed learning more about his mother. Something told me that over the years, he hadn't gotten the glimpses of the true Danica, the one I knew, the one I hadn't seen much of since her return.

"Really. She's got a fantastic ability of knowing what the

perfect gift is. The problem is that it's always something so specific, and she's so stubborn that she won't budge once she's set her mind on buying it. She always claimed that anyone could do a video game, a new phone, some CD's, and movies, but that kind of gift never meant as much as the ones you put more thought into. She was right." I didn't tell him about the photo of us she'd framed for my last birthday that we'd been together. The glass was the first to go, and the frame followed not too long afterward in one of my fits after she'd left, but I kept the photo in a box of mementos that contained all sorts of trinkets and photos of mine from my earlier years.

"She really is the best at getting presents, but she's not like that. At least, not now." That was a disappointing truth. "No one else is around this year. I want to make it special, but we've been through every store in this place, and I haven't seen anything that would be great for her."

With that, I decided it was time to pull out the arsenal from the dusty corner of my memory bank. "You know what? I have an idea."

CHAPTER 31

By the time we were finished, it was nearing four o'clock. I drove Jordan home with our gifts. Yeah, I had gotten her a few things myself. What can I say, Jordan's enthusiasm to my idea had been contagious.

When we arrived, I held my breath.

Jordan hissed. "Shit! I'm done for."

Danica leaned back on the trunk of her car, arms crossed over her chest, tapping her high-heeled foot with a look of disapproval.

"Follow my lead." I exited the car and stood beside it. He did the same, bringing his gifts along.

"Where the hell were you?" She looked at Jordan. "I got a call from your school at lunchtime saying that you hadn't shown up. And you…" Her eyes were aimed in my direction.

Before she could finish, I reached into the back of the car and pulled out a large basket. I walked up to her, pushed it into her arms and kissed her cheek. "Happy Birthday, Nica." Her look of surprise faded to tightened lips, and the lines in her face grew taught with frustration. "Well, aren't you going to look?"

Her eyes traveled between her son and I. "Let's take this inside."

Jordan looked at me with a grim look on his face as we followed.

She led us to the living room and sat the basket down on the coffee table. Her mouth opened, about to say something, but then she snapped it shut when I crossed my arms at my chest and nodded my head toward the basket. I got why she was mad, but Jordan had put so much of himself in this that she needed to cut him a break. On this, I wouldn't budge.

"Oh, all right." She huffed her submission without me having to say a word.

Danica peered through the contents of the basket, pulling out a box of pasta noodles, cans, bags of spices, wine, bread, movies I knew she liked, and a few other assorted items.

With humor in her gaze, she looked up at me. "What is all this?"

"I'm making you dinner," I said.

"Correction," Jordan said, *we're* making you dinner." Jordan grinned at me. "And this," he handed her the gift bag and gestured to the basket as well, "is why I wasn't at school today. I wanted to make today special. Happy Birthday, Mom." He kissed her cheek and I smiled when her eyes fused to mine and all the frustration left her, her eyes tearing up.

She rummaged through the tissue paper and looked inside. I watched as her eyes widened in surprise. Her head snapped up to Jordan and then me. "I can't believe you remembered." She pulled out the large box of truffles. Jordan nudged my side. When I turned to him, I winked at Jordan's grinning expression.

"Why wouldn't I?" I never forgot the place, having gone back more than a few times over the years. In our teens, when things were rough, and Pax and I couldn't pull it off, those homemade truffles were the one thing that could make her smile, make her troubles melt away. There's no way I would forget that.

"I haven't had these in so long, I'd all but forgot about

them." She opened the box and picked one out, but Jordan and I protested. "But…" One shake of my head and she dropped the sweet back in the box. "Fine." She grumbled.

"That's dessert," Jordan said.

I walked toward the kitchen. "I say we get started on dinner since the birthday girl seems famished."

With a celebratory fist-bump, the kid said, "You got it, hot shot."

Aside from opening cans and containers, Jordan wasn't much help in the kitchen. When he dropped the can of tomato juice, which exploded all over the floor and lower cabinets, his duties changed to cleanup. When he finished, I made him sit at the island and keep me company as I took care of the cooking, which meant I had to improvise. I was thankful to find that Danica had a full container of cream in the fridge.

We sent Danica off to relax, but she walked in when I was half-way through making the sauce. "Smells good."

"Shouldn't you be reading or something, Mom?"

"Aren't you the one that told me to do what I wanted since it's my birthday?" I eyed the exchange. After Jordan's nod, she continued. "Well then, what I want to do is sit right here and enjoy the action."

"Action, Mom?" Jordan looked at his mother like she was the furthest thing from cool.

She nodded. "I don't think I've ever known this guy to cook a day in his life." Her eyes crinkled at the sides.

"Things change," I said, and her lips tilted up to match the humor in her twinkling eyes.

When dinner was ready, I served Jordan and Danica, and walked back to the sink, pouring water for the dishes.

"What are you doing?" she asked. Jordan was eating with gusto while his mother had yet to touch her meal.

"I'm cleaning." I added the suds and made sure the water temperature was just right. "I made you dinner, but I'm not about to leave the dirty dishes behind."

"Come and eat." Jordan dropped his fork, his attention now on our conversation.

"It's for you. Enjoy it. I'll get something later."

"Jacob, sit down. You're being ridiculous."

"Jacob?" Jordan looked from me to his mother.

She nodded but didn't explain. "Sit down or I'm not eating." She sat back and crossed her arms at her chest like a pouting three-year-old.

"Your name's Jacob?" Jordan asked.

I turned the water off at the sink. "Yeah, but no one calls me that but my parents and your mom." Danica had engaged me in a staring match.

"That's my middle name."

I smirked at Danica. "I think I remember hearing your mother shouting it out once or twice," I said. Her eyes narrowed and so I gave in, serving myself a plate. "There, are you happy now?" I joined them at the table. "Eat."

"Much." She held the bottle of wine up. "Want some?"

"No, thanks." I kept my head bowed, and scooped up my first bite.

Jordan broke the awkward silence. "So, Mom, how was your day?"

She shrugged her shoulders. "Busy as always. Things are looking better in Austin though. Uncle Mike is doing great fixing things there."

"That's good." Danica nodded.

We settled on *American Pie* as the movie of the night. I didn't want to stay, but Jordan asked me to, and I gave in. What can I say, I'm a martyr.

Danica walked into the room with a bowl of popcorn and her box of truffles. She handed the bowl to Jordan who dug in as if he hadn't just eaten a full meal and gone for seconds. Where in the hell did the kid put it all?

"That's for you too. I suggest you get your fill before he eats it all. That was the last bag." She pointed to Jordan. "And this," she shook her box of truffles and plopped down between Jordan and me, "is for me!" Her beaming smile made me chuckle.

"And how am I supposed to get to the popcorn now?" I asked.

"You should have thought about that before I sat down." She popped a treat in her mouth, turned my way, and smiled with her lips sealed, making her cheeks bulge. I shook my head at her and returned her smile.

"Here you go!" Jordan passed the bowl no more than fifteen minutes into the movie. I looked down to find not even a handful left of the stuff. I leaned forward and looked at him in disbelief.

"I told you," she teased.

I grumbled. "Give me one of those." I reached for her chocolates but she slapped my hand away.

"Ask nicely and maybe you'll get one." She smirked. This picture was quite reminiscent of the old days.

"Pretty please?"

"Shh! Guys, I'm trying to watch the movie," Jordan whined. Danica shook her head, indicating the negative my way.

"Pretty, pretty please?" I whispered, leaning into her ear. Her smile broadened but she shook her head again, her face still facing the screen. "You're forcing my hand here," I warned. "I'll tickle you for it!"

Squealing, she set her box down and jumped up, darted over Jordan's legs which were up on the coffee table. Pleased with myself, I leaned forward, grabbed a truffle and popped it in my mouth before leaning back and crossing an ankle over a knee.

"Hey, give it back!" she said.

"Mmm…" I smacked my lips after swallowing the treat. "As good as I remember, but I think I ate one of your favorites."

"Not the caramel!"

"Guys!" Jordan looked up with exasperation.

I waved for Danica to come and sit back down, handing her the box of chocolates as a peace offering. When she sat with her gift on her lap, I leaned in. "I would never eat your caramel ones, Nica, that's just not right."

Rolling her eyes, she said, "Ever the gentleman." Next thing I knew, she held a truffle to my mouth and smiled. "Here." She didn't have to tell me twice. I took it from her, careful not to bite her fingers. As I bit into it, my eyes widened and I looked at her. Caramel. "It's the last one. I know they're your favorite too." She brushed her lips against mine so quick that I'd almost missed her sweet move. "Thank you for today."

I was speechless, so I nodded. She'd kissed me with her son in the room. Then again, I think it was safe to say that Jordan was so far into the movie that a bomb could have gone off and he wouldn't have budged.

Danica straightened herself and turned to watch the movie as if nothing had happened.

Over my shock, I wrapped an arm around the back of the couch and settled in for the rest of the show.

CHAPTER 32

When the movie ended, I turned to find Jordan smirking at me.

Slumped into the crook of my arm, Danica was asleep.

"What?" I asked at a whisper so as not to wake her.

"You like her."

"Of course I like her. She's a friend."

He snorted. "She likes you a lot, you know." His eyes cast themselves downward with a solemn look. "Don't tell her this, but she doesn't know I could hear her at night when she went to bed and cried herself to sleep. Since we've moved, she hasn't done that."

"Are you sure it's not because Bruce is gone?"

Jordan shook his head. "At first I thought it was because he was never home. But then I caught her in the bathroom down the hall after he'd been home and gone to bed." He seemed to be pondering something and then his eyes shifted and narrowed on me, but those green eyes danced. "I think it's more than that. And I think you have something to do with it."

Jordan helped me get his mother to her bed. Leaving her in

her clothes, I draped the covers over her and kissed her forehead.

She grabbed my shirt and pulled me toward her. I braced myself just in time with an arm on either side of her, so I wouldn't crush her.

I heard snickering from behind me.

I mouthed an, "It's not funny," over my shoulder.

"Jacob," she whispered in a dream-like state. My head snapped to look at her. She was still asleep, but she was mumbling. I leaned in closer to hear what she was saying and felt her nuzzle my cheek. "I can't do this alone, Jacob. I need…" Then she fell silent.

When her hands released me, I stood and she rolled onto her side, settling in with a peaceful sigh.

I brushed a wayward lock of hair out of her face. "I'm right here." *I've always been right here.*

Turning to leave, I realized I'd forgotten all about Jordan, but the kid no longer stood in the doorway. I shut Danica's bedroom door and breathed a sigh of relief when I saw the light on at the other end of the hall, where I presumed was Jordan's bedroom. With the door being shut, I knocked.

"Come in."

I pushed inward and peered inside. "Nice room." I admired the slew of sport and gaming paraphernalia plastered to his walls.

"Thanks."

"I'm heading out now. Lock the door?"

"Yeah." He seemed distracted, but I didn't want to pry. He'd been good at coming to me when he needed to talk. I turned to leave.

"Jake?" He caught up with me when I was at the front door.

"Yeah?"

He walked up to me, stopping about a foot away. "Thanks for today."

I smiled. "You're welcome, kid." Next thing I knew, he

threw himself at me, wrapped his arms around my waist. By the time my arms came around to return his gesture, he released me. *What just happened?* My voice gave away my failed machismo with a shaky, "Goodnight."

"Goodnight, Jacob." I heard the laughter in his words.

"It's Jake!" I said as I walked to my car.

"Hey!" I turned to face him with the driver's side door open. "I get your parents, but why my mom?"

I shrugged my shoulders. "She's just special, I guess." His chin jutted out in an understanding gesture. "Goodnight, Jordan."

He smirked from the doorway. "Later, hot shot."

"And lock that door."

He rolled his eyes. "Yes, Dad."

I knew that he was using the *dad* word in a sarcastic manner when he said it, but with each subsequent time, I found that I liked hearing it, along with his calling me *hot shot*.

A lot.

Maybe too much.

I let out a short laugh and shook my head. *You, a family man?* The idea, where a month ago seemed preposterous, had grown on me. Jordan was the source of that change, of that I was sure. Okay, maybe it was also the fact that he was Danica's son and at one point—one I was willing to acknowledge—I had pictured us having a family together.

I knew that Jordan wanted a father, or at least some kind of male figure he could bond with. It was in his eyes. If that wasn't proof enough, it was in the way he came to me when he couldn't go to his mother or any other member of his family. Most of all, it was in the way he hugged me tonight. He may have been a typical macho teenager, but deep inside, the child in him screamed for a man to be in his life in a consistent manner.

I made my decision as I pulled up my driveway. The

sooner I found out about Jordan being my son or not, the sooner we could all move on.

Tomorrow, I would go and enjoy myself at Pax's, and on Sunday, it was time Danica and I cleared the air.

As I unlocked my front door, Paxton's voice played about in my head, reminding me that I had a few things to tell her on top of finding out how she felt about me, and one request that could alter our life forever.

CHAPTER 33

I was a little late showing up at Paxton's. My feet stopped dead in their tracks the moment I made it out to the patio and found Danica sitting beside Alissa, hands animated as they talked about something, and then I caught the word *baby*.

Pax elbowed me. "Don't listen to them."

"Jake!" Alissa got up and I met her halfway for a hug. "You look," she eyed me from head to toe and back again, "better."

"Thanks." I offered her a soft laugh. "Where're the kids?" I asked, missing my usual leg tackle from Jasper.

"Jasper's at his mom's," Pax said over his shoulder as he tried to fire up the barbecue.

"And Jordan's spending the night at Trevor's." Danica smiled and babbled on. "I'm glad he's made a friend so quick, but it'd be nice if he put as much excitement into his house chores as he does socializing and sports."

"Don't forget girls," I added and leaned on the patio's ledge beside Pax. Her gaze snapped to me. "What? Don't tell me you didn't know that your son has a penchant for cheer-leaders?"

She huffed. "The short skirts, the lack of underwear, the slutty nature. All I need is for him to fall for one of those floozies."

Pax laughed, but I felt myself grow defensive. My body stiffened. "I fell for one of those once or don't you remember? She sure as hell wasn't a floozy or a skank." I held Danica's gaze with mine. Paxton's laugh halted, and Alissa leaned forward in her chair, biting back a smile. "She was my tutor, my best friend, and if you'd asked me at sixteen who I was going to marry—"

"He'd have said Heidi Klum." Pax gave me a shit-eating grin. I turned to him and slapped the back of his head before moving to the patio's railing, and leaning back on it. "Hey!" Alissa was giggling like a schoolgirl, and Danica graced me with a shy smile before casting her eyes downward.

"Needless to say, don't sell your boy short," I added. "He's a smart kid, and a good judge of character."

Our eyes remained fused to each other's until Paxton broke the silence. "Hey, Jake?"

"Yeah?" I turned from the ladies to him.

"You think you can run to the barn and grab the extra propane tank from the closet by the ladder to the loft?"

"No prob."

I was rummaging through the closet, the blasted propane tank evading my detection.

Okay, so I was preoccupied. I don't know what possessed me to be so defensive earlier, nor why I felt compelled to spill my guts in front of my best friend, his wife, and most of all, Danica.

"What's taking you so long?" I heard, making me jump and hit my head on a shelf. Falling forward, everything collapsed over and around me. "Oh shit, Jacob!"

I groaned, reaching up for my head, shaking it to rid it of spots floating across my vision. "Fuck, that hurt." I groaned.

Danica rushed to me and started pulling things off of my back so I could turn around. She tried to help me up, but I ended up pulling on her hand before she had the chance to brace herself, sending her toppling on top of me with a shriek of surprise.

"Oh my God, Jacob! Are you okay?" Her deer in the headlights expression was so priceless that I started to laugh a full out belly laugh.

"Leave it up to you to get me injured. At least there's no need for me to worry about getting sacked this time." She blushed at my mention of the championship football game where she had first told me she loved me.

Her forehead hit my chest and she sighed. The moment for laughing had passed when she fisted my shirt. "Nica?" She trembled when I ran a hand up the middle of her back. Backing away, she kept her head bowed, and her loose hair curtained her face, shielding me from it.

"Here." She stood up and presented her hand. This time, I managed to get up. "Sit down." She nodded toward the small stack of hay bales beside us, and I did as I was told.

She rummaged through the rubble on the floor. "What are you doing here?" I asked and at the same moment, she pulled out a first aid kit from the rubble.

"Pax asked me to come and check on you. You've been gone for fifteen minutes." She popped the kit down beside me on the bale and opened it.

"Really?"

"Mmm." She pulled out some gauze and an alcohol swab, and began dabbing my forehead. "It's just a scratch." I winced at the burning sensation the swab had brought. "Man up, you big baby." She smirked, keeping her eyes on the injury above my forehead. "Did you mean that?" Her hands ran through my hair, looking for any other injury or bump.

"Mean what?" I asked, playing stupid, forgetting that she could read me like a book. She bent forward, cupping my jaw and eyeing everything on my face except my eyes.

"Jacob, you know what," she said with an air of annoyance.

I bit my lip. "Yeah, I did." Taking a

deep breath, I continued. "And I need to ask you something."

"Then ask."

"I want us to run a paternity test on Jordan." She pulled back, shrank down to her knees in front of me, and looked away. That curtain of hair occluded her face again. I leaned forward and pushed it to the side, tucking it behind her ear. "Hey, I don't care what it says, all right? I haven't had very long to process things, but if he's mine, I couldn't be happier."

She looked up at me and a single tear fell down her cheek. "And what if he isn't?" she whispered and her eyes were aimed to something past my shoulder. "I-I don't know if I could handle it Ja–"

"I hadn't thought that far yet. But I'd hope that I could still be in his life somehow, and I'll be here for you too."

Her eyes came back to me. "But why? Why would you want anything to do with me? With everything I put you through..." She took a fortifying breath. "Paxton told me earlier this afternoon. I know what happened with you, after I left. I get it now, why you were so hostile when I came back to town. I understand your question from two nights ago, and I know you wanted me for sex." Her voice cracked with tears.

"Whoa, hold on a minute!" I shot up to my feet, almost knocking her off her knees and onto her ass. "I never said I wanted you for sex." It came out a little louder than anticipated. "I never signed up for a fuck buddy, nor have I ever wanted to play games with you. In fact, you made it happen, both times! Sure I went for it, I'm a guy!

"Did you know that when you told me you loved me for the first time, I was ready to call it a day and make you my forever? You said you spoke to Pax earlier. Do you really understand what your leaving did to me?"

She shook her head, silent tears cascading down her face. I wanted to brush them away, but I held back. This was my time to come clean, my time to paint the vivid picture of my side of things, much like she had done with giving me hers two days before.

"The day you left, the day Paxton came to tell me you were gone, was the worst day of my life. I loved you!" She whimpered at my words. "I went to find you. I saw the movers." I swallowed the lump that had grown in my throat. "For so long, I waited for the day you called, wrote, or came back, but you never did."

"Jacob—"

"I tried to get over you. I tried to forget you. I even tried a relationship, once, but I couldn't do it. So, I stuck to servicing my needs instead. That's why Nikki thinks of me the way she does. But despite your best friend's opinion of me, you came to me. You turned those blue eyes my way and used your charms, and I've never been able to say no to you." I ran my hands through my hair and fisted it.

"At first, I thought that I wanted what you did—a roll in the hay, no pun intended." I nodded at the bales behind me. "But later that night, I did something I haven't done since high school, since you and I were together. I let a woman spend the night." I closed my eyes and reopened them to focus on her tear-stained face. "I let you spend the night with me, Nica. And the next morning, you were gone with a note stating that it had been amazing. I felt used because amazing deserves the woman to be there in the morning. Amazing deserves a simple wake up call if the woman needs to leave. That's the moment where everything changed for me." I took a deep breath. "No one's made me feel that way before.

"The second time around, I gave in because I didn't want to stop at the one night. I fucked up by letting it happen. The punch to the gut was when you said that it had been fun. It became clear to me that that night meant more to me than it did to you. It solidified the fact that you wanted a fuck buddy, but I can't be that guy for you. It's why I got mad and left."

I paused to gather up my breath, my ass

falling back onto the bale, but I was far from finished. "You–"

"I never wanted that kind of relationship either," she whispered.

"Then why didn't you say anything?" I asked, my voice hoarse. "Would it have been so hard to tell me that you wanted more, or that you wanted to be friends?"

"I did," she said, "at Fairfax, remember?" She had. "When you didn't go for it, I tried a different approach. I never expected it to go that far."

My brow arched. "You mean you accidentally seduced me?"

"Well, that's..." She sighed. "I figured that if we connected on a physical level, that maybe you'd talk to me. Once I started, all I wanted was to wrap myself around you and never let go. Everything from fifteen years ago came crashing back." She wiped at the tears on her cheeks. "I still love you, Jacob. I always have." She shrugged her shoulders and shook her head.

She stood and turned to leave but paused after a few steps. Keeping her back to me, she said, "I've always been happiest here. After fifteen years, it took my son trying to get to know me to make me remember that. This is my home, Jacob: you, Jordan, Nicole, Paxton, and now, Alissa and Jasper too. You're my home, and if I have to settle for living in the same city and sharing friends, then I will.

"We'll do the paternity test. Just know that if you turn out to be Jordan's father, I'm not going to keep you from him. I fucked up. You know why I did what I did. I wish I could take back all those years of pain you went through. I wish I'd been stronger. Maybe then I would have found my way back to you, and we could have had a chance. But what's done is done, and I can't change a thing no matter how much I wish I can."

She resumed her retreat. I wanted to follow but I was stuck on a single factoid. *She loves me.*

The sound of a car engine however, had my ass flying off the hay bale and my feet in a sprint out the door. I pulled my car keys out of my pocket and ran for my car. Pax's feet slid to a stop over the gravel to see what was going on. "Where are you going?"

"To get my woman! By the way, you might want to re-think that shelving system in that closet, and I know what you were up to. Too damn bad I was so distracted to remember your barbecue runs on charcoal." I rubbed my head so he knew what I meant and jumped in the driver's seat. Turning the key over in the ignition, I gunned the engine and set off to follow her.

CHAPTER 34

The cloud of dust she kicked up in her racing off was fading fast. I sped up, but I still couldn't see her taillights. She couldn't have been more than a few minutes ahead of me.

When I got to town, her house was the first place I looked. Relief overtook my worry when I saw her car in the driveway. I parked on the side of the street and ran to her front door.

I knocked and waited

Knocked again.

After my third attempt, I turned to walk away. *Maybe she needs a little time.*

On the bottom step, my body froze when I spotted her. She was sitting in her car, her head resting on the steering wheel, her shoulders shaking as she cried.

I walked to the vehicle and wrenched the door open.

She startled and looked up at me in shock. "W-why… W-what–?"

I grabbed her hand and pulled her out of the vehicle, slammed its door, and pushed her up against its side. "Because, you didn't hear me out. Instead, you went off on one of your tangents and ran off. You don't get to run, Nica. Not this time." She bowed her head. A fresh wave of tears rimmed her eyes. "Look at me!" She met my gaze. My hands wrapped around the sides of her face while my thumbs tried their best at wiping her damp cheeks. "Let's try this again, shall we?" My lips were pinched, but she nodded. I sighed my relief. "You still love me?" A flash of pain flew through her eyes, but she didn't answer. "Danica, do you still love me?"

She took in a shaky breath before she answered. "Very much."

"How much?"

"Enough that I would do anything to make you happy, Jacob," she whispered. "Even–"

"Anything?"

"Yes, anything."

"Good. Now, listen to me carefully." She bit her lip. "You want to know what makes me happy?" I didn't wait for her answer. "You, Danica, it's you." Her breath whooshed out, fanning over my face. "You infuriate me, you confuse me, you make me crazy. I was floored with your news about Jordan which, I have to say, has me both excited and scared shitless right now. As much as you've fucked me up with your leaving, it took one night to make me realize that I can't live without you." Her body went limp with sobs and I clutched her to my chest, burying my face in her hair. "I can be myself around you, and know you'll call me out on my shit when it matters most. It's impossible to hate you, sweetheart. I should know, I spent fifteen years trying, and I thought I'd succeeded until you waltzed back into my life. I think people would call me crazy, but they don't know you like I do."

I moved back and took her face in my hands again. "You've changed. I've changed. But something didn't, and right now, it's worth everything to me. I've tried to move on too, Nica, tried to forget." I shook my head. "It didn't work."

That crooked smile made its way onto her face. "You're rambling."

"I know." I smiled back and took a deep breath to calm

my racing heart. "I need you, sweetheart… in my life, front and center. I've seen a lot of what there is out there and no one holds a candle to you, and I've just realized why that is."

"And what's that?"

"That I still love you too." There it was. I said it. "I don't think I ever stopped. I mean, I thought I had but, now, I know I didn't. God knows I–"

"Shut up!" she said and my mouth snapped shut. "Say it again."

I smiled and leaned my forehead against hers. "I love you."

"Enough to get past–"

I pulled my face away from hers. "Sweetheart, if we love each other enough, we'll work through anything. Anything else, we always have handcuffs and counselors."

The woman giggled. "Handcuffs?"

I waggled my brows. "Handcuffs." Then, my expression sobered. "I'm all in, Nica, the good, the bad, the great, and ugly. I don't want a short affair where we part ways. I want forever." I kissed her forehead. "You, me, and Jordan."

"Is this real?"

"Oh, it's very real," I said. "Sweetheart, I'm not letting you go again. I don't think I'd survive it."

"Good, because I don't think I can leave."

"Thank God! I thought those handcuffs would have to come out much earlier than planned."

Her eyes shone. "I'll have to remember that you've got those."

I groaned but was hushed when her lips captured mine, eliciting a moan from me. My hands let go of her face as they found her hips, and I pressed my body against hers.

I was first to pull away. "Maybe we should take this inside."

Leading me to the front door, she let us in and locked the

deadbolt. Fierce hunger was in her eyes when she faced me.

"Woman, you better be prepared for this." I took the few steps needed, grabbed onto her hips, and pulled her hard into me. "I'm going to be taking my time with you." I nuzzled the side of her face. "And then, I'll fuck you senseless like I know you like," I whispered into her ear. She whimpered and I felt her knees shake.

Picking her up bridal-style, I headed toward her bedroom. She kicked off her flats on the way.

I set her down on her feet, her delicate fingers rushing to unbutton my shirt. With every inch of skin she revealed, her mouth and hands tantalized.

Divested of my shirt, Danica kept her eyes on mine. My arms reached for the hem of her baby blue sundress. Over her head it went, and was added to our building pile of clothes on the floor. Revealed, she wore a matching set of blue lacy boy-cut shorts and bra. I took a moment to admire her.

My fingers ran down her bra straps, following the edge of the material until they'd reached the tops of her breasts. She arched toward me and I groaned. "I love this color on you." A hand slid around her waist, the other threaded through the hair at the back of her head, and I pulled her in for a hungry kiss while I guided her down to the mattress.

When her hands reached for my jeans, I backed off and stood at the edge of the bed. Her eyes were hungry as she watched me undo my pants and let them hit the floor.

"You're not wearing underwear!"

I laughed. "Condom?"

"No. Pill, remember?" Her voice had grown husky.

"Thank fuck!" My lips left a trail on her skin as I peeled her underwear down her legs. I moaned against her thigh. "So soft."

Her breathing grew heavy as I ascended her torso, skipping over her womanhood. I made sure to stop and pay tribute to the marks on her stomach. She watched me do so, a look of pure love in her eyes.

Making my way to her bra, I was thankful for the frontal clasp. Her cleavage spilled into my waiting hands the moment I released the garment.

She squirmed beneath me as I ravished her breasts with my mouth. I kissed up the middle of her chest, over her collarbone and then to one side of her neck, nipping the sensitive area below her ear.

She whimpered. "I need you in me, Jacob." I moved to the other side of her neck. This time, I pulled her earlobe with my teeth, generating a hiss and a, "You're killing me."

I laughed into her neck. "Are you ready, sweetheart?"

She moaned into my ear. "More than you know. Make love to me, Jacob."

I positioned myself at her entrance. Easing in, our eyes connected, and I watched as she felt me filling her. Her pupils dilated, her irises darkened to a midnight blue. Her swollen lips, made so from my kisses, drew apart. She was beautiful. Perfect. Always has been.

When I was buried to the hilt, I pulled back just as slow as I had entered her and felt her walls contract. I pushed in again, and stayed there, nuzzling her nose with mine.

"I love you, Nica."

"I love you too, Jacob." She lifted her head and kissed me slow and sweet, and I began to move deep inside her.

Hands caressed down my back. She grabbed onto my ass and met me thrust for thrust. Her eyes rolled back to a close when the first of her tremors started. Her breathing hitched.

I caressed her cheek with my fingertips. "Sweetheart, look at me."

When she did, whatever doubts, whatever worries, whatever walls had been between us, were gone. We were bared to each other on more than a physical level.

Our bodies moving in a synchronized dance as old as

time, she crested with my name on her lips, her eyes glued to mine, and that was my undoing.

Satisfied, my body hummed as I tried to catch my breath, my head buried in her neck, loving the feel of her wrapped around me.

I peppered kisses from her shoulder to her cheek and pulled back to see her face. Beneath me lay a sated woman; skin glistening, flushed, and warmth filling her eyes.

She gave me a peck on the lips, buried her face in my neck, and giggled. "This is better than any barbecue."

I agreed and rolled us over so I wouldn't crush her. "Speaking of that, what are we going to eat now?"

"We could always go back to Pax's and Alissa's." She bit her bottom lip. I reached to free it and she grabbed my wrist and kissed my knuckle. "With all the excitement, I left my purse there."

"I was hoping to have you to myself for the rest of the night, but I can't have you without your phone in case Jordan tries to call."

Dressed, all evidence of our tussle erased except for the flush of her cheeks and her swollen lips, I grabbed Danica around the waist and pulled her into me. I brushed her loose hair away from her face and pressed my lips to hers in a tender kiss.

"God, I've missed you," she whispered against my mouth, her hands cupping the sides of my neck, thumbs rubbing the edge of my jaw.

I groaned. "You can show me how much when we get back."

"Then let's not waste time." She kissed my chin and slipped from my arms, heading for the stairs.

CHAPTER 35

Forty minutes later, we pulled into my best friend's driveway. The look of shock on Paxton's face as he opened the front door was replaced by that cocky smirk of his. "I see you caught up to her."

"I forgot my purse," Danica said.

"Is that what they call it these days?" Paxton snickered. "We waited over an hour and a half on you two. Figured that you'd both be MIA for the rest of the night, so we ate." He pulled back and let us in.

"Honey?" Alissa stopped mid-stride and eyed Danica and me with a wide gaze. "You're back."

"She forgot her purse," Paxton said with a hint of laughter. "You guys hungry?"

Done with the eating portion of the evening, Danica grabbed our plates. With a quick kiss to my cheek, she went inside, Alissa following suit with the rest of the tableware.

Paxton's knowing smile made its appearance. "So?"

I smirked. "How're the trails? I'm feeling for a ride."

"Nu-uh." He shook his head. "You're not getting away so easy." Seconds later, we heard squeals coming from inside. Pax looked from the house to me and his smile turned into a grin. "Well, I guess that says it all. So, you told her?"

"Told her what?"

"Don't play dumb with me, Jake. She's been stuck on you for years. You've been stuck on her for just as long. Please tell me that you've told her you love her."

"I told her, but how'd you know how she felt?"

"It wasn't rocket science. I mean, the first thing she asks when I see her has something to do with you. Every time you were mentioned, she'd perk up and then a dark cloud would wash over her. You've had the same reaction over the years whenever you heard her name. That's why I told you to talk to her; you two needed answers before anything else. And frankly, I was sick of the doom and gloom thing you both had going on."

"Thanks for the interference, Dr. Phil." I laughed. "I can't believe I fell for your propane errand."

Pax grinned. "You're happy?"

I returned his grin. "Without a doubt."

"Good."

"What are you two grinning about?" Alissa came back out, Danica not far behind.

I grabbed my woman, spun her around and sat her on my lap. I wrapped my arms around her and set my chin on her shoulder.

Alissa stood behind her husband, hovering, with her arms around his neck. He peered up at her and she leaned down to give him a quick upside down kiss. "If you're feeling for a ride, take the wheeler. Get it stuck, you're on your own. Me and the missus have plans."

"We do?" Paxton nodded to his wife.

"Babe, I don't have the right clothes," Danica whispered in my ear.

"Oh, but you do, sweetheart." I felt her shiver of anticipation at my words. "So what do you say we leave these two to do their thing and we go do ours?" I waggled my eyebrows.

"Whoa!" I turned to look at Allie who'd caught on to my double-entendre and was fanning her face. "Go for the wild adventure, honey. Something tells me you won't regret it."

I roared with laughter when I saw my best friend's expression.

"Adventure?" Pax pulled Allie around so she landed sideways on his lap with a squeak. "If you're feeling adventurous, baby, I think I can help you out." I didn't need to hear that, but I was glued to the scene as he pulled her face toward his with a hand to the back of her neck and laid a slow one on her. That feeling of envy wasn't there any longer.

I felt my face being turned and my lips came into direct contact with Danica's. I wanted to beg for more, but she put her hand over my mouth to shut me up. "Let's go before I jump you right here." She nuzzled my jaw. "These two are about ten seconds away from getting it on out here and watching them is making–"

My dick twitched to half-mast and I lifted her up off my lap, shot to my feet and grabbed her hand. "Where are the keys?"

"Kitchen counter," Paxton said over his wife's lips. "When you get back, leave them on the work bench and don't come in. Better yet, leave your purse in the car because I'm locking the doors."

"Yeah, yeah!" Danica and I said at the same time.

Pax rolled his eyes. Alissa laid her head on his shoulder as he studied us. "I'm glad you guys are back together. It's where you belong."

I couldn't agree more.

CHAPTER 36

I pulled us over in a secluded part of the trail. Having Danica's body pressed up against mine, feeling her rub up on me with every bump on the way, was wreaking havoc on my senses. With her death grip, I doubted that the space between us had seen much air until now.

I cut the engine and pulled off my helmet.

"Why are we stopping?" she asked as she pulled hers off as well. The color in her cheeks made her look more beautiful than ever. "I thought that we'd hurry this up and go home, and, you know."

I got off the four-wheeler, lifted to sit her side-saddle, and positioned myself between her legs. Her breath fanned up onto my face. "I don't think I can wait that long." I nuzzled her cheek. I grabbed the back of her knees and pulled her hard into my groin. She grabbed on to my shoulders in an effort not to slip off the seat. "That body of yours, rubbing up against my back and ass with each bump, has made it damn well near impossible for me to see straight. I figured we'd stop before we hit a tree."

She feigned shock with a dramatic gasp, but the mischief in her eyes told me that she was along for the ride. "What do you suppose we should do?" she asked as I kissed her neck. "I could suck you off right here, but that's too easy." I groaned at her choice of words and nipped her jaw. "I could lie down in the mud, and let you fuck me until I've scared all the critters away with my screams, but I doubt you'd appreciate the detailing job to your car afterwards." She beamed and shivered in my arms when I licked the seam of her mouth. "Mmm. I know, you could ram your cock into my wet pussy right up against that big tree over there." She seemed to purr the words, and it took everything in me not to lose my footing.

"Fuck, baby!" I growled. "With the way I'm feeling right now, you'd have no skin left on your back if we did that." I bit down on her earlobe. She hissed at the sensation. "How 'bout right here on this machine?"

Her sultry laugh poured out. "I like it."

Sitting with my pants unzipped, Danica freed me from my jeans, straddling the machine with her back to the handlebars. Without warning, she pushed her underwear to the side and dropped herself hard, sheathing me in one fell swoop and a loud moan.

"Fuck, that's hot." I buried my face into her cleavage. "There's so much I want to do to you. I don't think a lifetime will ever be enough."

"Let's start with this." She bobbed up and down with some help from me, as I gripped her hips to control her movements. "We'll work our way down the list."

"I like you're way of thinking, sweetheart, but we'll have a teenager in the house." I licked the length of her neck. "I doubt he'd enjoy hearing us."

"So we have our challenges." She arched back, gripping my shoulders harder.

"I can feel you're close."

She bit her lip and focused on my face. "I think trying to stay quiet when people are around might be fun."

I laughed and gave her a quick kiss. "Are we into exhibitionism, Ms. Withers?"

"I-I…" This was it. She was about to burst. "Oh, yes!

Harder, baby! Oh God, Jacob! Help me ride you harder!"

My balls tightened right up. The way she gave herself over to me, her explicit words—everything—was intoxicating. I leaned her back onto the handlebars, lifting her hips so I could gain greater depth and freedom of movement.

"Fuck, Nica!" I thrust hard into her, bottoming out each time.

She cried out with abandon. "Jacob! Yes, Jacob, just like that!" Her head tilted back, my head burrowed into her cleavage. Through the fabric of her dress, I bit down on one of her nipples. The scream of passion she let out sent the birds in our area scattering through the treetops. The vice-like grip her sweet heat had on my length had shards of light and dark exploding behind my eyelids as I gave into my release, letting her pussy milk my length until the last of my tremors faded.

Pulling out, my ass settled on the seat and I tugged her forward to take the pressure of the handlebars off her back. She collapsed into my chest.

With a fistful of her hair, I pulled her head back so I could see her face. "Woman, that was–" She cut me off with a ravenous kiss.

"Very satisfying," she finished for me as she pulled away enough so that she could tuck me into my pants and do them up.

I nodded, giving those irresistible lips of hers a soft peck. "There's a clearing up ahead, how about we turn around there and head back?"

"I think that'd be a good idea." She smirked, reached down between us, and rubbed my package through the denim.

"You're insatiable!" A half-groan, half-laugh escaped. "And I thought I was bad."

"Oh, you haven't seen anything yet." She winked and got off the wheeler. Jamming the helmet on her head and handing me mine, she got on the front of the machine. "I'm driving."

The ride back had been more enjoyable than torturous for me. I'm not sure I could say the same for Danica however. If I had it pegged right, her squeals were more from me groping at her tits and pinching her nipples than from the thrill of the ride.

Every time I did something to her that incited a spurt of lust, the wheeler would either slow down or speed up.

Back at the barn, she chucked her helmet on the workbench along with the keys and stalked toward me. "You," she started and grabbed onto the front of my shirt, "have a very odd way of letting a woman hurry your ass home so she can give it to you good and proper."

I threw my head back and laughed. "Sorry, sweetheart." I kissed her nose. "I just can't seem to help myself around you."

We rode in companionable silence to Danica's house, her hand tucked on my lap with my fingers playing over her palm.

"I have to ask," I said. "Where'd the friskiness come from?"

"Call it years of pent up frustration and curiosity." She looked at me and smiled, but with a brief look at her, I detected hidden misery in her eyes. "I've never been like that with anyone. You make me crazy. Then again, you can attribute some of my ideas to some books I've read over the years." My brows rose toward my hairline, but I kept my gaze on the road. Was the woman into reading those erotic romances that I've seen at the drugstore checkout? "I love it when you're rough. I adore it when you're gentle. It's like you know how to play with my body without me saying any-thing at all," she said, staring out the passenger side window.

"Interesting." I gave her another quick glance. She'd turned to look at me. "It's how I feel when I'm with you. No other woman has ever been able to make me lose control like that."

"Good. Because I'm the only one you'll ever have from now on."

A normal guy would have felt nervous. A player like my-self should have freaked at her declaration, but instead, my heart swelled and butterflies of anticipation fluttered in my stomach.

It had taken me over fifteen years to figure out that there'd be no other woman for me but Danica. At least I fig-ured it out. Some don't get that luxury.

"About those books…" I began.

I followed Danica through the front door, up the stairs, and into her bedroom. My heart raced as I watched her shed her dress, bra, and underwear and headed into her en suite bathroom. Moments later, I heard water running and I fol-lowed the sound.

In the large glass enclosure, there she was, naked, wet, and irresistible with the steam rolling off of her as it caressed her skin.

I proceeded to take my shirt off and shed my pants just as quick. Sneaking into the stall, I wrapped my arms around her.

She laughed. "I was wondering if you'd get the hint." She turned in my arms, wrapped a hand around the back of my neck, and pulled my head down to hers.

"Just try keeping me away," I said against her lips.

She grinned. "I would never."

Reaching to the side, she grabbed the bar of soap and be-gan to run it over the front of my body, bringing my skin up to a full lathered mess. The feel of her small hands on my heated skin felt amazing.

She went around and began doing the same to my back. As she rinsed me off, I felt her lips over my spine and her fingernails running down my sides, and then… "Hey!" I whirled around. "Y-you bit me!" Danica was giggling. "You bit my ass!"

It didn't hurt. Well, it stung, but it was a pleasurable sting—a surprising one at that.

"I couldn't help myself," she said, all demure-like. "Just like with this." She ran her hand down my chest and headed south until she took hold of my swollen shaft. I was as hard as a steel rod.

She dropped to her knees and proceeded to lick up my length and then around the rim of the head. My head lulled back as my arms jetted out to my sides to brace themselves on the shower stall walls, and I widened my stance.

"You're so good with that devil mouth of yours," I said. "I could never get bored of this. I… oh… ugh…" I groaned. "So good." I was sounding more incoherent as she continued, sucking one of my balls into her mouth while pumping her hand up and down my length. She slid her tongue into my tip's crease and the sensation had my knees knocking, my senses reeling. She was going to make me come in that generous mouth of hers, and there wouldn't be any other option. "Fuck!" I felt my climax building one minute, and seconds later, I was gushing, feeding her my very essence. She moaned around me, bringing forth another bout of smaller tremors as I throbbed between her lips.

My chest was heaving, my eyes felt heavy, but we weren't done. When she regained her footing, I pushed her against the stall's tiled wall and crashed my lips to hers.

I trailed my mouth down her body, alternating between kisses, licks, and bites. Her nails dug into the skin of my shoulders, and I revelled in the power that I held over her. She was helpless in my ministrations, and it was how I wanted her.

"Oh, sweetheart, this bare pussy of yours drives me

wild." I petted her in a way that had her arching her pelvis toward my face. Lifting a leg over my shoulder, I pushed those nether lips apart and flicked my tongue over that swollen clit of hers. She was ready for me.

Wrapping my lips around her hardened bud, I thrust a finger deep inside her, stroking her greedy heat, bringing forth a series of moans. I trailed my inserted digit on that bumpy pad inside of her until I felt her shudder.

The one leg she stood on was about to give way, so I pulled my finger and face away from her core and helped her wrap it over my shoulder so she sat with that beautiful cunt of hers straight in my face, and went back to work.

I feasted on her like a man starved. My fingers worked their magic until she begged for me to stop, but I was relentless. She came for me so hard and fast that I pushed her for one more.

I could feel her pushing my head away and it generated a laugh, causing the vibrations to flutter all around her clit, and that's when she exploded a second time. Her thighs tightened like vices around my head.

"No more! No more!" she pleaded.

I pulled my face back so I could see the pleasured yet desperate look mirrored in her eyes. I continued to stroke her to ease her down from her high.

Being gentle, I lowered her legs from my shoulders, bringing her down until she straddled my lap. I smiled when I took in the sheer look of dazed bliss covering her face. Her breath was still labored, but no longer coming out in pants. She seemed off into her own little world. I was impressed that I was capable of inducing such effects.

"Sweetheart, let's get you dried off," I whispered in her ear, reaching up for the shower controls and turning everything off. I got up, making her keep her arms around my neck to help her to her feet in the process. I was humored when I found my woman unable to walk on her own due to the weakness my pleasuring had left her with. I reached out of the shower and grabbed the two towels that hung there. Wrapping one around her body first, I did the same with mine next.

I sat her down on the toilet and grabbed her hair brush.

"I can do that." She reached out.

"Let me."

She didn't argue.

Afterwards, I carried her off to bed where we spent most of the night talking and discovering more about each other's bodies. It's safe to say that we didn't sleep much, but who was I to complain? We were making up for lost time.

In the early hours of the morning, I succumbed to exhaustion. With my arms wrapping around Danica, she snuggled closer into my side, and I let sleep take me away. It had been one hell of a day.

CHAPTER 37

After some fooling around, Danica argued that we needed to hurry and get out of bed before Jordan got home and found us in a compromising position.

So here I was, cooking bacon in nothing but a pair of my workout shorts and a t-shirt, while Danica was washing my mud-spattered clothes from yesterday.

Cool fingers slid beneath the front of my shirt as her front pressed to my back. "I'm nervous."

Her confession made me set my fork to the side, remove the pan from the heat, turn off the burner, and face her. "Are you?" She nodded. I grabbed her hips and backed her into the island across from the stove. Lifting her so she sat on the counter, I cupped her cheek with my hand and brushed my lips over hers. "Sweetheart, I'm sure Jordan will be fine." I tried to reassure her further with another kiss that turned hot, wet, and sinful.

The front door slammed shut.

"Mom?" Jordan's footsteps were now just outside of the kitchen entrance. I backed away and Danica jumped off the counter. She reached up and wiped something off my lip.

"Jake?" Jordan came into the kitchen. "Mom, what're you doing?"

Blushing, she pulled away from me but I wouldn't have

it. I wrapped my arm around her waist, keeping her at my side. "Well, uh…"

"What's going on?" her son asked.

"What's going on is that I've made breakfast," I said with nonchalance. "Sweetheart, how would you like your eggs?" I asked, kissing Danica's cheek.

Jordan's mouth parted and then he grinned. "I'd like scrambled."

"Scrambled is fine," came next from Danica.

"Got it." I turned toward the stove.

With a quick backward glance, my woman looked like a deer in headlights, and Jordan seemed like he was enjoying it as much as I was. The teenager walked up to his mother, kissed her on her other cheek and asked, "Miss me?"

She cleared her throat. "Of course. How was Trevor's?"

"Fun," he said as I got to work on the rest of breakfast while mother and son chatted.

Danica disappeared to the laundry room after breakfast, and with Jordan's help, he and I cleaned up the kitchen.

"So, you and Mom, huh?"

"What do you mean?"

"Come on, hot shot." He smirked and crossed his arms at his chest. "I'm not stupid. Ever since we moved here, you two have been hanging out."

"And?"

"Are you banging her or not?"

My head snapped in his direction. "Excuse me?"

"Well, are you two, you know… doing it?"

"I don't feel comfortable with where this conversation is heading."

"Okay then, how about this? What's going on with you and Mom?"

I couldn't lie to him, and he was old enough to be privy to my intentions. "I love your mom." The kid chocked on his remaining sip of juice. "I know it's a shock, but–"

"Hardly! I knew that you cared for her. I mean, you cooked her dinner, hung out with me, took me shopping for her birthday gift, and you carried her fat ass to bed the other night."

"Hey now, your mom doesn't have a fat ass!" I said.

"So you've been checking it out, huh?" He laughed. I shook my head at his antics. My grin couldn't be helped, and the room filled with silence before he continued. "So what now?"

"We take our time, see where it goes. How do you feel about that?"

"You must really love her if you're asking me about my feelings. Bruce never did. I think that if you hurt her, I'm coming after you, though." He wore an exaggerated tough guy demeanor. "I mean it, hot shot. I know where you live."

I laughed and presented him with my fist. "Deal." He bumped it with a smile. "If I hurt her, I'll let you get the first swing in."

As he leaned against the counter, I could have sworn I saw a glimmer of hope in his eyes. "So, you're going to, like, be here all the time now?"

"What would you like to see?"

"I want to see my mom happy."

At that moment, Danica came into the room and met my gaze. I winked at her teary smile. "Oh, honey." She rushed to hug her son. "I am happy."

"Now you are," he mumbled into her hair.

I waited for the moment to pass before I asked him the same question. I knew he was holding out, what with the brief shadow that crossed his face before his mother joined us.

"What would you like to see aside from your mom being happy, Jordan?"

He hesitated. "This is stupid." He set his mother aside so he could make an escape.

I gripped his shoulder to stop him. "Nothing's stupid if it's got you bent out of shape."

"You'll think it's stupid."

"I promise, I won't." I lifted my hand from his shoulder and held it, palm out as if swearing an oath.

"Well…" He made eye contact with me. "I want this." He pointed to all three of us in a circular fashion. "I mean, I have a family, but it's just Mom and me. I want what you and I have."

"You mean our friendship?"

"Yeah, sort of." He cleared his throat. "It's just…" He sighed. "I think it's cool that you and I get along great and stuff, but that you're able to call me out on things. You care and you're not afraid to remind me or correct me about how I treat Mom. You're kind of like a dad—a cool one. Bruce and I never…"

He didn't have to finish. A soft breeze could have knocked me over I was so off-kilter by his words. I didn't mind the idea of being Jordan's father, biological or not, that much I was sure of, because loving Danica meant having Jordan with her, and that wasn't a hardship at all. I never realized, until now, that how Jordan felt—what he wanted and what he thought of me—would hold that much importance. His words meant the world to me.

Jordan knocked me out of my reverie as he started to exit the room. "I'm going to go do some homework."

Danica's hand clutching mine was what prompted me to say something. "Jordan?"

"Yeah?" The kid turned to face me from the kitchen entrance.

"I think you're pretty damn cool too. And for what it's worth, any man would be lucky to call himself your dad."

The boy acknowledged me with a simple nod and held my gaze as my woman plastered her front to mine in a tight hug.

Jordan laughed and strode away.

"Are you okay?" Danica asked when we heard Jordan's bedroom door shut.

I held her closer and rubbed my cheek against the top of her head. "Perfect."

"Good," she said, as she leaned back and got on her toes to deliver a kiss to my chin. "That went better than I thought it would go. I love watching the two of you together. You're so similar."

"Really?" I saw some of what she meant, but she seemed to see a lot more.

She nodded. "Over the years, I noticed certain mannerisms, some expressions… they reminded me of you. I've never been able to find traces of that guy in him. I don't know if it's because I choose not to be reminded of that part of my life or–" She looked down, haunted by the awful memories.

I grabbed her chin. "Stop it! I fell for him before I found out he could be mine. If he is, and even if he isn't, I'll be right here, sweetheart. You're mine, which makes him mine."

"You can't say that until we know for sure, Jacob," she whispered. "Things can change."

"I can and I have. I meant everything I said yesterday. I'm all in." I squeezed her to me. "I want us to know because it'll give us the closure we need, and the answers that Jordan will be able to have so he can find his place in the world." She nodded. "Now kiss me like you won't see me for the rest of the day."

"You're not leaving are you?"

"I'll have to some time, sweetheart, but I don't plan on leaving until later." I leaned toward her.

"Then let me show you how much I'll miss you." She smiled and met me halfway.

Her kiss was urgent, fiery, and demanding. I loved every bit of aggression that she put into it. Grabbing her firm ass, I lifted her onto the island counter-top. Her hands rushed for the hem of my shirt, and when her fingers touched my heated skin, I stopped her hands and pulled back.

"I want this as much as you do, baby, but we can't do this right now. Not in the open." I chased my words with a peck.

"Come with me." She returned my chaste kiss, and I gave her enough room to jump off of the counter, take my hand, and lead me to the laundry room where she shut the door behind us. She turned to me with a sly grin. "Better?"

I laughed into her neck, nipping at the soft skin below her ear. "Devil woman."

CHAPTER 38

"You could stay." She nuzzled my cheek, pressing her body into mine after we made our way to the door. I hated leaving Danica and Jordan after a fun-filled day together.

"As tempting as it is, I don't have clothes, and I've got that important meeting tomorrow, you have work, and Jordan's got school."

With a promise of an early morning run to kick-start our day together, I left.

The following morning, I cursed my alarm clock for waking me so early, but then I remembered why.

I hadn't slept much the night before, missing a certain five-foot-six woman with hair the color of a raven's, eyes as blue as sapphires, and the warmth that she provided.

As my feet hit the landing, I heard the doorbell.

I greeted Danica. "Hey."

"Good morn–" Her words halted. "You look exhausted, what's wrong?"

"It's your fault. I missed you in my bed."

"Oh, honey." She came in, patted my cheek and leaned up for a kiss. "Maybe we should go back to bed instead." She hung a garment bag on the newel post. I took notice of her tight running shorts and tank top that did everything to accentuate her assets.

"Oh, we can go back to bed all right." I wrapped my arms around her, settling my hands on her ass. "But I'm not going to be doing much sleeping."

Her eyes sparkled. "It's a good thing I brought my office clothes, huh?"

"Well, if you wanted to move in, why didn't you ask?" I laughed at my pun.

"Moving in?" She snuggled into me. "That's a very appealing idea. This castle could use a few extra occupants."

I loved that she saw herself living a life with me in this monstrosity of a house. "How many would you say?"

She shrugged her shoulders. "No more than three or four?"

My brow furrowed. "Three or four?" Was that including her and Jordan?

The question on my face made her giggle. "Two on top of us, Mr. Bachelor-for-Life."

"If we keep getting busy like we have been, I'd say that we shouldn't have a problem filling those rooms when the time comes." I kissed the top of her head before leaning back and tilting her head, so I could see her smiling face. "As for me being a bachelor, I've advocated that throne, sweetheart."

"Well put, counselor. Now let's get you to bed so we can practice that theory of yours, shall we? Maybe you'll have some time to rest too."

I gave her a dramatic sigh of relief. "I thought I'd have to do you here in the entrance-way." I spanked her bottom, my grin getting wider with her giggle before laying a hot wet one on her.

Hurried to my room, Danica had me with my shirt off, and was down on her knees, working my shorts toward my ankles. She pushed me onto my bed, then disposed of her own clothing, exposing pure, porcelain flesh that begged for my touch.

Crawling to me from the edge of the bed, she straddled my hips, her hands on my chest for stability with one of her sensuous smiles that boded of erotic things to come. I took control and flipped her rough and fast, onto her back. Her eyes went wide, and her pupils dilated.

"Looks to me like someone wants it rough," I teased. "I'll apologize now if you're unable to walk in those fantastic heels of yours later."

She lifted her head and licked a trail up my neck. "Honey, just fuck me already. I want you inside, hard."

I nuzzled her neck. "God, I love that filthy mouth of yours," I said, but I didn't make a move.

"Jacob, now!"

I waited until she was about to say something else, and then I shoved my cock inside her, to the hilt. A guttural moan rumbled in her throat as I teased her, running my length against that sweet spot inside her.

Kneeling on my haunches, I lifted her hips and picked up speed. I was enthralled with watching myself disappear inside her heat. It was an erotic sight that urged me to keep up with my frantic pace.

She came undone, screaming my name until her voice ran hoarse. Sweat beaded off our bodies. Tension rose deep inside, starting at the base of my spine, sending tingling sensations from my stomach straight to my balls.

"Now, my love," I slowed my thrusts. "I'm giving it to you my way." Dropping her bottom to the mattress, I covered her body with mine, leaning on my forearms and concentrated on slow, steady, and thorough.

She was still riding out her first orgasm when the second one hit her just as fierce as the first.

I hushed her erotic cries with my mouth, capturing, feeling all of her as her tremors took me over the edge with her this time. Her legs gripped my waist like vices, and her arms came around my shoulders, holding me to her, wet skin sliding against wet skin as I slowed us to a stop, and I tucked my face into the crook of her neck.

After a while, Danica's legs slid down the back of mine. "You might be right," she whispered. "I think I might have a tough time walking in those heels today."

I lifted my head to find a very flushed, lips swollen, eyes glittering woman who was the epitome of satisfaction. Pride swelled within me.

"But you'll have me massaging those aches and pains away later." I winked.

I escorted Danica out to her car, opening the driver's side door.

"Oh, I forgot to mention…" Danica turned around before she got in. "Jordan's got a doctor's appointment at lunch. He thinks it's part of his routine physical but when I booked his appointment last week, I asked for the DNA swab to be taken in case you decided that you wanted to know."

I nodded. "Okay."

She smiled as she pulled out a small box and piece of paper from her purse, and handed them to me. "Will you be there?" Her smile held a certain note of anxiety. "I know it was presumptuous of me, but I figured that I'd pick up a swab for you too, and–"

I stepped toward her, cupped her cheek and pressed my lips to hers. "I'll be there," I said against her mouth. Her body relaxed and she leaned in, wrapping her arms around my neck for another kiss that I pulled away from before we got too out of hand. "I'm already regretting sending you off, please don't make it harder. I love you, and I'll see you at lunch."

That temptress smile of hers came out again and she shrugged. "Worth a try." I pressed a hand to her stomach, indicating that she should get in her car, and shook my head at her antics. "Right. I'm getting gone and I'll see you in a few hours. When Jordan asks, we're going with me inviting you to lunch with us."

"Okay, sweetheart. See you."

With the test tube containing the swab and the DNA from my cheek in hand, I did my business with the clerk at the front desk, and then sat down in the waiting area.

Danica and Jordan arrived a few minutes later.

"Hey, hot shot." Jordan smiled at me as I walked toward them. "Small world." Danica smiled at me from behind him.

"Not really, your mom invited me to lunch."

"Cool."

"Thanks for coming." She brushed her lips against mine.

"You're welcome." I kissed her temple. "So, by the end of the week?" I asked in a whisper as we walked to the front desk, and Jordan found himself a seat.

"That's what they said when I picked everything up," she said, smiling at the clerk, and handed over Jordan's health insurance card.

"Please take a seat. The nurse should be right along to bring you into the exam room."

"Maybe we can celebrate at the ball," I pondered aloud as we went to join Jordan who was already seated.

"What ball?" she asked.

"I forgot to mention it with everything that's been going on. Every year, Standhope has–"

"Standhope, as in the charity?" I nodded. "How'd you get tickets? They were sold out before I got to buy one this year." She pouted.

"Well, you're in luck. Stan's my one client. He gives me two tickets every year because I help him out. So, what do you say, will you be my date?"

She pressed her lips to mine. "I'd be honored."

"Mom, sheesh!" Jordan whined.

"Jordan Withers," the nurse called.

"Let's go, Jordan, I want to eat and get your butt back to school before your next class."

"Do I have to?"

"Yes!" His mother and I said at the same time.

We turned and looked at each other and broke into laughter.

Jordan groaned. "You two freak the hell out of me with this say-the-same-thing-at-the-same-time thing you've got going on."

"Language," I warned.

"Yes, Dad."

The nurse stopped Danica and Jordan. "Your father can come too if he'd like."

"Oh, he's not my dad."

"I'm sorry. It's just… Well, you kind of look like him. Then again, you look a lot like your mom too."

Danica turned to look at me, biting her lip. Jordan turned to study me, and my eyes froze on him.

He looked me from top to bottom in an assessing gaze, and a glint in those green eyes that told me he was pondering something. Just as quick as this scene took place, it ended with Jordan shaking his head, and following the nurse. Danica and I shared one last look—the one that said that we both hoped that Jordan was wrong. The desperation I felt in that moment for those results to prove that I was his biological father was immeasurable.

CHAPTER 39

The week seemed to fly by as Danica, Jordan, and I fell into some kind of routine. During the day, I spent most of my time at home, working, and in the evenings, I'd hang out with both of them. I loved our time together, and often I found myself wondering how I could have ever fathomed a life without these two relationships that now dominated my existence.

By Friday, we still hadn't received news about the DNA results. Danica was antsy, and I wish I could say I was doing better, but I wasn't. Whenever our minds wandered toward the topic, I tasked myself with keeping us both distracted. Needless to say, sex had been one of our favorite methods to accomplish said distraction.

The ball was scheduled for tomorrow night. Jordan had plans to stay over at his friend's again, and I was looking forward to having my woman to myself.

I walked into Withers International to surprise Danica with an early lunch, catching her as she was backing away from the reception desk.

"Why hello, gorgeous," I whispered in her ear, spun her around and kissed her right there in front of all to see.

"Get your filthy paws off my daughter!" I heard bellowed behind me.

Danica jumped, and I turned to face the man, keeping an arm wrapped around her waist, as my woman exclaimed, "Daddy!"

"Mr. Withers." I approached him, dragging Danica along beside me. I held out my hand. "It's good to see you again, sir."

He huffed, ignoring my hand. "I wish I could say the same for you." He turned his disdainful gaze from me, and narrowed his sights on his daughter. "Danica, what's this fool doing here?"

"Daddy, I swear–"

"What? He broke your heart. He tried to steal this company from under us and–"

"What?" I asked.

"Jacob, Daddy's just talking out of his ass." She looked at him, her face pale, lips held tight, and eyes that glowed daggers in her father's direction. By then, we'd gained a small audience in the form of employees getting up to take in the action over their cubicle walls. "And for the record, Daddy, you should maybe think about retaining the services of a new lawyer. The only reason why we won in court–"

"Nica, it's okay." I squeezed her closer. "I get that the man never liked me, and I see that it's not about to change."

He snarled. "You're damn right about that one, you bastard."

"What's the matter with you? He threw the case so you could keep your precious company!" She looked at her father with incredulity. "Did you forget whose heart you broke when you made the decision for all of us, years ago? I told you that I loved him, and I still do. Now, I suggest you accept that, because I'm not going anywhere, and neither is Jacob.

"He's a respectable, honourable, and loving man, and you ought to be happy for me to have been able to find that twice in a lifetime." She snorted her disgust as she looked around. "If you don't mind, this isn't the place. I'm done here. Come and find me when you're ready to discuss things like a proper adult. Let's go home, Jacob. Liz, in case you haven't caught that, I'm taking the rest of the day." Before I could move, Danica stormed off following the receptionist's nod of assent. With one last look toward her father, I followed her.

Danica didn't say much on the ride home, but I could feel the simmer of her rage radiating off of her in pulses.

I parked the car and turned toward her. "What do you say we go for a run? I have my workout bag in the trunk."

She looked at me with eyes glistening. "I'm sorry. It's the same old thing with him." She started to exit the car, and I followed. "In his eyes, I'll always be his little girl, but this stifling of his has to let off at some point. I mean, I'm thirty-four for crying out loud!"

"Sweetheart, he does it because he loves you." I grabbed her hand and walked us to her front door.

"I know." She looked down with her keys dangling in her hand. "I just wish he could see what kind of man you are."

"And what kind of man am I?" I smirked, pulled her into me for a one-armed hug, and took her keys from her.

"Didn't you hear me earlier?" She laughed. "Then again, I wasn't going to start labeling the more obvious traits."

"Like?"

"You're going to make me say it, aren't you?" I nodded and kissed her forehead. "Fine." She sighed. "Aside from having a god's body, a tongue for sinners, and arms of an angel, you're downright sexy, and quite possibly the best lover I'll ever be able to imagine."

I shrugged my shoulders. "I suspected as much."

The grin she sported after her admission fell, making the

one I was trying to fight off grow, thus giving my attempt at teasing her away.

"Didn't you say something about a run?"

$$\textit{CHAPTER 40}$$

I was busy enjoying my view from behind when Danica stopped dead in her tracks. In an effort not to plow into her and send us toppling to the ground, I grabbed her waist. We stumbled a few steps, but recovered. Looking past her, her father sat on the front steps, waiting for us. He was holding something in his hands.

The man got to his feet and approached. "Here." He handed the item to me. I looked down at the wrinkled thing and realized that the envelope had already been opened—and a long time ago at that, judging by the creases, the stiffness of the paper, and its discoloration.

"What's this?" I looked from him to Danica. Withers didn't answer, and Danica shrugged her shoulder with a shake of her head. She looked as curious and confused as I was.

I peeked into the envelope and pulled the pages from it.

I read the document.

Paused.

Reread it in its entirety, taking in the date of the document, and paused once more.

My heart drummed out of my chest at what I saw. "What is this?" I lifted my gaze from the papers to the man who handed them to me. Rage built up and I felt my blood simmer. "Is this a joke?" I held the papers in one hand and shook them in his face. The man had known the truth—for ten fucking years! "You sick son of a bitch! You're as low as they come, you know that? You knew!"

"Jacob?" Danica rubbed my arm in what she must have figured was a soothing fashion.

I was seething so much that I couldn't answer her, let alone calm down. Instead, I pushed the papers into his chest, turned, and walked toward my car.

"So you're going to walk away and prove me right?" he asked.

"Jacob, what's going on?" Danica asked. "Where are you going?"

"I have to get out of here," *before I kill the fucker,* I finished in my head.

"I told you he wasn't the type to stick around," Withers said to his daughter.

I spun around, my anger bringing forth one hell of a headache. I marched the ten or so steps to stand in the man's face. "I'm not leaving because of what's on those papers, or is that how low your opinion of me is? I'm the filth from the wrong side of the tracks, amounting to nothing, resolving to being a deadbeat, is that right?"

"Well, it does sum it up quite well don't you think? You don't measure up, son. You never have."

"Don't call me son!" I spat as if his endearment left a foul taste in my mouth. "I have a father, and I can damn well guarantee you that he would have never done this!" I pointed to the crumpled pages he held against his chest. "Danica, I'm sorry, but I need to get out of here before I do something we'll both regret."

"What's going on?"

"I think you better ask him." I bent down and kissed her cheek. "I love you. I'll be back. I just need to cool off. Just so we're clear, Withers, I'm not a man without." I opened the driver's side door, gave Danica a quick look before looking her father in the eye with intent. "But you're about to be."

As I was about to step foot inside my car, I noticed that Danica's old man had blocked me in with his SUV. Slamming the door, hitting the fob to lock up, I pocketed my keys, and took off running without a backward glance.

My blood was pumping, the adrenaline was flowing, and I hoped that by the time I reached my house that my fury would manage to dissipate.

With each thump of a foot against the pavement, thoughts reeled about in my head.

A decade, the man had known the truth and he hadn't told a soul. All of that time had passed when I could have known that I was a father. All that time spent being miserable and that man was responsible for it.

He had almost ruined three lives, and for what? So he could keep his daughter for himself? I snorted as I rounded the final turn to the street my house was on. *Highly unlikely.* Withers had pawned Danica off to Spalding the minute he saw a great business venture.

The reality of my life felt strange. I was elated to have an answer after this entire week, albeit, not from the source it was intended to come from.

I was a father.

Fucking hell!

Thrilled and terrified at once, I battled with figuring how Danica and I were going to break the news to Jordan. Who knew how the kid would take it, but there was one way to find out—and there wouldn't be any holding back when the time came.

It wasn't until I reached my driveway that it hit me. If I was livid at the news, I could only imagine Danica's reaction when she found out that she'd been betrayed by her father.

My worry about Danica's reaction and my urge to be

there for her surpassed my anger. I turned around, and sprinted back toward her house. There was no way that she would be dealing with all of this alone. Not when the man she idolized and vetted for all these years had betrayed her in the worst way.

CHAPTER 41

When I arrived at Danica's, a loud crash came from inside the house and I made a dash for the front door.

"How could you?" Danica's voice shook with fury, and was followed by yet another crash of what sounded like glass. I shut the front door behind me and moved toward the sound of their voices.

"Sweetheart," her father said.

"Don't call me that!" The woman was stark raving mad, and her words held a trembling quality that told me that she was crying.

"For the tenth time, Dani, would you let me explain?"

"I think those papers explain more than enough, don't you?" I heard doors slamming. "Ten years! Ten years, Daddy! Ten fucking years! You knew and you never said a thing!"

I entered the room. "Nica!"

I found Withers in the corner, cowering, surrounded by broken shards of glassware and porcelain. Danica was at the opposite end of the room, by the cabinets. I suppose I should be glad she hadn't gotten to the knife drawer yet.

Her tearful eyes met mine, and I hurried to her, as she collapsed in my arms. "Why?" She sobbed into my chest, and I gave a vehement look at her father as I tightened my arms around her.

"Because he wasn't good enough for you," he said. "Bruce—"

"You're going to throw that vermin into this conversation," I interrupted him. "After what he's put you and your kids through? Have you lost your ever-loving mind?"

"Now you listen here!" His face turned a deep crimson. "You two were too young to be having kids. I didn't agree with her choosing someone of your kind."

"Excuse me? What's that supposed to mean? My family might have lacked for funds, but we worked hard for what we have." I took a deep breath. "I doubt that my going out of my way to study and make ends meet so I could see myself into a scholarship, and through years of college and law school, in order to make something of myself as something less than worth being proud of and respected."

The man stood there, not one word, so I went on. "And don't you think for one minute that I would have let your daughter fend for herself had I known all these years. I would have been glad to work multiple jobs and lose sleep to make sure that she got through college. I would have made sure that my son had everything he could have ever wanted for." Danica's body went solid and I tightened my grip on her.

"I see now that no matter what I do, that you'll never approve." Danica's arms clutched at my waist with everything she had. "Now, I suggest that you get the hell out of here before I throw you out myself. You've done enough damage to last us a lifetime."

"Just you wait one minute! This is—"

"No! I've heard enough! I won't let you attack Jacob, Daddy. I want you to leave."

"You heard her," I murmured against her hair, kissing it.

"But—" he started.

"Don't! Leave now and don't come back. And for the

record," she paused for effect, "I quit! I quit you. I quit your precious company. I-I quit it all! You can take my shares and shove them where the sun doesn't shine because I don't want a part of any of it. You've controlled enough of my life, and it stops now."

The man didn't try to protest, despite his evident rage at the situation. I sure hoped that he was mad at himself more than anyone else, because he only had himself to blame.

He walked past us and out of the kitchen.

Seconds later, a crash from the hallway was heard. Danica looked up at me, her eyes wide with worry.

"Shit!" I cursed. "Stay here." I went to see what was going on, thinking that the man had chucked a piece of art or some vase in a fit but it wasn't so. I found the man sprawled on the floor, clutching at his chest, his crimson color turning to a purple shade. "Danica, call 911!" I rushed to the man's side and knelt down. "Are you okay?" The man's breathing was shallow and wheezy. He was reaching out for me. I could see his lips, begging me to help him, but the words never materialized. "We're getting you some help. Just lay still and try to keep calm."

When the man passed out and his breathing ceased, fear overwhelmed me. I was thankful for my knowledge of First Aid and CPR, but I'd never imagined that I'd have to use it someday, least of all on the one man that I loathed about as much as he disapproved of me. Despite those facts, my moral compass dictated my actions.

I tilted his head back, thus opening his airways. Without thinking, I pressed my mouth to his and breathed air into him.

Next, I began chest compressions.

"Come on, man, stay with me!"

For what felt like an eternity, I continued with the breathing and compressions. Danica was kneeling on his other side, holding his hand. The look of guilt on her face was what kept me going. I would do anything for her—including saving a man I despised with all my might so my woman would have a chance at unshouldering her guilt.

The paramedics arrived about twenty minutes after his collapse and carted Withers off. Danica was beside herself with an overwhelming load of emotions, and I was out of breath, exhausted, sweaty, and numb. Too much had transpired in so little time that it was as if I'd shut down due to emotional overload.

"Let's get to the hospital," I said.

"I have to call Mike."

"I can do that." I pushed a stray strand behind her ear. "Why don't you go change and I'll take care of it. The number's on your cell?" She nodded and handed the device over. "Go, sweetheart."

"What about you?"

"Don't worry about me. I'm fine." I found and dialled Mike's number when she reached the top of the stairwell.

One ring… two… On the third, Michael Withers picked up. "I was wondering when you'd call, stranger." I could hear the smile in the man's voice.

I cleared my throat. "Mike. It's–"

"Jake?"

"Yeah."

"Is everything okay with my sister?"

"She's fine. It's your dad."

The man cursed. "I knew this trip was going to be too much for him."

"He's in the hospital, Mike, and it doesn't look good."

"I'm on my way on the next flight out. And Jake?"

"Yeah?"

"We need to talk."

I groaned and ran a hand through my tousled hair. "Why am I not surprised?"

After a few more words, the man disconnected, and I

leaned forward, my ass against the wall and elbows to my knees to wait for Danica.

An hour later, we were sitting in the family waiting area when the doctor came to inform us that Danica's father had suffered a moderate heart attack, which required him to remain in the hospital over the course of a few days to regain his strength.

The physician stated that the man was comfortable and asleep, and when he offered to take her to his room, she declined. It was clear to me that she might be worried about her father's health, but she wasn't ready to face him just yet.

"Let's just go home," she said. "Jordan will be home from school soon, and who knows when Mike will show up."

"Are you sure?"

She nodded. "Visiting hours last until later, and I can't go in there right now and hold it together."

On our drive home, Mike called to let us know that he'd be arriving in a couple of hours.

Danica and I rushed to get the mess in the kitchen cleaned up in time to hear the front door open and close as the last dustpan filled with debris hit the garbage can.

"Mom? Jake?"

"We're in the kitchen, sweetie." Danica let out a loud tension-filled breath.

It all hit me like a tonne of bricks when my eyes settled on him and his beaming smile.

My son!

❧ <u>CHAPTER 42</u> ❧

I watched as Jordan and his mother bantered back and forth while she made dinner for all of us and Mike, who was late, but had promised to be there to eat. I found myself smirking like a fool despite my worries.

Would it all be okay when Jordan found out?

He was a teenager, not a young child that could be convinced with simple explanations. The story was a long one, and it needed to be told from the very beginning. There was bound to be a slew of questions, explosive and angry moments, but I hoped that the kid would take it all in stride. Jordan accepted me as 'Jake the hot shot lawyer' and his mother's boyfriend, but would he accept me as his birth father?

For me, it was easy, it was simple. I knew the truth. I was able to digest the news of what had happened in increments. It wouldn't be that way for my son.

My son...

So many years I could have spent, but missed, watching my child grow up—nearly sixteen years of a life lost because of his grandfather. It pissed me off to no end. I felt cheated, and I could only imagine how Danica felt—let alone fathom how Jordan would feel when he was in the know.

I didn't want for his relationship with his mother's father

to be strained, but I had no control over that. The man had ensured a bitterness to hang in the air between all of us when he made the decision to play God and keep the truth to himself.

Knocking me out of my jumbled thoughts, Jordan called my name. "Jake?" I smiled at the teen sitting across from me at the table. "Are you all right?"

I cleared my throat. "I'm fine."

"You look like you've got a lot on your mind." I looked at Danica who gave me a tight-lipped smile. "Is it because of what happened to Granddad?"

I nodded. "Some."

"Why do I get the feeling that you're both hiding something?"

His mother wore a sad expression.

"Hello?" came from the front door, putting an end to Jordan's question, and filling me with a sense of relief that Danica and I had gained some reprieve.

"Uncle Mike!" Jordan got up and rushed to the man.

"What's up, dude?" Mike hugged him. "Jake." He shook my hand, then walked over to his sister and took her in his arms for a bear hug. "Sis." He backed away and cupped her face in his hands and kissed her forehead. "You look great. How's he doing?"

"He's fine, from what they've told me. I couldn't go in." She sighed. "Can we talk?"

I watched as Mike eyed his sister with an assessing gaze. "Jordan, do you mind giving your mom, Jake, and I a minute?"

"I'll be in the living room." He grumbled something about him not being a little kid anymore as he left the room. Little did he know, he was about to grow up in a hurry when we broke our news.

W ith the coast clear, Danica reached for the top of the

fridge, pulled out the envelope, and pushed it over the counter toward Mike. I closed in on her and wrapped my arm around her waist.

He eyed the envelope and then looked up, his gaze moving between me and his sister. "What is this?"

"Did you know?" Her voice was shaky.

Mike took the envelope and pulled out the papers. He read them and then looked at her, his brows drawing together. He looked down to read them again and then looked at me. "You're– but–" His color paled and he cleared his throat. "Who's is this?" He turned the envelope to find his father's name and address on its discolored front as an answer. His eyes widened. "He's known all this time?" Danica and I nodded. He looked down at the papers once more, his hand rubbed down from his forehead to pinch the bridge of his nose. He sighed. "Mom must be rolling in her grave right now. She'd be furious if she knew that he knew all along."

"Dad and I had a spat at the office and I walked out on him." Danica proceeded to explain the events of the day to her brother as I remained silent through their exchange. "I took Jordan in for his physical on Monday. They have the swabs. We've been expecting the results all week. They haven't come yet, but Dad had these." She nodded toward the papers abandoned on the counter. "I think he's been carrying them around with him all this time, or maybe he's had them in a safety deposit box somewhere. With the amount of times we've been in his safe over the years, there's no way he could have kept them hidden."

"Jordan doesn't know that I could be his dad." I cleared my throat. "That I am his dad."

"You're my what?" We jumped and turned to find Jordan standing in the kitchen's entrance, looking pale. "What's going on? Mom? Uncle Mike? J-jake?"

"Sweetie." Danica made to step toward him, but he shook his head and took a step back. "You need to sit down."

"No!" he said to his mother. "No more secrets! I knew you were hiding something!"

"I promise I'll tell you everything." Danica's calmness was impressive. "Please sit down."

Jordan gave in and did as he was instructed. His eyes were glued to me, his jaw was tense, and his fists where clenched so tight his knuckles were white. My boy was mad, and all I wanted to do was shield him from the pain he was about to experience.

CHAPTER 43

History came to repeat itself in the way of words. Jordan sat and listened and when he asked questions, we answered as best we could. For once, I was glad that Mike was there, because Jordan didn't allow for either Danica or myself to get close, let alone comfort him.

"When did you find out?" His anger was now redirected from me to his mother, but even that was fading fast as the story unfolded.

"We found out today," I said looking at Danica. "That swab you had on Monday was used to see if you were mine. Those results aren't back yet, but–"

"So where'd those papers come from?" He pointed to the envelope.

"Ten years ago, Granddad ran some tests." Danica kept her voice soft. "I'm not sure as to how he got Jacob's DNA, but–"

"So, he's known all this time?" If I thought that Danica's look of betrayal had been bad, it had nothing on the one Jordan sported. Seeing it in the face of an adult is one thing, but seeing it in a child's eyes—my child's eyes—it tore at my soul.

Within seconds, he went from looking like a teenager that bordered adulthood, to a three-year-old child who needed both his parents to mend his broken heart. "Why did he do that?" he whispered. "He knew I hated Bruce. All the times we talked… He lied to me?"

Danica and I couldn't bear saying the word so we nodded. It still looked like we'd sucker punched him in the gut.

"I'm sure Granddad will answer your questions when we go see him later," Mike said.

"I don't want to see him." Jordan's tone brokered no argument.

"That's fine." Danica supported his decision and reached forward to cover the top of his clasped hands with hers, and he let her. "Are you okay, baby?"

He shook his head. "I think I might be in shock. My grandfather is a manipulative son of a bitch and–"

"Watch it, kid!" I said with authority and his head snapped up to look at me.

His eyes watered. "And I have a dad?"

I felt my eyes copy his reaction as I nodded. "And I have a son." It felt great to state it out loud, so much so that I felt like yelling it from the rooftop.

We let those words hang in the air for a moment, digesting the tumultuous emotions that reeled through each and every one of us after what I could consider our first family meeting.

"So what happens now?" Jordan asked.

"Why don't we just keep going the way we are—that's if you're okay with that?" I said. "There's no rush."

"I thought that we'd all move in together since you're always here anyway," he said.

Did he mean that?

Had anything changed between us aside from the obvious fact that he was of my blood?

No, but I knew the battle hadn't yet been won. What he'd come to learn was far too much for him to wrap his mind around in such a short amount of time. I know I hadn't digested everything as of yet.

Danica seemed as surprised with her son's comment as I was. I squeezed her shoulder. "How about we take it easy for now, let Granddad recover, send him home, and then we can talk about a move?"

"Sounds smart to me, and I'll stick around so that the old man leaves when he should," Mike said. "Who knows, I might find me a good woman too while I'm here."

Danica harrumphed. "If you did, you'd have to move back, dear brother."

"It wouldn't be so bad, would it?" he asked. "I've been thinking about relocating now that I'm practically done with the reorganization."

"There's just one problem," she said. "To find a good woman, you need to keep her for longer than a night, which reminds me… We'll talk about that later. Now, who's hungry?"

CHAPTER 44

Mike was alone when he left for the hospital.

Danica and I stayed behind with Jordan, too bitter with our son's reaction to his grandfather's betrayal. Instead, we settled in for a night of movies.

Jordan came into the room with two bowls of popcorn.

I couldn't help but laugh. "What, are you incapable of sharing?"

"I just figured that you'd enjoy more than a handful this time around," he said.

"Now boys," Danica said, "sit your butts down, this mama wants some cuddles. Jordan, is everything all set for you to be spending tomorrow night at Trevor's?"

"Yeah."

Before we knew it, both movies were over, and Jordan had gone up to bed. Mike had returned with the slight smell of liquor on him. It was evident that he'd been to see Ben over at Fairfax.

"How's Ben today?" I asked.

"Same old miserable man," Mike said. "I know it's hard for him with losing Candice and all, but the man needs to get laid already. It might make him feel better."

"Mike!" Danica smacked him on the arm.

"You know it's true," he said.

"You're an insensitive jerk, you know that? Ben's always been a sweetheart. Some lucky woman is bound to snag him soon enough when he's good and ready."

"I agree with your sister," I said. "The man's coming around." Danica cuddled further into my side and Mike settled in at the other end of the couch.

"And how about you?" Danica asked her brother. "When will you stop being a pessimist and settle down? You know we're not all like Tracey."

The man scoffed. "Dani, I'd rather not relive the hell that woman's put me through. So, if I choose to have my fun without settling, I'm fine with that." Mike's brows arched, his gaze meeting mine when I rolled my eyes at his declaration. "What?"

I chuckled. "It's just that it's all too familiar. Shit, I was just like you before your sister rolled back into town." I smiled down at my woman. "I thought I'd moved on, swore off relationships altogether after she left. It was a one-nighter every now and again. I knew something was missing, but I just didn't know what. In the end, it wasn't pretty."

"What changed?" he asked.

"I realized that none of them were your sister." My eyes met his again. "You can't fuck a woman out of your head and heart." Danica punched my shoulder. "I'm sorry, sweetheart, it's crass, but it's true. I had a lot of anger buried deep inside, Mike. It wasn't until your sister gave me her side of the story that I was able to understand and move on." I kissed my smiling woman's forehead. "Then again, I had to be willing to listen to her first."

"And there's the bomb about Jordan," he added.

I nodded. "I can't say that the news didn't blow me away. I was convinced that I'd be a bachelor for life, and now here I am with a family." I smiled and shook my head at the thought. "I never realized I wanted kids so damn bad until I found out that Jordan might be mine. I'm floating on clouds right now, knowing that he is. To be honest, even if he weren't, it wouldn't change the way I feel about him, either."

"That's pretty deep for you," Mike said.

"Yeah." I chuckled. "But what I'm getting at is that it's clear that our situations are different. I'm not going to sit here and pretend I know everything that's happened, because I heard the Cliff's notes version from Ben and your sister, but with the way you're behaving, Tracey wasn't the one for you. If she was, she wouldn't have run around. I didn't expect for your sister to come back into my life, and if I were to guess, the woman you're supposed to be with will find you when you least expect it. Trust me, when you figure it out, it'll hit you like a shot between the eyes."

"I'd like to say that I believe you, but I can't. Life isn't about fairy-tales—it's messy, it's complicated. It's a lot of work is what it is. At least, it's how it was with my ex."

"I wouldn't have believed me a few months ago either," I said.

Danica snorted. "Tracey was a conniving bitch who couldn't keep her hands off of what wasn't hers."

Mike's laugh was void of humor. "I'm glad you feel about as much love for her as I do, sis."

"I'm glad she's out of the picture," she said.

"So what's going on with you two?" Mike asked, but looked at me. "I had to calm Dad down tonight because he was on one of his rants."

"He can rant all he wants." Danica gave a dismissive wave of her hand. "I'm not going anywhere, and neither is Jacob. Dad knows this. We're happy, and we're together."

Mike groaned. "He said you quit your job, that you want to get rid of your shares. Why would you do that?"

"He's taken advantage of me all of these years, Mike. He plotted behind my back, manipulated me to get his way. I'm sick of it. I want to show him that I don't need him. That I could have made my way without his involvement. I don't think there's a better time for me to do that than now."

"I can't seem to wrap my head around why he'd hide those results from all of us." He ran his hands through his hair.

"Aside from being a control freak, your guess is as good as mine, big brother."

CHAPTER 45

I woke up with my woman in my arms, my son in his bed in a bedroom down the hall, and a wonderful realization. I was home.

"Good morning, sweetheart," I whispered into Danica's hair when I felt her stir.

"It is." She backed her ass into my crotch.

I hugged her tighter, and rubbed myself on that wonderful derrière of hers. "You shouldn't do that." I teased her further with a nip to her ear. "We could be liable for waking the entire house."

"I'm more curious as to what you'll do to me to ensure I stay quiet." She giggled into her pillow. "I'm not sure if I can wait until tonight."

I flipped her onto her stomach and climbed over her, spreading her legs with my knees. "With the way you just misbehaved, I should punish you." I nuzzled her neck, and then nipped where it met her shoulder.

"Punish?"

"Yes, punish." I pulled her head back by her hair, twisted it to the side, and kissed her hard. Letting go of her tresses, I let my hand roam down her satin covered body, and pulled her panties to the side. I slid a finger into her hot folds. "I love that you're always so wet and ready for me." She moaned. "For your punishment, I want you to be quiet. If I hear a sound coming out of you, let's just say that tonight might be full of surprises." She groaned.

I guided myself to her heat from behind, loving it all the more when she arched her ass up toward the ceiling for me. My restraint failing, I slapped her tush. Staying true to my word, she remained quiet despite jumping at my loving smack. Slowly, I slid in.

I groaned in her ear. "You feel so much tighter like this. I don't think I'll last long. You should know that I don't plan to be too gentle with you either." She released yet another moan. "Quiet." She nodded and bit down on her lower lip.

An hour later, I was downstairs, whipping something fresh up for breakfast while Danica took a shower.

"What smells yummy?" I turned to Jordan who stopped dead in his tracks, a look of confusion strewn across his face. "Did you spend the night?"

"I hope you don't mind. I'm making crêpes." I put the bowl of fresh fruit I had just prepared to the side, and got started on the simple syrup. "How'd you sleep?"

He shrugged his shoulders, taking a seat at the island counter. "Okay, I guess."

"Having a hard time digesting everything?" He nodded. "Trust me, I felt the same way when I found out I might be your dad. Give it some time."

"Where's Mom?"

"She should be down any minute."

"Morning." Mike stood in the kitchen's entrance, half naked in running shorts and still sleepy.

"Dude, put some clothes on!" Jordan said.

"I agree." Danica came waltzing in beside her brother, and cuffed him across the back of the head in a playful manner.

"Hey!" He rubbed the back of his head.

"We don't eat at the table half naked in my house. Put a shirt on," she said.

"And hay is for horses!" Jordan egged his uncle on.

"And I'm hung–" He was cut off by an elbow to the gut by none other than his sister. "Okay, all right. I'll give you that one, my bad."

"Remember that," Danica said.

"It's not like I didn't know he was going to say that he's hu–" I smacked the back of Jordan's head. "Ouch!"

"Just because you know what he means, doesn't mean you get to repeat it." I shook my head at him, and managed to stifle my laugh, but the smile couldn't be tucked away.

Danica shook her head at us and came up beside me to grab a cup of coffee. "I can get used to you cooking." She kissed my cheek. "It smells amazing."

"By the way," Mike began, "you might want to think about soundproofing your walls whenever you guys move in together."

"Damn!" Danica hid her face in my chest while I tilted my head back and laughed.

"Why should you–" Jordan's eyes grew to the size of saucers. "Oh! Ew! Gross!" He headed out of the kitchen.

"Keep thinking about it that way for the next ten years!" I called out to him as he flew out of the kitchen.

CHAPTER 46

With Jordan dropped off at Trevor's, Mike spending most of his day at the hospital, and Danica floating from one place to the next to get ready for tonight's ball, I headed home to relax, tend to a few work-related tasks, and get ready.

By the time five o'clock rolled around, I hurried to my car, and rushed over to Danica's. The sight I was met with had me in a temporary heart-stopping stupor.

Clad in a pearl-gray gown that seemed to have been sewn onto her body, as if made with her figure in mind, she looked ethereal. Her hair was curled in large, soft twirls with the front half pinned up. The bodice was a form-fitting halter that was cut in a modest "v", hinting at her cleavage, but keeping her covered, while the length fell to the floor in a pool of silk-covered organza that seemed to flow with her body's every movement.

I gave her the signal to twirl for me and lost my breath when I discovered that her back was bare, the dress starting at her lower back, bordering the edge of respectable, and indecent.

I gulped, wondering how the hell I could have gotten that lucky. "You look amazing!"

She gazed down at herself then met my eyes. "You like?"

"I love." I brushed my lips against hers so not to smudge

her makeup, which she had kept subdued and natural. "Sweetheart, you're going to turn heads tonight."

She grinned. "So will you."

The champagne was flowing and the music played a series of ballads, which Danica and I danced to, before Stan and his wife made their approach.

"Jake." Stan stuck out his hand, which I shook. "It's good to see you." The man's eyes floated to the woman on my arm. "And who might this lovely angel be?"

"Danica Withers." She presented her hand. Releasing mine, he took it. "It's a great pleasure, and I'm his girl-friend." I was surprised at her labelling me with a title, but I found that I rather much liked it—and looked forward to being able to call her something more than my girlfriend in the near future.

"Did I just hear right?" Stan's wife asked. "I'm Hope by the way." The two women shook hands. "It's very nice to meet you, Danica."

Danica gave her a beaming smile. "Likewise."

Stan eyed me with an arched brow. "You date?"

"Not really," I said.

"Not anymore." Danica looked at me, and I grinned. "Long story short, we used to date in high school. We've… reconnected since."

"She's the one that got away." I kissed the side of her head. "And she's stuck with me now."

"Well now, Danica, I suppose we should expect you at more of these events in the future," Stan said, and I didn't miss the note of approval in his words.

"Of course! I know you hear this all the time, but what you guys do amazes and inspires me," she said.

"We may be the faces of Standhope, but there are many more that make us who we are," the man said. "So many from the communities we work with are involved with every aspect of our projects.”

“You should think about portraying that. Putting a variety of faces to your platform would enhance the relations you have within prospective communities, and increase your support,” Danica said. “I work in public relations so if you ever need–”

“I love that idea!” Hope jumped in.

“You’ve got a deal!” Stan stuck out his elbow toward her and nodded toward the dance floor. “Jake, this one’s a keeper. What do you say, pretty lady, care for a dance?”

I laughed. “Don’t I know it.” I released Danica’s hand from my elbow. “Go ahead, sweetheart.” I turned to Hope and offered her my arm. “How about we show them how it’s done?”

She smiled. “You’ve got a deal, counselor.”

CHAPTER 47

The hotel's private terrace was decorated in fairy lights. Candles in crystal holders lay on the center of each table. As warm as the evening was, no one seemed interested in acquiring fresh air.

With a penchant for dramatics and tremendous flare, Stan sought out consolation from Hope as I pulled a giggling Danica away from the dance floor, after three dances with my client, who seemed taken with her.

"Where're we going?" she asked.

"Not far." I patted her hand after wrapping her arm around mine. "I just want you to myself for a minute, it's getting a little stuffy in there."

Her brow arched. "What are you up to?"

"Nothing." I was quick to say.

"Jacob?" She stopped walking altogether, pulling me to a halt.

"What? Can't a man take his woman out on a terrace where no one is around and indulge in–"

"Are you sure that's all?"

"What did you think I was doing?" It was my turn to eye her with suspicion.

"Well…" She peered down in a sheepish manner.

I started to laugh. "Oh, sweetheart." I searched her eyes,

which required me to cup her face and tilt it back. "If I were to pop the question, it wouldn't be here. You know how I like to do things."

She grinned. "I remember the first time you asked me out. I still can't believe you didn't end up in detention for it."

I laughed. "Me neither. I was a dork."

"No you weren't." She pressed her front against mine. "As overboard as it was, I loved it. I fell in love with the football jock that wasn't afraid to make a fool of himself, remember?"

"And what of the man that stands here tonight?" Our faces inched closer.

"He's surpassed that young boy by miles, Jacob. Although, you're not the same guy you were in high school—you're so much more now, and I'm so proud of who you've become. It might have been fifteen years, but I feel like despite that, it's like we've never missed a beat, with the exception of gaining a son, tougher skin on our backs, and wisdom."

"I feel the same way." My mind floated to my being a father.

"If you're thinking that you're not going to cut it as a dad, think again, hot shot." She winked.

"How'd you know that's what I was thinking?"

"In case you haven't noticed, I know you." She cupped my cheek. "I've never seen Jordan so attached to anyone else, other than Dad and Mike before. If he doesn't love you yet, he's falling. Sure it won't always be sunshine and rainbows, but we'll work through it. I love you more for the concerns you have, but there's no need to doubt, Jacob—you're a natural. I see the love you have for this family and I can't be happier right now."

I crashed my lips to hers and poured the emotions that were reeling through me. When I pulled away, I leaned my forehead against hers. "Thank you." I gave her a soft peck.

"You always know what to say to calm me when I start losing my head about something."

"You make it easy, counselor." She winked. "And you don't lose your head often."

"True."

She grinned. "Now, kiss me again like you just did. I think tonight might be a nice, slow night."

"Sweetheart, you're forgetting something," I whispered by her ear.

"Mmm?"

"I have plans for you." I kissed her jaw. "My enjoyment will be…" I kissed her neck and she opened for me. "Very…" I kissed the other side of her neck. "Very…" I nipped her earlobe. "Thorough." Her body quivered in my arms, and I knew that I had her where I wanted her. "Dance with me."

"Out here?"

"Out here, where it's just you and me, without the envy, without the looks. I may be proud of the woman I have, but I'm sick of everyone's eyes devouring you when I'd rather be home doing it myself."

CHAPTER 48

Since Mike was returning to Danica's tonight, we'd made the decision to stay at my place. After parking the car, I went to open the passenger side door. Danica took the hand I offered, and I escorted her up to the house.

"Are you tired?" I asked as I stuck and turned my key in the deadbolt.

"No." I guided her through the doorway and shut the door behind us. "I would love to get out of this getup though."

I smirked. "Then let's do that then, shall we?" I pulled her toward the kitchen, and out onto the back patio.

"What are you doing?"

"Stay right there and wait for me." She nodded and did just that while I rushed inside.

Soft music now played on the outdoor speakers. I fetched the champagne out from the fridge and poured us a couple of glasses. Still standing where I left her, minus her heels, which she'd kicked off to the side in my absence, I said, "Come here." It came out more as a command, but my desired outcome was achieved. Danica's back straightened and she followed through. "Follow me." I walked away with our drinks and headed up the small set of stairs that led up to the balcony.

"This is off of your bedroom, isn't it?" She looked around. "This is gorgeous!"

"I figured that you'd appreciate it." I set our champagne flutes down on the ledge of the Jacuzzi.

Her eyes were glued to the tub. "I don't have a swimsuit."

"Sweetheart, it's just you and me." I began to strip, her eyes leaving the tub to ogle me. Naked, I climbed over the edge and sat in the hot water, turning on the jets. Danica's eyes had darkened, and I found myself giving her another command. "Strip."

Without question, she licked her lips, looked around her for reassurance that no one was watching, turned her back to me, and began to take off her clothes. I watched as the fabric pooled at her feet in one graceful movement, leaving her wearing nothing but a gray lace thong.

I groaned. "That will have to go too." She peered at me over her shoulder, her eyes glimmered with wickedness, and then she shimmied out of the small piece of fabric.

The sight of her ass when she bent over could have knocked me onto my knees had I been standing. *Tease.* "Sweetheart, come here." She walked toward me with purpose, a devilish grin splayed across her lips.

I stood and gave her my hand to help her get into the tub, enjoying the jiggling movement of her breasts, and sat her down sideways across my lap. Running my fingers downward over her breastbone, she sighed and leaned her head back on the ledge of the tub.

"Now, I'm beginning to think that you like me overpowering your decision making."

"You'd be right." She sighed, keeping her eyes closed and letting me do as I willed to her body. My fingertips didn't leave her skin as they ran an indiscernible pattern. "I love not having to think. I love that I can trust you." She opened her eyes and stared into mine. "You always know what I want and need."

"So you like not having a choice?"

"No." She lifted her head, shifting to cup my face in her hands. "I love taking over and controlling you in bed. I love the feeling of power that comes with it, but I love the other side just as much."

I grinned. "Great answer." I didn't want a woman that did what she was told, one that took, and never demanded in return. I knew that Danica was the right one for me, but I also craved to know how far I could go with her. "Are you willing to give yourself over to me tonight and let me call the shots, just like this morning?"

She giggled. "You're starting to sound like one of the Doms in my books."

"Okay, now, you've got my attention." I chuckled. "I knew you liked your sexy books, but Doms and BDSM?"

"I stumbled upon it by mistake." She bit her bottom lip. "A girlfriend loaned me a book, and once I started reading it, I couldn't put it down—next thing I knew, I owned the entire series." Her hands fell from my face to land on my chest. "I'm not into the whole whips and blood, or anything extreme. I just like the edge to it all from time to time. Or at least, I think I would." She shook her head. "I don't know."

"So you're curious?"

"What are you getting at?" She sounded nervous. "Are you asking me if I want to be tied up, spanked, and whatever else comes to mind?"

"Precisely." I ran a finger between her folds. Her head fell to the side onto one of her shoulders, her eyes shut. She relaxed into my arms and I heard her quick intake of breath. "I remember your reaction to me biting your nipples on our first night together. The way you reacted to my slapping your ass this morning. How hard you come when I give it to you rough. I know you love it gentle, and your reactions are explosive, but..." I inserted two fingers deep inside her and listened to her moan, her eyes snapping open, glazed, only to begin rolling shut again. She fought it off and kept her eyes on me. "There are a lot of things I want to do with you—to you. The question is–" I swallowed hard, mesmerized at how well I could play her body, as if it were my own instrument, "Will you let me?"

"Please." Her hips arched into my hand in an act of begging.

I pulled my hand away from her, running it the entire length of her upper body before sitting her up, manoeuvring her so she straddled my thighs, my hardened cock poking her ass, with her back to my chest.

Her head fell back onto my shoulder.

"There's something I've wanted to try." I began petting her pussy again. She was limp in my arms and I had to wrap my free arm around her to keep her against me. My hand left her heat and traveled down the side of her thigh to its underside. I loosened my grip on her enough so I could run my hand over her ass. I felt her cheek twitch beneath my palm. "Have you ever…?" I let my question trail.

"Only toys." My body stiffened in surprise. She noticed. "I told you once, I had to compensate."

A finger found her puckered rosette and rubbed over it a few times. The vixen pushed her ass into my hand. I cleared my throat. "What kind of toys?"

She turned around to face me, straddling my waist. Wrapping her arms around my neck, she smiled that lascivious smile of hers. "You know…" she nipped my jaw, "plugs, dildos, that kind of stuff."

"How about one of these?" I pulled out my surprise, which, earlier in the day, I had stashed in the small storage cabinet built into the tub.

She laughed. "Honey, that's a plug."

I grinned because she didn't know what else I had planned. "I know, but have you ever had double penetration?"

She shook her head indicating the negative. "Just a plug and clit massager."

I licked my lips, loving her overtness. "Well then, you're about to."

She may be nervous, but the darkening of her eyes told me that she was excited too.

I lifted her to her feet. "Bend over and spread your legs."

She held on to the edge of the tub, doing as I requested, while I primed her for my taking.

The sight of that ass of hers, bare to the elements and the bedazzlement that now protruded from its puckering hole, made me hungry for what was coming.

I positioned myself behind her and guided my aching cock to her entrance, rubbing it over her bare lips.

"Are you ready?" As soon as she nodded, I began to push in, amazed at the sensation of tightness all around me, which caused me to take my time and savor the feel. "Christ, you're so ready for me."

I must have been going too slowly for her own liking because with one swift push, she rammed herself into my crotch, thus swallowing my cock whole.

"Fuck!" I growled into the back of her neck, my grip tightening on her hips.

With slow and sure thrusts, I began to move in and out of her. Her moans were like music to my ears, and when I felt her clench me, I reached over for the controls I had hidden to the side prior to entering her.

"Oh, God!" she screamed out as soon as the vibrations hit. "What the fuck is– Oh! Oh, God!" I smirked, speeding up my strokes and adding my fingers to dance around her clit as she was forced to take it all.

My cock felt the vibrations coming from her ass, and it felt amazing. It was my first time using a vibrating plug, and I have to say that I was looking forward to a repeat session.

"That's right, take everything I'm giving you," I whispered into her ear. "One day, I'll bury my cock inside–"

"Jacob! Fuck! I..." Her words cut themselves off. I could feel her pulsing muscles as she fell into her first climax. Relentless, I kept thrusting, a bit more forcefully now, pushing her toward the edge without her first wave of bliss dissipating. "Again, I'm coming again!"

I growled. "Fuck, I love this." This time, I intensified the vibrations, and it took her to a whole new level of bliss.

Her body stiffened and her upper torso shot up against my chest. My arms went to support her against me, allowing one to clutch a breast, tweaking its nipple before switching to the other.

When she rolled into her third orgasm, she started pleading. "This is insane. I can't take any more." With how much she shook in my grasp, I believed her.

I turned the plug off and drove her home, forcing her to bend forward again, my hand on the back of her head to keep her in position, while my other hand pulled her hips back into me every time I thrust forward.

When my balls tightened, I never expected to achieve near blindness.

My load came hard, fast, and loud, extending her climax, and I remained aggressive with my thrusts until the last of my tremors died down.

I pulled out of her, holding her upright, and proceeded to pop my well-used toy out, leaving it to the side for washing later. I pinned her against me, and guided us back to my seat, panting, exhausted and speechless. I turned her so she straddled my thighs and she leaned into me, nuzzling the crook of my neck with her hands on my chest.

"Sweetheart, you're amazing." I rubbed her back. She mumbled something. "Huh?"

She lifted her head enough for me to see the awe strewn on her face and said, "Three fucking times," before collapsing into me again.

I let my head fall back to the tub's edge and laughed.

CHAPTER 49

After the Jacuzzi experience, we'd relaxed in each other's arms, sipping our forgotten champagne. Before we knew it, we were in bed, wrapped up in our bodies one last time.

It was slow.

It was sweet.

It was pure bliss.

I wanted to show her how I felt, make her know how indispensable she was to me, how I needed her in every way a man could ever need a woman. She owned my heart, my soul—all of me.

As the remnants of our climaxes ebbed, I moved to lie on my side, hovering over her. Wrapping her hand around the back of my neck, she pulled me down to kiss me with unbridled passion.

"I love you so much," she whispered over my lips.

I smiled down at her. I couldn't hear those words enough. "I love you too."

Rolling over onto my back, she draped herself over my side, her head in the crook of my neck, and her hand on my chest, tangling her legs with mine.

"Can we just stay like this?" she asked.

"Like what, naked?"

She laughed. "Just like this." She lifted her head and looked at me. "Happy."

"It's what I plan on doing." I gave her nose a peck.

"Okay." She set her head back down, but I sensed there was something else on her mind.

"What's going on in that head of yours?"

She let out a long breath. "I'm feeling a little impatient, is all."

"About?"

"About moving in together. About starting over." She shook her head subtly before lifting her head and meeting my gaze. "I'm not sure. I know we said we'd wait but it feels like–"

"Like it's the right thing to do, even though everything is going at lightning speed?"

"That, but I have this feeling." Her expression darkened. "Like something's going to happen if we don't."

"What do you mean?"

"It's just a feeling I have. Maybe I'm just worried because we were pulled apart once before, but–"

I put my fingers to her lips and gave her a chaste kiss. "Nothing's going to happen. I won't let it. It's you, me, and Jordan from now on. I have a plan, but if moving in together right away is what you want, I'll start moving my stuff tomorrow."

"That's not happening." Her expression went from dark to determined. The twinkling in her eyes showed me that she had something up her sleeve. "I'm renting the house we're in, and let's face it, this place is much more suitable for a family and then some."

"It is."

"So you're okay with this?" she asked.

"I've been okay with it since I told you I love you." I cupped her cheek and brought her face closer to mine. "If I can have you and Jordan every day, I'm going to. It's more than I'd like to admit, but this back and forth business of ours over the last week has been getting to me."

"Is that all?" She laughed and nuzzled my nose.

"That, and the fact that I'm going to marry you someday, very soon." I winked at her.

"I like that idea." Her words brushed my lips.

"So when are we telling Jordan?" I asked.

"Tomorrow." She settled against my side with a yawn. "After he gets home from Trevor's?"

I felt my lids grow heavier. "Hmm. It'll be great."

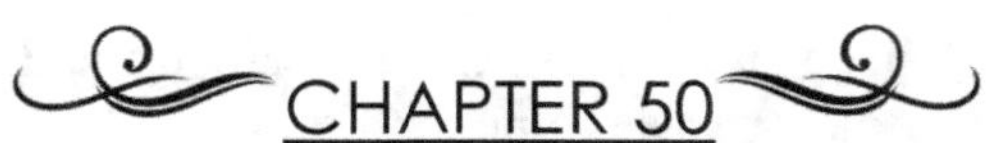

CHAPTER 50

Disappointment surged when I woke up in bed alone.

I listened and couldn't hear a thing beyond the walls to my bedroom.

As I left the room in search of my woman, I found her in the kitchen, bent over with her head inside a cupboard. Her gray thong poked out from beneath the dress shirt I had worn the night before, which she was now using as a nightshirt.

"I hope you're on the menu." I chuckled. She jumped up in surprise and turned to face me. Her hair was up in a messy bun and she couldn't have looked better. I cornered her against the cabinets, wrapped my arms around her and crooked my neck to give her a kiss.

"Good morning," she said between pecks.

"Morning." I trailed kisses down her neck.

"Breakfast?"

"Mmm…" I nibbled at the tender skin by her ear. Her hands gripped my shoulders. Lifting her up, I twirled her around to sit her on the island's edge. "I thought I was already having that."

"You should eat." Her breaths were ragged.

"Oh, I plan on eating." I pulled back smirking. "Right now as a matter of fact." I proceeded to unbutton her shirt, baring her flesh. My lips trailed down her body, following each button as they were released. "Lay down, sweetheart, the buffet's served."

Danica had come hard, and I had lapped her up like a man deprived of sustenance. I kissed up her body and leaned in over her. She didn't waste time, and grabbed the back of my head, laying a juicy one on my mouth, licking my bottom lip before pulling away.

"Mmm. I love the way I taste on you."

Hot damn!

Her hands reached between us and her smile grew to a full grin when she realized that I was in nothing but my underwear. She began to pull at them.

I groaned against her neck. "What are you doing?"

"I would have thought it obvious. I'm hungry too, and you need to get yours."

I laughed and pulled back to look at her face. "Hungry, huh?"

"Well, yeah." She was getting frustrated because her arms didn't permit her to get my boxers low enough. "A little help?" I shook my head. "No?"

"No."

"Why the hell not?" Forget frustrated, now she was insulted.

"Because this morning was for you, that's why." I brushed my lips over hers before helping her sit up. As hard as it was, I walked toward the coffee machine.

"I don't think so!" Her bare feet hit the tiled floor. Next thing I knew, my back was up against the counter, my hands on the ledge of it, my underwear down around my ankles, and her ravenous mouth was sheathing my cock.

"Fuck!" My head fell back. As much as I love my morning java, this was so much better than coffee!

CHAPTER 51

Breakfast had been filled with an exchange of goofy grins, reliving our earlier morning exploits in our minds. Danica was one hell of a match, always giving as good as she got.

When we were done with the breakfast cleanup, I drove her home.

"Are you coming in?" she asked from the passenger seat.

"I want to, but I need to call Pax, and I have a few things I need to do before we make the move official. Do you want me to pick up Jordan while I'm out?"

"That would be great."

She gave me the Callaghan's address and sent me on my way with one hell of a kiss that ensured I'd be thinking about her until I returned.

Before putting the car in drive, I grabbed my phone and hit Paxton's number.

"Hey, buddy," he said. "What's up?"

"What are you doing today?"

"Nothing. We're just laying low." It was typical of my best friend. I had always been the social butterfly, and Pax, the homebody.

"Just what I was hoping to hear. Listen, I need a favour. Can you meet me at my place as soon as you can? And bring the family."

"Give us a couple of hours. Jasper and I have been tinkering around in the barn, we need to clean up," he said. "What's this about?"

"I'll fill you in when you get here."

Next on the agenda was to go fetch my son. I drove to the Callaghan's and hurried to the front door.

"Jake?" Jordan came to the door looking confused. "Why are you here?"

"Picking you up. I know I'm early, but I need your help with something before I take you home to your mom."

"My help?" he asked. "Couldn't Paxton help you out, or Mom?"

"Nope, I need you for this." I grinned.

He grinned back. "Let me get my things."

After a quick catch-up session with Clara and Marty, while Trevor helped Jordan get his stuff rallied, my son and I drove to my house in relative silence except for the hum of the radio in the background. Jordan was the first to break the silence. "So, aren't you going to tell me why I'm your number one guy?"

"You'll see when we get to my place."

"I like it there," he said. "It's so much cooler than our place. Because it's a rental, Mom treats it like a museum."

Smiling, I asked, "So what did you guys get up to last night?"

"Went to a movie and hung out."

"No ladies?" I asked.

He rolled his eyes. "No, no ladies."

"Too bad."

"I asked Jenna out at school yesterday," he threw in.

"And?" The grin that spread onto his face said it all. "She said yes, huh?"

He blushed. "Yeah."

"My son's got a hot date!" I chuckled when he snickered at my teasing elbow nudges.

"So not cool." He shook his head, but still hadn't lost his grin. "I was hoping to be talking to a friend, not my dad."

"My bad, but I can be both you know."

I parked the car, and was glad that Paxton hadn't arrived yet. It meant that I still had some time to talk with Jordan. The kid had been accepting of everything that had happened so far, and I hoped he'd be on board with what I had to run by him.

After our talk, which had gone better than I thought it would, Jordan and I headed back to Danica's house, finding her in the kitchen.

"Hey, Mom." Jordan walked over and kissed her cheek.

She turned and wrapped her arms around him in a hug. "Hi, sweetie." She looked over at me, and I nodded my head. "Can we talk to you for a minute?"

"What is this, Consult-With-Jordan Day?"

Danica gave me an inquiring look, which I brushed off.

"Just sit down." I nodded toward the couch. "Your mother and I want to run something by you."

"What's going on?" He looked between his mother and me as he took a seat.

"How do you feel about us living together?" I asked.

"I said I was fine two days ago. Nothing's changed, if that's what you're worried about."

I grinned. "Good to know. How about you guys moving into my house?"

His brows furrowed. "What happened to waiting for Granddad to get out of the hospital?"

Danica came to my side and I hugged her. "Your dad and I talked it over last night, and neither one of us want to wait. I know it's fast–"

"So when's the move?" he asked.

"I hope you slept well last night, because we were thinking today," I said.

"This day keeps getting better and better." He was smiling like a loon. As if I knew what was coming, I let go of my woman, and the kid came at me for a man hug, released me, and then hugged his mother. I couldn't help the urge to ruffle his hair. "Hey, man!" He pulled away from his mother and tried to fix the damage.

"Go pack!" I said.

I excused myself and headed to my house, finding Paxton and his crew pulling up behind me.

"Uncle Jake!" Jasper took a running leap at me once he got out of the truck.

"Hey, buddy." I ruffled his hair. I laughed when his nose scrunched up. "How strong are you?" I crouched down to his level. The boy flexed his arms for me, and I squeezed the tiny four-year-old's biceps. "I think I can use someone like you on my team. As for you two," I stood up and looked between my best friend and his wife, "it's mandatory."

"Care to share what's going on that requires my son to have muscles?" Paxton's arms were crossed, his eyes assessing me.

"I've asked Danica and Jordan to move in. And they've agreed. I need your help to bring their stuff over, and since I know you're a sucker for a good steak and cold beer–"

"What?" His tone bordered on incredulity. "Okay, you and me need to talk." I looked at Alissa and Jasper, and none of them looked like they were bothered with my news. If anything, they looked excited. I nodded toward the house so he would follow.

Paxton shut the front door behind him, leaving his wife and son outside on the front lawn. Before I could get a word in, the man lay into me as he paced the entrance hall. "Have you gone and lost your mind? You haven't even had the paternity test yet. What if Jordan's not yours?"

"He's mine."

"Like I said–" His head snapped in my direction. "What?"

"He's mine, Pax. Did the swab on Monday. The results aren't in, but her old man beat us to it—by ten years no less. I don't know how he managed, but he's got the paperwork to prove it."

The man was in shock. "He's known all along?"

I snorted my disgust. "Without going into specifics, yeah."

"Holy shit!" I nodded. "So what's the rush with moving in?"

"What is it, Pax?" I studied him. "One minute you're rooting for us, and the next you seem against it, and then you're back at it all over again. Look, I know it's fast–"

"Don't get me wrong, I'm happy for you. It's just…" He looked as if he was mulling something over. "Wow! Okay, never mind what I think. It's fast, but I'm not one to talk. You've known Danica most of your life."

"So you'll help? I want them home, Pax. It's time we live the life we should have had this entire time."

"Count us in," he said as my cell rang.

"Hold that thought." I scrunched my eyebrows when I recognized the number. "Hello?"

"Dad, you have to come quick." Jordan didn't sound so good. "It's Mom. Bruce was here and now she's hysterical. I don't know what to do. I've tried to call Uncle Mike, but his phone is off." The kid became more panicked as he went on.

"Jordan, calm down. I'll be right there, okay? Whatever it is, it'll be fine." I wondered if this was the something bad that Danica had had an inkling about.

"Dad, hurry."

"I'm on my way." I hung up and looked at Paxton. "I've got to go. I need you with me and I think it's best if we leave

Alissa and Jasper here. Her ex was over there.”

“What’s going on?”

“I’m not sure, but whatever it is, it’s got my woman twisted like a pretzel.”

“What the fuck man!”

“Let’s get out of here.” If that bastard did anything…

CHAPTER 52

I parked the car, turned the ignition off and pocketed my keys. I jumped out and ran for the front door, Paxton bringing up the rear. My eyes settled on my woman, taking in the bruising that was forming on her arm. The rage was immediate.

"What the hell?" I rushed to her, cupped her cheek and looked her over, my gaze settling on her face. Her eyes were wild with panic. "Sweetheart, what's wrong?" I pulled her into my chest and she gripped the front of my shirt. Why did it feel like she was pushing me away, even though she was holding on? When she didn't answer, I prompted her again. "Nica, what happened, what did Bruce do?"

"It's gone!" She gave me a rather unladylike snort.

"What's gone?"

"The company, Jake, it's all gone!" Her body tightened in my grip, and within seconds, she pulled back and pushed me away. With a step back to right myself, I saw that her eyes were aflame with the fires of fury. "How'd he do it, Jake? What did you do?"

Well that's not good. She must really be pissed at me if she's called me Jake twice. She never called me by my nickname.

"What do you mean? I didn't–"

"Bruce came by to gloat about my signing over my portion of the company." When I didn't say anything, she continued. "He said Dad signed his over earlier today and he's got Mike's signature too."

The bottom fell out of my stomach. "He what?"

"What did you do?"

"I didn't do a damn thing! You were there when the judge ruled." Her gaze remained accusing. "You saw the papers with your own eyes before they were filed, Nica. Christ, you read them and had your lawyer review them. If anything's changed, then it's not my doing. The ruling was sound, they're your shares. Bruce can't take them from you, not without the appropriate paperwork."

"He says he owns it all! He showed me the damned papers, Jake! What I don't get is why you lied to me."

"Lied? Where's this coming from? I never lied to you, Danica."

"Those papers have your signature on them!" She looked at me with heartbreaking betrayal. "When were you going to tell me you're still his fucking lawyer?"

"Are you shitting me? I haven't had anything to do with that man since our day in court, and you know that. Think about it." I walked past her, running a hand through my hair, muttering, "Damn hot-headed women."

"Bullshit! Is that why you left earlier, so I would be alone when he showed up, so you wouldn't be found out?"

I pinched the bridge of my nose with my thumb and forefinger and turned to face her once more. *Remain calm*, I reminded myself and took a deep breath. "Sweetheart–"

"Don't you sweetheart me, Jake Landen." She pointed her index into my chest, and all I could do was look down at it.

I grabbed her by the shoulders and gave her a small shake. "That's enough!" Her eyes rounded. "Now, you will listen and listen well."

"I wasn't done!" I halted further words from her with a shake of my head and a growl. She gave.

"I have two clients. You know this since you've met both: Stan and Anna. Bruce is a client's of BDS&M. If you remember, I was assigned to him at the very last minute. I haven't had any ties or contact with Bruce or anyone from the firm since I left." *Except for…* "Fuck… Brent."

"Who's Brent?"

"Townsend, his original lawyer. Remember?" I asked. "But he wouldn't be involved in this. He's the only one I've spoken to since I left. We're friends, I know him well."

Her tone was laced with disbelief. "So one of your friends is fucking me over?"

I shook my head, trying to process everything. "Brent wouldn't be involved in this. He represents whomever he represents, but he draws the line when the lines blur from legal to crooked.

"Someone like Bruce would have taken his business elsewhere after what happened. His name was dragged through the mud. With how things went down, Brent would be his last choice for a lawyer, even if he'd stayed with BDS&M." I reached for Danica's hands. "Sweetheart, I would never do anything to hurt you. I've never lied to you, and I'm not about to start now. Deep down, I know you know that."

"I don't know that." She pulled her hands out of mine and backed away, shaking her head. "I don't know you at all." That statement sent my emotions into overdrive. She failed to notice the hit she delivered since she realized there was another man standing in the room with us. "Paxton?"

"You know he's telling you the truth, Dani," Pax said. "And that bullshit you just spouted about not knowing him, that's a lie and you know that too."

"What are you doing here?"

"Helping you move." He gave her an awkward smile. "Surprised?"

"A little, yeah, but I don't know if it's such a good idea now." She sounded defeated.

"Pardon?" I blurted.

"I don't think we should—"

"I can't believe this! What happened to being with each other? What happened to you loving me, to us working through the ups and downs together?" I waited, but her answer never came. "I can't do this if you believe that I've betrayed you. Dammit, Nica, I love you! But maybe you're right. Maybe you don't know me at all. And that makes me the fool again." I turned to look at Paxton. Beaten, I shook my head. "Fuck this shit, I'm out of here. If anyone needs me, I'll be at home."

I was halfway to my car when I heard footsteps. "Jacob, wait!" I paused mid-stride but forced myself to keep moving. "Jacob!"

"I can't do this right now, Danica. It's clear you—" Before I could finish, she pulled on my arm to twirl me around and launched herself at me, fusing her lips to mine. I tried to keep my emotions in check, but I couldn't. I tried to keep my body from betraying me, but my arms wrapped themselves around her, and I returned her kiss, albeit hesitant.

"Don't go," she whispered against my mouth. "I love you. I'm so sorry, Jacob. I don't know what came over me." She stepped back and settled her forehead against mine, a look of disbelief crossing her features. "I must be crazy to think—"

"Yeah, you are. You're my world, Nica. You and Jordan. I want a family, a wife, a married life filled with more kids. I want all of that with you. Why would I jeopardize that?"

Her eyes teared up. "Jacob…"

"Listen to me. If you don't want to move today, I understand, but I need to hear you say that you believe me when I say that I would never hurt you, or else, what the hell are we trying to build here?"

"I believe you." The look in her eyes told me that she was convinced. "Can you take us home, please?"

Home. I smiled down at her. "In a minute, I have something to do first."

"What's–" I cut off her words with an aggressive kiss.

When we pulled apart, our breaths were labored and all I wanted to do was take her somewhere where we could be alone. "We can go home now. And when we get there, you can damn well bet I'll be making some phone calls and find out what Bruce is up to."

CHAPTER 53

Jordan lay on his bed, listening to music, his clothes folded, but lying beside a large suitcase at the foot of the mattress when I walked in. He sat up and gave me a concerned look. "We're not moving anymore are we?" His tone denoted his disappointment.

"Who told you that, and why is some of your stuff still packed if you thought that you weren't moving?"

"When Mom flew off the handle, I figured that things were done between you two. I came in here and started packing, thinking that you could at least take some of my things with you. I wanted some of my stuff to be at your place for whenever we hang out."

My heart swelled at the knowledge that my son still wanted me to be part of his life, even if things didn't work out with his mother. "Son, your mother is upset and she has a damn good reason to be. I know I'm mad as hell." I brushed a hand down my face and sighed. "Something's going on with Withers International." His eyes narrowed on me. "I didn't do anything to be caught in this shit storm, but somehow I am. And as for moving, we're still on."

"Okay."

I put a hand on his shoulder. "Are you sure you're okay?"

"Yeah."

"Okay. I'm going to go see if your mom needs help, and then we'll head back to the house as soon as everything is packed and loaded."

Paxton showed up with his new truck, having left earlier with my car. Alissa helped out with the kitchen things while Jasper helped Jordan with the rest of his room. The men handled the boxes Danica had stored in the garage but never unpacked, and loaded them up first.

"What about the furniture?" Paxton asked me.

"Not hers. The company furnished it. They use this place for relocating their professionals."

"So it's just boxes?" Pax asked.

I nodded. "Just boxes."

Danica was busy giving the place a once-over when Jordan walked into the living room declaring he was done. Paxton, my son, and I loaded his boxes while Alissa entertained Jasper, chasing him around the front yard.

My woman came out of the house with a box I relieved her of. "That it?"

"The last one," she said.

We smiled at each other. "You ready?"

"You know I am." She kissed my cheek.

"Then let's go home."

"Home," Jordan said with a smile of his own as he came to a stop between us. "So, hot shot, how many rooms do you have in that place anyway?"

"Five. You can pick whichever one you want, but I'm sure you wouldn't mind the one with the bathroom, though."

"Dude, my own bathroom?" I nodded. "It's mine!"

CHAPTER 54

After storing Danica's kitchen boxes in the garage, I showed Jordan the bedroom I'd mentioned earlier. The kid fell in love with the space and its dark gray walls.

"I'll be in here for a while," he said, pulling out his iPod and speaker base from a backpack to set it on the six-drawer dresser as I set the last of his boxes on the floor.

I turned to him. "Got a minute to spare?"

"Sure. What's up?"

"I've been trying to figure a way to say this since that morning you found out that your mother and I were together."

"What?"

"When I said that any man would be lucky to call themselves your dad, I meant it. To find out that you're my son, I can't put into words how—"

"Dad, I love you too."

"How'd you—"

"You ramble when you're nervous." He chuckled. "I noticed it this morning after you brought me here, and the day you took me shopping for Mom's birthday."

My breath escaped with a whoosh and Jordan smirked at my reaction. "Can't get anything past you, or your mother. But so you know," I approached him and stopped when I was a few feet from him, "I love you." The kid launched himself at my chest and this time around, I didn't hesitate. My arms went around him, and to hell with my machismo— I kissed the top of my son's head and held him as if he were a little boy. "I've loved you since before I found out you were mine, Jordan. I need you to know that you're not here because your mom is. You're here because you belong here, with me."

"Okay."

We released each other and took a step back. "I should let you get yourself settled in and make sure that your mom and Alissa have what they need."

My son gave me a quick nod and set to work.

I found the ladies already busy, making room in my closet and dresser for my woman's belongings. Smiling at the sight, I let them be and headed downstairs toward the den. On my way, I caught sight of Paxton playing catch with Jasper in the backyard. I would have liked to have done the same with Jordan. I felt the twist of my heart, but I had other things on my mind. Things I needed to get to the bottom of.

When I reached the den, I picked up my cell and dialed.

"Brent, here."

"Buddy," I said, but not in my habitual enthusiastic way.

"Holy hell, what's wrong man?"

"Something big." My tone remained clipped and serious. "I know you have nothing to do with what's going on, but I need your help."

"What's up?"

"What do you know about Bruce Spalding?"

"Aside from him being a crook?"

"Precisely."

"The day you left, he stormed in here like he owned the place. I'm shocked you didn't see him on your way out. The man claimed he was set up, caused a raucous, and left, taking his business elsewhere," Brent said.

"Any word on if he's found someone new?"

"Yep, and you're not going to like it. Clark Duncan"

I slammed an open palm down hard on my desk. "You've got to be fucking kidding me!"

The conversation drew to a still, and Brent ended the silence before it swallowed us whole. "Jake, are you in trouble?"

"I need to know what I'm dealing with first." I sighed. "And I need a favor."

"Name it."

"You know that investigator you hire from time to time, the one that's got creative ways of doing things?"

"What about Steve?"

I bit my lip, pausing to make sure that this was my best course of action. "I need his number."

"What's going on?"

"I can't talk about it right now, but I'll fill you in soon."

"All right man, I'll text them over."

"Thanks." I hung up the phone.

Clark Duncan—the name sent bile rising up my oesophagus. The man was by far the dirtiest player I've ever had the displeasure of coming across in my career.

When my phone beeped its message notification, I didn't waste time and dialed the investigator who picked up on the first ring. I introduced myself, mentioned Brent's name, and left him to it with a detailed account of what I needed him to look into.

A few hours later, Steve called back. "I hope you have something for me," I said, instead of greeting the man with the traditional hello.

"You're not going to like what I have to say." I held my silence, waiting for the man to continue. "With my preliminary checks, everything looks legit from the surface." I was expecting a "but," and I wasn't disappointed. "But, I think there's something there. They're small things, almost undetectable if you're looking too quickly. Someone's going through great lengths to cover their tracks, but they're being sloppy about it."

"Yeah, and shoving the blame on me." I grumbled. "He's got Duncan working for him." The man groaned. "I need you to figure out how Spalding got our signatures. I don't care if Withers signed his damn life away on his portion, but I know for a fact that Danica never did, and I'd be willing to stake my career that her brother didn't either."

"Yeah. So, how deep do you need me to dig? It wasn't too hard to locate what I just gave you, but to have it hold up in court, I might need to… I know Brent told you how I work, Landen. There can be some backlash when you're going up against a prick like Duncan."

"I know." I sighed. "As long as it's admissible, that's all I care about. I'll deal with the rest. Danica's had enough, and frankly, so have I. It's time to end this."

"Got it."

I hung up and dialed Mike next.

An hour later, I stood by the barbecue, grilling steaks when my front door slammed shut. Mike had arrived. He found us all on the back patio, the gang laughing, most of them oblivious as to the chaos that brewed around Withers International. Even Danica seemed to have forgotten the grim events of the day, and was enjoying herself. The man came to a halt just past the French doors and our eyes met.

"Grab a beer." I nodded toward the cooler.

The man popped the top off his drink and chugged half of it. "You got a minute?" he asked.

"Sure. Pax, you mind keeping an eye on the food for a minute?"

"No prob."

I led Mike into the den and indicated that he sit down.

"Why's your name all over this?" he asked.

"Because that's what they want it to look like. Bruce has the paperwork to prove that you've all signed over your rights. He popped by your sister's earlier today to gloat. Have you been to the offices yet, signed anything without reading it through, seen something suspicious?"

He shook his head. "After your call, I headed over there. Couldn't get past security. In my business, you don't sign anything without reading things through."

I weighed my options internally for a short while. I could pay Duncan a visit, but I wanted something tangible from Steve first. Showing my cards this early on could be suicide.

"So what do we do?" Mike asked.

"I've got answers coming." *Just not fast enough.* "For now, let's get back out there before someone starts wondering what we're up to. I think I'm going to need a word with your old man too."

He nodded toward the leftover boxes of Danica's that were in the corner of the living room as we passed by on our way to join the others. "You sure about this?"

I couldn't help the grin. "More than anything in my life."

Mike chuckled and clapped a hand to my back. "That's all I need to hear. Take care of her."

"You know I will."

Everyone had gone home and I hadn't heard back from Steve as of yet. I was getting antsy. Fresh out of ideas, my brain was exhausted from the events of the day.

Jordan was watching TV when I came into the living room and sat at the other end of the couch.

Danica let herself drop to the couch between Jordan and I. "There, dishes are all done, and I'm exhausted." She yawned. "Did you talk to Mike?"

"Yeah. He had no clue until he left the hospital to swing by the office and check on things before dinner. Security didn't let him through."

"It doesn't make sense…"

"If there's any proof of doctoring or forgery, Steve will find it, along with whatever else we need for the courts." I didn't have the heart to tell her that I thought that Spalding might be holding something over her dad's head. That feeling I had when I lost to them in court was back again as I replayed Danica's elation and her old man's subdued joy and relief when they won. If my suspicions were right, and Bruce had something on Withers—it would explain why Danica's ex was going through great lengths to take over when his first attempt hadn't worked. "For now, I think we just need to relax." I pulled her into me and kissed the top of her head.

She snuggled into me. "Who's Steve?"

"The investigator I hired to look into things. Brent uses him from time to time. I'm not a fan of how the man works, but we're up against people who are known to play dirty. I wasn't left with much of a choice."

Her brow furrowed. "Is there any way that this could backfire on us?"

"Not really. If anything, I'll be the one bailing him out of jail, but I doubt it'll get to that." I smirked. "I can't say I wasn't warned, but Steve's the best that I know, and he'll do what he needs to do to get the results we need without any of us getting into trouble."

She groaned and pinched the bridge of her nose. "We should have pushed for the damn charges. None of this would have happened if we had."

I was in complete agreement. "That would have been a novel idea."

"I'm going to bed," Jordan announced.

"We're right behind you." I turned to Danica. "Go on. I'll lock up and be right there."

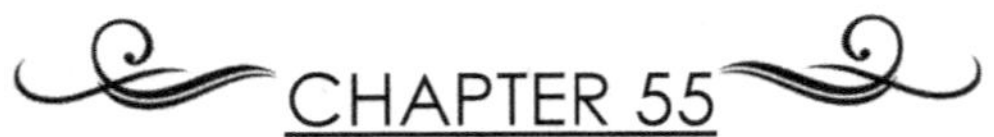# CHAPTER 55

I woke up earlier than usual. Leaving Danica to sleep, I got out of bed, went to the washroom, and jumped in the shower.

When I got to the kitchen to make coffee, Jordan was already up and about, reminding me that today was Monday.

"Isn't it a little early to be heading out to school?" I asked.

"I have soccer practice before class on game days." He took a bite of toast. "Trevor's mom is picking me up. We still on for tonight?"

I grinned. "Nothing's changing my mind."

"Why not do it like every normal person?" he asked.

"Your mother deserves so much more than that. Besides, it's how I do things."

"You're crazy, you know that?"

"Yeah, but I'm not about to change now. Have a good day while I try and sort this whole mess with your grandfather's company out."

"You do that, hot shot." He smirked. "Tell Mom I love her."

Popping the fresh bowl of fruit, toast, and compotes, along

with coffee, on a tray, I brought everything upstairs. Danica was still asleep.

I set the tray on the bedside table, stripped down to my underwear and crawled under the sheets. I watched the fluttering of her lashes and smiled at her serene demeanor.

My fingertips traced the contours of her face, her high cheekbones, her narrow jaw, her tiny nose, and those pink lips of hers that I could spend hours delighting in. She was beautiful, but it was what she held inside of her that meant the most.

Danica was a fierce woman. One that would do anything for the people she cared for. She was run by love, devotion, and loyalty, and not by her pocketbook, which if you haven't figured out yet, left her without financial worries. It was the simple things in life, the tiny acts, the smiles, the looks, and the affection that mattered most to her. It was the same for me.

As I thought back on my life, the last fifteen years had left me feeling shameful for being so dense about how a relationship could brighten the darkest of days. I had been superficial. Now that I had it all, I knew that bachelorhood wasn't a life I was cut out for.

In the span of weeks, my past had collided with my present. The course my life was on was derailed and sent in a different direction. Leave it up to Danica to turn my life upside down and right side up, reshaping it into something extraordinary. It was a life I wouldn't trade for the world.

I had come to terms with the haunting of my past.

I had rediscovered my feelings for Danica.

I'd become a father.

So much had happened in so little time. Yet, with no hesitance, albeit, a bit of anxiety, I was embracing it all, and if someone came along to take any of it away from me, I knew I would fight—to the death.

I rolled onto my back and closed my eyes, lost in my reverie. A series of kisses on my chest made me open my eyes and the face of the woman I loved filled my vision. Those blue orbs of hers stared back at me.

With one look she ensnared me. Fifteen years apart and we couldn't make it work with anyone else. There was no denying that we were meant for one another.

"Hey." She brushed her lips over my chin. "Why so deep in thought?"

I cupped her cheek and she pressed it further into my palm, those sleepy eyes of hers coming to a close, savouring my touch. "Just thinking. It's been one hell of a ride since you've been back, hasn't it?"

"You have no idea." She smiled. "But I'd do it again, in a heartbeat."

"Jordan's left a message with me, for you." I pecked the tip of her nose. "He loves you."

She looked over at the clock and her eyes widened. "Wow, I was exhausted!" She took notice of the tray of food and her brow arched. "Breakfast in bed?"

"I figured we could lay low today, unless you have other plans." I sat up, and she did the same. I moved the tray and brought it to sit between us. "What do you say?"

"I think it will be a day to remember, so long as we don't miss Jordan's game tonight. He said they're supposed to have something beforehand."

"Yeah, he mentioned that yesterday. I'm excited." I grinned.

"He is too, in case you haven't picked up on that yet," she said with emotion. "It's his season opener and his father will be there to see him play." I nodded. "He plans on joining football next year, you know. He played in Austin, but we moved here after tryouts. Although you two haven't met until now, there's so much of you in him, Jacob. Things that I didn't see until you came back into my life."

"Including my name." I grinned.

She blushed. "It was a way to keep a part of you with me. I never once forgot you."

Neither did I. "Did you know that it's a Landen family tradition to use the father's first name as the son's middle?"

She shook her head and smiled. "I had no clue. What do you do if you have a second son?"

"We'll give him my middle name."

"Nathaniel." She let the name roll off her tongue and then grinned. "I like it."

"You remember?"

"Of course I remember. What do you think girls do when they have a crush on a boy?"

"I don't know, run around chasing them to try and steal a kiss?"

She giggled and smacked my thigh. "That was you and Paxton, not me."

"I know. You should know that even though we got together in our senior year, I think you captivated me around the same time Paxton held you, and I kissed those sweet lips of yours in fifth grade."

"Yeah." She looked down to the bowl of fruit, grabbed some cantaloupe and pressed it against my lips. "I know we played it off as a joke, but the fifth's where everything changed for me too. You gifted me with my first crush that day, Jacob."

"Wait a minute… first crush? There were more?"

She laughed. "Leave it up to you to worry about not being the only man aside our son, my brother, and father on my mind. Yes, there were other crushes."

"Damn, I thought I had you since that day at recess." I laughed.

"Jacob, do you want to hear about this or not?" She took a bite of her toast.

I pressed my lips to her forehead. "Go on, sweetheart."

"In grade five, there was Jacob, the kid who liked to tease by chasing me around the schoolyard.

"In grade nine, I was the rich dork, and some girls thought that they could mess with me. This boy came swooping in, the popular kid with the hero complex. He saved my butt from what could have been an embarrassing first day of high school." I smiled.

"In grade ten, a boy asked me for help. He confided in me that his parents wouldn't be able to afford his tuition, and that the only way he could make his dream happen was if he got a scholarship. So, I helped him out. He deserved it, and we traded favors. I still can't believe I became a cheerleader because of him." She winked at me. "But I also understood, in that moment, the effects of persuasion those emerald eyes of his had on girls.

"In my senior year, the football starting quarterback had been the only person to pick up that something was wrong. After practice, he sat down beside me on the bleachers, not saying a word until I was ready to talk. The Sadie Hawkins dance was around the corner, and I was upset because the idiot I had asked not only rejected me, but had done it in a public, and in a vicious manner. After spilling my guts to him, the jock told me that I was beautiful and that any guy was crazy to turn me down. He said that it was a guy's job to ask a girl out and that the whole concept of Sadie Hawkins was ridiculous. He also told me that he would have never said no had I asked him."

"And then you asked him." I chuckled. "And he did say yes."

She nodded. "Four. I've had four crushes in my entire life, Jacob, and they've all been on you. Although…"

"What now?" The woman was playing with fire. I never thought I had a jealous bone in my body, but it turns out that I do when it comes to her.

"Yeah, there's definitely a fifth." She gave me a wry smile. "There's this man who pretty much risked his career to save my father's company when, with everything I've put him through, it would have been understandable that he let us fall. He loves my son as much as he loves me–"

"Come here, woman." I grabbed her face and gave her a

lingering kiss. She tasted of strawberries and honeydew mel-on. "I love it when you get all soft and corny."

"Well it's nice that I can be the woman every now and again." She giggled and tried to get away by jumping off the bed.

"Why you little!" I laughed with her, moved the tray to the side, our breakfast forgotten, and pounced off the mat-tress to chase her. It didn't take much effort to catch her, and once she was over my shoulder, I brought her back to the bed and dropped her onto her back. I covered her body with mine as she laughed, and my heart warmed at the sound. She'd been doing a whole lot more of that as of late, and in that moment, I made a personal vow: for as long as we were together, I would make sure she laughed at least once a day at my hand. "I'll show you."

"Show me what?" Her palm cupped my cheek.

"Just how much of a man I am." Her breath caught, her laughter ceased, and her eyes went wide.

CHAPTER 56

The day hadn't gone as planned, but after speaking with Danica, she agreed to speak with her father and find out what was going on.

I followed her into the man's private hospital room. His pale complexion and frailty didn't deter from the presence of power he always exuded.

Mike got up from his father's side to greet us. With one glance in our direction, Mr. Withers turned his head and looked toward the window.

"I'll leave you two with him." He squeezed his sister's shoulder. "Got anything?" he asked me when Danica moved toward her father.

"No, you?"

"He's not talking." Mike gave his father a brief glance. "Let's hope your guy finds something."

"I don't think we'll be here for too long." I eyed his sister. "I doubt that this is about to go down very well."

"How is she?" He looked toward Danica, who was sitting by her father's bedside, being ignored by the man. I pulled him toward the hallway and spoke so as not to be heard.

"She's mad as hell, but she made the decision to come here on her own. She has an ax to grind, and he's got answers he needs to give. Arguing is what landed him here in the first place, which has me a little concerned, but I'll be damned if she doesn't get what she's owed with all the hell he's put her through over the years."

"I hear you." I could see that the man was torn between his two closest relatives. "I've got to say that I'm impressed with you, Jake. Contrary to my dad, I knew that you were a good guy and all, but I never thought that you'd do all that you have. From what Ben's told me over the years—"

"Like I've said, your sister is the one I needed all along. Jordan's a plus. No disrespect intended, but I want to throttle your dad for knowing my kid's been miserable and he didn't do a damn thing all these years."

"I'm not happy about it either." He patted my shoulder. "I need some coffee. I'll catch up with you guys later."

I approached Danica who sat by her father's bedside, and came to a stop behind her. "Mr. Withers, how are you feeling?"

He scoffed at my inquiry.

"Daddy!" Danica warned.

"What?" He turned to look at his daughter. I saw the ice in his eyes when his gaze turned to me. "Come to finish the job?"

"That's enough!" Danica stood abruptly. "I've come to see you and find out how you were doing, and you're going to lay there, not say a word, and attack Jacob after what he's done to keep you alive? I can't believe you!"

"Sweetheart, it's fine." I squeezed her shoulders. "He can say whatever he damn well pleases, but in the end, he's going to be listening to everything I have to say."

The man's expression was one of smugness. "Is that so?"

I held his gaze. "For the sake of redeeming your daughter's and grandson's faith in you, I hope you choose to listen."

I wasn't backing down.

It worked.

He looked over at Danica and reached out for her hand, but she backed off and settled against the front of my body. My hands went to her hips and squeezed. As quick as the man's eyes took in my gesture, they met his daughter's again. "I only meant to protect you." His voice was soft. "I knew you loved him, but he wasn't right for you."

"And you were the judge of that?" The anger simmered in Danica's tone. "You said so yourself." She swallowed hard. "In court, that day. You were impressed with the man Jacob's become. You can admit it to me and Mike, but why can't you admit it to Jacob's face?"

"It's true." He paused to give me a fleeting look, and then turned toward her once more. "He did impress me. I never thought he'd amount to much to be frank, and you know how much I dislike to be proven wrong."

"You behaved like a ruthless, spineless… a heartless bastard, just for the sake of your pride?" I squeezed her side again and she covered my hands with hers and squeezed back. "I feel like I don't know you, Daddy. Jordan doesn't want to see you. All those heart-to-hearts you two had… You didn't just betray me, you betrayed your grandson when you chose to keep the truth from us. Do you have any idea what I went through all these years: the shame, the guilt, a marriage based on lies, just so I could see my son be happy with a father figure, to please you? I sacrificed everything!"

The man's face grew red with fury. He exploded. "I was there, dammit! That was enough, wasn't it? I helped you with your finances. I looked after Jordan when you had school and work. I was there when you graduated and when you couldn't find a job. Who gave you that first job when you were still green under the collar? Who saved you from the worst mistake of your life? It was me, baby girl, me!"

"Our son is not a mistake!" Danica shoved my hands off of her and I backed up. The tension radiated off of her like a wildfire. Sure enough, she sent the chair flying back a few feet as she pushed it out of the way to bend over his prone position in a fury.

"That's not—"

"Jacob and I aren't a mistake!" She got nose-to-nose with him.

"Dani—"

"Let me clarify a few points, father." She straightened. "You helped me financially, and this we both can agree on, but that's where it ends. Mom was the one who looked after Jordan, Dad, not you! It was the same way when Michael and I were kids. You were too busy with your precious business. Why do you think he and I got involved? I can't speak for my brother, but it wasn't my first choice for a career. We wanted you to be proud. We wanted to be around you more, especially after Mom died. You were there when I graduated college because it looked good on you. I never told you this, and I let it pass because I was happy at *WI*, but I found out about your little phone calls to my prospective employers. You gave them cause not to hire me!

"No matter that, I spent the years not knowing this fact working my ass off trying to make something of myself for you to be proud of. It's what I've always done." She paused to take a breath. "Have you ever been happy with anything I've done? Hell, have you ever been happy? Is this what it's all about, that I want happiness and you can't stand the thought because you're miserable?"

He lay there, his mouth opening and closing, trying to get a word in edgewise with no success, as his daughter kept speaking.

"I will never trust you with my family again." Although her voice had gone soft, it left little of her anger out. After a moment of silence, Danica appeared to be collecting her thoughts. "You need to tell me the truth, once and for all." I sensed that this was the calm before another storm if the old man didn't deliver. "You owe me that much."

His nod was slight, but it was there. "Okay, what would you like to know?"

"What's going on with Withers International?" she asked, and I came to stand beside her, one arm wrapped around her waist. "Did you sign anything that would give Bruce the right to take over the company?"

"No."

"So, you didn't know that Bruce took over the company?" The man's jaw tightened and his eyes seemed to be everywhere but on his daughter. He shook his head to indicate the negative.

My body grew tense. "He's lying to you, Nica."

The man's head snapped in my direction. "Mind your business. This is between me and my daughter."

"That's where you're wrong. Your daughter is mine and whatever concerns her, concerns my son, and thus me, because, unlike you, I protect what's mine. You're hiding something. I don't know what it is, but I suspect that Spalding's got something on you that you'll sacrifice your kids' livelihoods to protect yourself. So what is it?"

"Landen–"

"Let me tell you what I know to be facts, from our day in court." I continued. "The judge's ruling was sound. I've seen the documents. I'm not an idiot like you would prefer me to be, and I can't be walked all over like you've done, and are still trying to do with your daughter." I took a deep breath to calm myself down. "Now, I'll ask again, what does Bruce Spalding have on you?"

"You wouldn't understand."

"Try us, because from where I'm standing, aside from Mike, you've already lost what you have of your family," I said. "What's the harm in trying to salvage what you have left?"

"If I've lost it all, what's the point? I'm a dying man, Landen, my heart's not good."

"Cut the woe-is-me bullshit, Withers," I snapped.

"Thanks to that deal, my son and daughter will be more than financially stable for the rest of their lives without having to work again."

Danica grumbled. "What deal? What did you do?"

"I had papers drafted up," he started. "I don't know how Bruce pulled it off and got his hands on the drafts, because this heart bullshit happened before I could get anything finalized."

Danica's voice reverberated off of the room's walls. "You can't do that!"

"It's done," he said with finality.

"Illegally?"

"Doesn't matter."

"But Mike loves working for Withers'. Y-you… You can't do this to him!"

"It's done, Danica!" the man said with a tone that brokered no argument. "Bruce's lawyer came to see me yesterday morning with the final copies and I signed them."

"But it's illegal." Danica's voice had gone whisper soft.

"It won't appear that way to a judge," her father said. "And I know you'll never bring this to court."

"I'd beg to differ. My name is on those papers, my signature, that of your son's and daughter's. Those are forged documents."

"And you can prove it beyond a reasonable doubt?" He gave me a stern look and a confident smirk.

"I have someone looking into what can be done as we speak."

The man recoiled in his bed, his eyes widening with surprise. "What have you done?"

I hypothesized aloud. "I guess things aren't as smooth as they could be, huh?"

"Dani." The man reached out to her, but she didn't make a move toward him. "You need to make sure that this sticks, Dani."

"Why, Daddy? You worked so hard to make WI what it

is. Mike and I suffered for it. Mom too! And for what, so you can give it up?"

The man hesitated. "Yes."

"What's he got on you?" I demanded.

"Doesn't matter."

I growled. "What's he got on you?"

With a sigh, the man came clean—blowing my mind. Spalding had an ax to grind with Old Man Withers, all right.

From money disappearing, to Withers' use of an external forensics accountant, he discovered that his former son-in-law was embezzling to keep his own business ventures afloat. This wasn't news to me. I had discovered that for myself.

"What else?" I urged him.

"Withers International kept leaking funds even after we caught on to Spalding," he said, and Danica nodded. "Turns out the man's far smarter than I ever gave him credit for."

Danica's father proceeded to confess his gambling problems. "I was going to pay Spalding off so he would leave you alone in the divorce. I didn't have the money, so I took it, shuffling things in the accounts so it didn't look suspicious, and buying me time to put it back."

"No!" Danica said.

He nodded. "I did, and I lost it all. That's when he came after the company. The divorce was supposed to be foolproof. I would sign over my portion, he would win yours in the divorce, and then because Mike is Mike, he'd hand over his portion, since he wouldn't want to be part of an outfit with his sister's ex. I knew you both worked for me because it was a family operation. I'm not blind."

"And then Jacob came into the picture," Danica added for her father.

He nodded. "Bruce found himself a great lawyer. I was shocked when you walked into that courthouse, Landen." He met my eyes. "What we didn't predict was that you'd throw his case and the company would stay with us." He snorted. "That was a gutsy move, and because you made it, I knew that you had looked into Spalding and his workings. I have to say that I admired your stunt to keep WI in my family's hands."

"What happened next?" Danica asked.

"Bruce didn't get what was owed to him," I answered for her father.

"Right."

"So why didn't you just leave it at that?" she asked.

"Bruce was willing to do anything to get what he wanted. It's why I hired the man in the first place. He's ruthless, a go-getter, and held promise for *WI*," he said. "If I didn't find a way to get him the company, he was going to leak everything. I couldn't face Michael, you, the board which you know is filled with people who've been around since before you were born. They may not be blood, but they're family too. I couldn't face that."

"Why not? Wouldn't it be better for them to know than go to jail?"

"I don't care about a damn cell. I'd rather lose the company to the man than go down, and bring you and your brother along with me. You don't get it, sweetheart. What you've been seeing at our last two quarterly board meetings hasn't been accurate."

"W-what do you mean?"

"We're going under," he said. "You and Michael think we're downsizing in Texas, but in reality, I'm planning on pulling up shop. We're not consolidating our offices, there won't be a smaller, more familial feel. In fact, there won't be a Withers International to speak of in the next few years, because Spalding will dissolve the rest of the company now that he owns it outright."

Fuck! "So that's why Mike's talking about moving here."

I hypothesized aloud. "There's no job for him there any-more."

He nodded. "I reassigned him here."

"I have one last question," I said. "Why'd you pin the legal work on me?"

"I didn't. No one double-crosses Bruce, or so I found out the hard way," he said. "He knew you fucked him over in the divorce. He was pissed."

I nodded. "Understandable."

"He also found out that you were with his ex."

"Okay…" I said, urging him on.

"That's it."

"That's it?" I felt like a parrot.

"His name was dragged through the mud, Landen," he said. "He might have been struggling to keep things afloat with his own businesses, but he's lost millions more after the divorce when some of his deals decided to pull out at the last minute."

"And that's Jacob's fault?" She had been so calm and quiet that her outburst made me jump.

"Princess," he said.

Her body tensed and the arm I had wrapped around her back tightened. "Don't you dare call me that! I'm not your princess, your sweetie pie, your anything. You allowed Bruce to drag an honorable man's name into this because of a personal vendetta. You took my son away from his father for ten years, and now, you've taken away my father." She shook her head. "That's not what a father does to protect his kin." Her voice ended on a quiver. I tried to gather her in my arms, but she slipped from me and rushed from the room before I could stop her.

I made to follow.

"Landen?" I turned to face Withers, relieved to hear Mike's muffled voice trying to console his sister out in the hall. "Do you lie?"

"No, sir. I left the firm that represented Spalding because I couldn't work with people that would do that."

"Good." He looked away before training his gaze on me again. "Take care of her, will you? She's got her mother's soul."

"And her father's temper." I gave him a tight-lipped smile. "Listen…" I approached his bedside once more. "I need you to know a few things, because I don't know when or if we'll see you again. I'm leaving that decision to your daughter and our son.

"I know your daughter, but despite all of the years that you've had with her, I don't think you know her at all. She's forgiving and gives so much of herself, to a fault, and you took advantage of that.

"Before you upped your family and disappeared, I respected you, and had you not been that hard of a man, I doubt I would have strived as hard as I did to get to where I am today. What I'm realizing now is that the man that I held in such esteem for so many years, a man I wanted approval from because I loved and looked to a future with his daughter, a man I saw as having so much determination, respect, and dedication to his family, was nothing but a sham.

"As for me risking my career by throwing my case to the dogs, I did it because it was the right thing to do. You kept my son from me for ten years because of your issues, not to mention, your dislike of me. What does that say about you as a father—as a grandfather? I'm not trying to sound disrespectful here, but from where I'm standing, your daughter turned out amazingly well, and it wasn't much thanks to you. Your wife must have been a gem, and I wish I'd had the chance to thank her for that beautiful woman out there that's gifted me with so much already."

"Landen–"

"By now, you're realizing that I don't care what you think of me. But being the man that I am, I believe you deserve to know that I plan on marrying your daughter. I will spend the rest of my days making sure that her needs are met, that her dreams come true, but most of all, that she's happy. The same goes for Jordan." I paused to let my words sink in some. "Get well, Withers. I'll be in touch, but I can't say the same for your daughter or my son."

I walked out of the room to find Danica sitting on one of the hallway chairs. Mike stood to greet me.

"We have answers," I said.

He gave me a curt nod. "We'll talk later, she needs you right now."

I sat and wrapped an arm around her shoulders and nodded towards the hospital room I had just exited. "I wouldn't go in there right now if I were you. Let him stew."

He nodded. "Go on and get her home."

"You coming to Jordan's game tonight?" I asked.

He grinned. "Wouldn't miss it."

CHAPTER 57

Bronson-Smith High was a place where friendships were forged, relationships came and went, and memories to last a lifetime were created. I peered down the stands, excited that the bleachers were packed to the maximum, and pleased that we had arrived in time to snag our seats.

Danica's emotions had run amok throughout the afternoon. Not once had I left her side, doing everything I could to console her. During a particular bout of tears, I promised her that Spalding wouldn't keep WI. I wasn't quite sure as to how I'd accomplish that feat—only that I was determined to find a way.

But now, waiting for the game to begin, she was smiling, excited and proud to be part of our son's first game of the year. I shared in her sentiment, relieved that we could put the events of the day behind us for a while. I had more important things on my mind anyway.

I saw an older couple walk by and yelled out to the familiar head of salt and pepper hair. The crowd parted and they climbed up the steps to join us.

"Mom," I kissed her on the cheek, "Dad." He shook my hand.

Mom sported a beaming smile, her gaze fused to the woman who sat at my side. "I'll be!" She pressed a hand to her chest before opening her arms to the younger woman. "It's so wonderful to see you again, dear. How've you been?"

"Good, thank you, Mrs. Landen." She returned my mother's hug and looked at me, winking when Mom pulled away.

"I'm so glad to hear," she said.

Danica sat in her seat and patted Mike's thigh. "This is my brother, Michael."

When my mother moved to Mike, my dad took Danica's hand and bent to kiss her cheek. "I'm so glad to see that you're back in the picture. I never thought this guy would find another one like you."

Danica laughed and I gave him a warning look. "I'm glad he hasn't found anyone else either." This made Dad grin.

Knowing I had somewhere to be, since the game was about to start, I excused myself.

The announcer was paid off, Jordan and the boys were anxious to get going, some of them a little green with nerves, and I was raring to go.

The boom of a voice could be heard over the crowd. "Ladies and gentlemen, may I have your attention please! We have something special to kick off the night, but first, in true Bronson-Smith High tradition, it's time to announce our honorary guest who'll lead us into tonight's game with a cheer!"

In case you're wondering, the payoff was for the announcer to call my name. It wasn't a hard sell once I let him in on my plan.

The mascots taunted each other, and the crowd was rowdy. It didn't matter what sporting team you were on at Bronson-Smith, the student body and their parents rallied together.

BSH alumni stood behind their players. The euphoria of the crowd grew contagious and I fed off of it.

Summoned to join the announcer on the sidelines he said, "Jake, the stage is yours."

I looked up at the stands to find Danica and my mother cheering and waving. I chuckled at the sight, but it was Danica that held all my attention now.

She was there every time I opened and closed my eyes, every time I dreamed, every time I looked into my past. She was there in my present, and the only one I cared to see in my future, along with Jordan.

I beckoned the whole team forth with a wave of my arm as I accepted the announcer's mic.

"For those of you who remember me from high school, you know that I was known for some outrageous stunts. Well, it appears that I've lost my touch." I paused to let the laughing crowd calm down. "My apologies, but an oldie will have to do by way of a cheer tonight. So boys, you know what to do—on three," I said, and winked at Jordan, who couldn't stop laughing and shaking his head at my shenanigans.

"Utterly mental," he lipped.

Surrounded by the boys, circled around me with their arms laced around each other in the way of typical team camaraderie, I took a knee. I counted to three with my fingers and watched each and every beaming face that was there to help. Holding the mic up to the boys, they yelled it at the top of their lungs. "Marry him, Nica!"

An audible gasp from the crowd was followed by dead silence.

If the crickets were out, they could have been heard.

Within seconds, the crowd roared with cheers, and the boys backed off, leaving me alone, front and center as they lined up behind me.

On bended knee, the ring in hand, I looked up to where I knew she was. Everyone around her was standing, yet she was frozen in place, sitting with her jaw dropped. My parents were hugging, with my mother jumping up and down in her seat. Mike was trying to get my woman to her feet so he could escort her down the bleachers. I stood to watch.

The mascot made his way toward the stands and collected her at the bottom step. She looked at the matted furry creature as if she'd contract a communicable disease if she touched him, but gave in.

The closer she got, past and future blurred into the present, and a surge of emotion began to overwhelm me. I felt like a teenager at his homecoming game, and this moment sure felt like my homecoming. It might have been fast, but it was right. I felt it in my bones.

A hand squeezed my shoulder and I turned to the side. My son stood there with a grin rivaling mine. The crowd chanted and cheered to the point that I couldn't hear myself think. Then again, there was no need to think—I already knew what needed to be said.

She came to a stop in front of me, shock still strewn over her face. She brushed off the mascot's gloved hand and scrunched up her nose as she looked at him. "You stink!" The team erupted in laughter, along with the crowd who managed to pick up her words through the mic. She looked around and blushed.

I handed the mic to Jordan who held it for me so I could grab Danica's hand. She looked as if she was ready to bolt. "I thought it fitting that I waited until we were at our beginning to give us a suitable end.

"Fifteen years ago, you told me that you loved me on this field." I paused to let the crowd get over their reaction. "Fifteen years later, we're back where everything began… before it was taken away. So this is me, picking us up where we left off, with a little excess baggage." I looked to Jordan and winked.

"You already know the rest, sweetheart. I love you. I've only ever loved you, and you know that I'm the only one for you. We've had a rough go over the years, you and I, haven't we?" She looked toward her shoes, tears streaming down her face and nodded with a small smile. "I once told you that I was ready to pack it up and make you mine after we graduated high school. After fifteen years, I finally have the chance to ask you. I'm a patient man, sweetheart, but I'm all tapped out of patience. So…"

I took a deep breath and a knee once more, turned to the boys with a nod, and another chorus of "Marry him, Nica," broke out.

My heart raced at a staccato pace. Her eyes held mine and she smiled. "Yes," she whispered, and I couldn't help the grin.

"Louder, Mom!" Jordan said, laughing in the mic. "I'm pretty sure everyone would like to know your answer." The crowd cheered their agreement.

"Yes!" She threw herself at me. The stands went wild as we kissed and I slid the ring on her finger. Jordan waited until we were standing again before giving us our hugs. "You are so your father's son." She hugged him tight, taken over with a bout of teary giggles.

"I think I might have to hit you up for some pointers, Dad," he said. "That was fun."

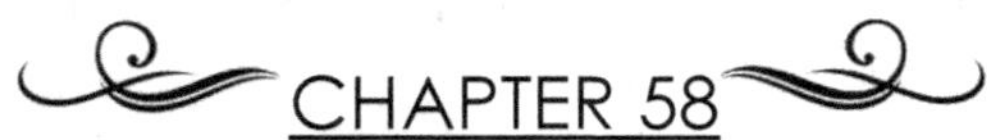

CHAPTER 58

The Jaguars won, although Kent was convinced that their win was because my stunt had thrown the reigning state champions, four years running, off their game.

When Danica, Jordan, and I arrived home, we were welcomed by more than my parents and Mike. Paxton, Alissa, and Jasper were standing there in the family room.

As soon as the congratulations were done and over with, Mom and Dad saving theirs for last, I reached for Jordan and wrapped my arm around his shoulders. "I've got two people that you need to meet," I said, and when we drew close enough, Jordan's steps halted.

My son looked between the older couple and myself and said, "T-they're…"

"Your grandparents—my parents," I said. "Mom, Dad–"

"My goodness, Jacob, he looks just like you!" Mom said.

"Explain," Dad said, "now!"

Danica jumped in and curled her front around my side. "It's not his fault."

"We didn't know until a week ago unofficially," I said.

"A week?" Dad said. "You've–"

"It was official as of this afternoon," I said.

Despite the depressing events of this morning, there had been some good news: the lab results had come in. If there was any question as to the legitimacy of Withers' decade-old results, they dissolved when the courier arrived.

"It's true," Danica said. "Please don't be mad at Jacob. I didn't want anyone to know until we knew for sure."

"Dad, it's a long story, and right now's not the best of times to explain the lengthier version of it." I squeezed Danica tighter to me.

Dad's hard expression melted away, his eyes remaining stern, traveled from me to Danica, and his gaze softened when he studied her. "I have a feeling this story isn't going to be something easy to digest, is it?"

"I'm sorry," she said.

We turned to find my mother approaching my son, their eyes having yet to leave each other. The woman cupped his face in her hands, she smiled at him. "So much like your father," she whispered and then leaned in to kiss his cheek. Before she could pull away, Jordan pulled her in for a hug and buried his face in her neck, and I felt my heart stutter. She didn't hesitate to wrap him in her arms, either.

I felt Danica bury her face in my chest, and when my eyes met my father's, the man was grinning. "I came into tonight thinking I'd enjoy a soccer game, only to find out that my son is settling down, and I have a fifteen-year-old grandson," he said, somewhat chocked up. Mom giggled and pulled away with Jordan releasing his grip on her to turn to my father. He stuck out his hand but Dad, being Dad, grabbed my son by the shoulders and pulled him in for a man-hug. "Welcome to the family, son," he said, and the emotion in his voice couldn't be missed.

With the last of the visitors gone and Jordan off to bed, I watched Danica as she tidied the kitchen from across the room, feeling lucky that she'd agreed to be my woman for life.

When the last of the bottles had been trashed and glasses

stowed in the dishwasher, I grabbed onto her hips and turned her to me, kissing her forehead. "I love you."

"Love you too." She leaned in and pressed her mouth to mine. "Now," she whispered, "do you think you can manage to take your fiancée up to bed? It's been a long day, and I've got some serious plans for tomorrow."

"And those are?"

Pulling back, I could see that devilish twinkle in her eyes. "I'm going to be busy making sure my husband-to-be's needs are met." She winked and leaned over to my ear and continued. "Over and over and–"

I put my shoulder to her stomach, in a fireman's hold and smacked her ass, eliciting a giggle. "It's off to bed with you, woman." I flipped the deadbolt on the front door and rushed her up the stairs.

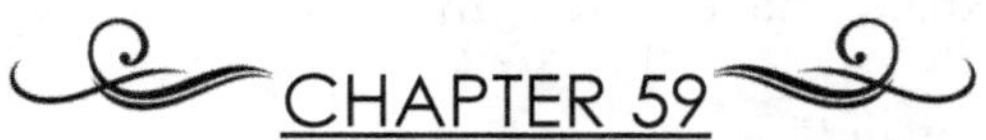

CHAPTER 59

Everywhere she touched, kissed, and licked set my skin ablaze.

Too bad it was all a dream.

I woke in a sweat, and my cock was as hard as it's ever been. I cried out when I felt a sinful mouth swallow my shaft whole. Within a minute I was exploding and the pleasure didn't stop there.

It wasn't a dream!

I felt her skin to skin, sliding her body over mine as she pulled the sheets down from covering her head. She climbed up my body with more of those heated licks and kisses until our eyes connected when she reached my chest. Her hand was still between us, making sure that I stayed erect by pumping my length. It was enough to keep the fire stoked beneath the pot she was stirring.

"Good morning." She smiled that innocent smile of hers and kissed me hard on the lips. "Nice dream?" Innocent, my ass!

"I'll show you." I bit her bottom lip and flipped her over. "I hope you enjoyed that, because I'm about to make you see those same stars that came flying through here minutes ago."

"I'm counting on it, counselor."

I crashed my lips to that smart mouth of hers in a punishing kiss before pulling back. "That's one hell of a fucking wake up call, woman." I entered her hard. Her loud cry of passion had me grinning down at her. "That sounds about right. I should tie you to the bed for that stunt."

"Do whatever you want to me, I'm yours," she said on a choppy exhale and I pulled myself out and plunged right back in.

"Say it again!"

"I'm yours!" I plunged back into her and waited. "I'm yours, Jacob." I retracted and plunged again, and as we continued the pattern, her voice grew hoarse from how loud she became. For the first time since buying my house, I was thankful for soundproof walls.

I kept fucking her until I felt her pussy clamp down on me like a vice, her words ceasing to make sense, turning into rambles of incomprehensible things.

I prolonged her bliss by thumbing her clit. Her cries mixed with her whimpers, moans, and guttural grunts. The array of sounds that she emitted made me wish that I wasn't about to come again. By the time she reached her second climax, I went along with her for the ride, our bodies moving in perfect synchronization at the pinnacle of our release.

I rolled her over so she lay on top of me, my length still inside her. She ran her left hand over my forehead, brushing my hair out of my eyes, and that's when I spotted the sparkle. I seized her hand and took a look at the diamonds I'd put there less than twenty-four hours ago. The fact that my ring was the only thing she wore made me want to ravage her again, but a certain appendage of mine had other ideas. A little rest was in order.

I kissed the knuckle, over the band. "God, I love you."

Her face held a look of adoration and her smile widened to a grin. "I love you too." She leaned up to deliver a soft kiss.

My cell began to ring and I looked at the caller ID. "It's Steve." She rolled off of me and I sat up.

"You get that and I'll go make us breakfast." Giving me a quick peck, I watched her get up. "Stay here, I'll be right back."

Her intent wasn't lost on me. "Hello?" I groaned into the phone as I watched her slip into her robe, covering all that delightful porcelain skin.

"You all right?" Steve asked.

"I'm fine, what'd you find?" I asked. "By the way, I've got some information to share with you too. Might make your job easier."

"Old man Withers is involved," he said.

"Fuck! I was going to tell you the same thing."

"There's something else."

"Go on." I listened as he told me everything.

CHAPTER 60

By the end of the call, I knew I could hold on to the promise I had made to my fiancée. It would take some work, and there would be some downsizing needed, but Withers International would live to see another day, a year, a decade. It would all depend on Mike and Danica.

With a bit of digging, Steve got his hands on enough information that a judge would have no problem overturning the notarized contract, as long as Mike and Danica both were willing to lay testimony. I doubted that would be an issue.

Along with the aforementioned information, Steve located forensic proof of Withers' and Spalding's perjury and embezzlement. Suffice to say that both men would be seeing the inside of a cell when all was said and done.

As for Duncan, I figured that with his more than questionable track record, and the reputation he'd gained in the courtroom, the least that would happen to the guy was that he'd get disbarred. I was leaving that to the authorities whom I was hanging up with when Danica had returned with breakfast.

It was safe to say that Danica had been all too happy to indulge in her own voracious method of thankfulness. It goes without saying that our breakfast could have been considered a brunch with how thorough she had been with her thank yous.

We were sitting around the table at dinner when Jordan came out with something that both shocked and delighted me. "Mom, I want to do something, and I need your help, but you might not like it."

Her brows narrowed. "What's that?"

His face bode a look of business. After a deep breath, he went for it. "I want to change my name to Landen." He looked at me and smiled.

"Are you sure?" I asked at the same time Danica said, "I figured I'd ask you about that when we got closer to the wedding."

"I'm sure. It's not that I don't like my last name; it's just that it's not right. Once you guys are married, you'll take his name and…"

Danica grabbed my hand and squeezed. "When do you want to do this?"

"Tomorrow, after school, maybe?"

"Okay." She smiled and shrugged her shoulders. "I guess I'll be the one out of the Landen name."

"Not for long." I leaned over the table and gave her a quick peck on the nose. "I'm hoping to convince you to marry me less than a month from now."

"Doing things at hyper speed, huh?" She laughed.

I nodded. "Gotta keep up with the pretense, right?"

Jordan laughed.

"Then, I have a proposition for you," she said.

"And what's that? Name it and it's yours."

"I want a baby."

Jordan cringed. "Uh, guys? I'm right here."

She turned to her son. "And what do you have to say about it?"

"About what? A baby?" She nodded. He shrugged his shoulders. "Cool, I guess."

"There you have it." Danica looked back at me. "So what do you say? A baby within the year?"

"I think I would love you that much more to see you grow round with our baby," I said.

"Then it's settled." She clapped her hands together. "We get married a week from next weekend and–"

"And you live happily ever after." Jordan rolled his eyes.

"We," she corrected.

"Yeah, yeah, yeah…" He rolled his eyes again, and I couldn't help but laugh. "I'm going to my room. Behave."

I laughed and arched a brow at my woman. "Behave?"

"You think he knows about, well, you know?" She watched our son's retreating back.

"Sweetheart, the kid's fifteen." I pulled her up and against me.

Her coloring went from red to pale. "Great! My kid is talking about sex," she whispered into my chest before looking up at me. "I think we're in trouble." She bit her lip. "Are you sure you really want a baby?"

I wrapped my arms around her. "With you, I'll have a whole football team if you asked me to." The horror on her face made me crack up. "Just kidding. Yes, I want another baby with you. I was an only child, and I don't want that for Jordan—and I never pictured us ever stopping at one. I wasn't around to see my first-born grow up, and based on him alone, I know that every other child will be fortunate with you as their mother."

"They'll be lucky to have you as a father, Jacob. You're a natural at it. How about we get to practicing?" The look on her face told me that she was dead serious about it too.

"Haven't you had enough woman?" I whined in a playful manner.

"Never," she said. "Then again, a nice bath and some cuddling TV-time in bed with you is just as appealing."

"Are you telling me that the TV is as interesting as I am?"

"Maybe." She curled her lips inward to keep a straight face.

"Maybe?" She nodded. "I'll show you maybe." Her body shivered at the intent in my words and I reveled in the power I held over her.

CHAPTER 61

Danica was bound and blind. I abstained from the gag, wanting to hear her. And perhaps, I wanted to make use of that mouth of hers too.

"Baby, I'm about to ravage you from top to bottom." She licked her lips and her bare breasts rose and fell at a faster rate.

I leaned forward, fisted her hair in my hand and pulled her head up. She let out a moan, her breath fanning over my face. I kissed her hard, bringing forth a feminine groan.

Lowering her head back to the pillow in a gentle fashion, I began to trail kisses from the side of her neck and her collarbone, tweaking her nipples with my thumb and forefinger, rolling them.

I trailed my hand to her stomach, my lips following close behind, tracing her stretch marks. "I never told you what these do to me now that I know that Jordan is mine, have I?"

"No." Her voice was hoarse and charged with eroticism.

I fanned my fingers outward and ran them over her hips and kissed her navel. "Baby, they make me hot. Knowing that we created a life is fantastic, but the fact that you carried him, nurtured him, kept him safe, means more to me than you'll ever know." I moved my kisses around her torso, her moans filling my ears, and I could hear the jingling of the cuffs. When I pulled away, her lower torso made to follow as her hips arched up off the bed. "I love the way you respond, the way your body begs without you having to say a word. But when you do, baby…"

"Jacob, please."

"Please what, sweetheart?" I hovered over her pussy, breathing air onto her glistening folds. "Tell me what you want and I'll give it to you."

Another whimper came out of her. "I want…" I helped her along with gliding a finger into her slick core, licking that engorged clit of hers. She arched her pelvis into my face. "Yes!"

I pulled away and kissed her inner right thigh and listened to her groan. I nipped her with a bit of aggressiveness and she yelped, her arms jarring against the shackles again. I matched my bite on her other inner thigh, branding her. "You're mine, Nica."

"Yours," she said. I latched on to her nub with my mouth and penetrated her with two fingers. A few thrusts of my digits were all it took to send her over the edge.

The chorus of moans that followed was nothing compared to what I knew I was about to hear when I slid inside her—and I wasn't doing that with her bound.

As her climax ebbed, I moved lower and undid the silk ties around her legs. "I need your legs wrapped around me," I said against the skin of her ankle as I soothed the flesh.

"Please."

"I need your arms to hold me, to touch me when I get inside you."

"Yes." She hissed as I hurried to get the shackles undone around her wrists.

Soothing the skin from the harshness of the steel restraints that had held her, my face hovered an inch above hers. "Now kiss me, sweetheart." My face hovered less than an inch away from hers.

Her arms wrapped around my shoulders, a hand glided

into my hair, and her lips fused to mine. She didn't reach for the blindfold. Oh, how I loved her total submission. It amazed me how she can give herself over like that, considering her love of taking hold of the reins.

I released her blindfold and pulled it away before pulling my mouth from hers. She blinked her hooded eyes a few times. "I want you to keep your eyes on me, sweetheart. I want to see everything." I positioned myself at her entrance, holding my cock to stroke her clit with it. Her hypersensitive body quivered with each pass.

Her words came out breathless. "Make love to me, Jacob."

It tortured me to enter her at such a slow pace, but damn was it ever a sweet pain. The feel of her tight core's rhythmic clenching around me made me grind my teeth, and just about threw me over the edge.

Holding her eyes with mine, I buried myself to the hilt, our bodies becoming one.

One word came to mind when we climaxed, calling each other's names.

Happy.

EPILOGUE

I was blessed. Here I was, surrounded by friends and family.
A little over a year since marrying the love of my life, I
would be lying if I said that I didn't love her more today than
I did the day I married her.

Today marked Jordan's seventeenth birthday.

Let me catch you up on what's happened since Danica
and I married…

W ithers International is now owned by a brother and sister team: my wife and the most hilarious brother-in-law
you'll ever know, Mike.

Duncan was disbarred, as I'd predicted, while Bruce
Spalding was sentenced to two years in prison. It's not
much, but it was better than nothing.

A month after his release from the hospital and weeks
prior to our court date, Danica's father passed away from
heart failure in his Austin home. Mike had been on the line
with him when their argument went silent. Danica's brother
had disconnected the call and notified the paramedics since
he'd been in Jacksonville at the time.

Despite the volatile relationship between father and
daughter, Danica had a rough time overcoming her loss. The

two never mended things, but had remained civil for the sake of our son who, despite his parents' encouragement, had given his grandfather the chance to explain, but had chosen to decline every other request for visits.

Jordan adjusted well, what with his falling out with his grandfather. Suffice to say, he found solace in his friends, his parents, and he enjoyed spending time with my parents. His Nana and Grandpa couldn't be more pleased to dote on him whenever the mood struck.

Paxton and Alissa had a baby girl—a honeymoon baby—and a few weeks ago, no more than four months after their new arrival, they discovered that they were expecting again. It was unexpected, but they were both overjoyed. An overprotective Jasper was not only boasting about his "little princess" at every turn, he was demanding that his parents give him a brother this time around.

It wasn't until we were in Alissa's hospital room, visiting with Paxton's family, and their new addition was in my arms, that I'd turned to my wife and wondered when our turn would come. A week later, I came home after meeting with a client. My crazy woman ran out the front door, waving a white stick, yelling "We did it!" like a madwoman before she launched herself at me and I had to catch her, using my car to prevent us from toppling to the pavement.

As for me, my law business was thriving, and I've expanded my practice from family law and got back into business law all over again, but for one sole purpose. I am now the head legal counsel for Withers International. It took a lot of begging and convincing on Danica's and Mike's parts, but I caved one night when my sexy vixen of a wife subdued me with those cuffs of mine.

"What are you smirking at?" Danica asked, pulling me from my thoughts.

I kissed the top of her head. "Nothing."

"Walk with me?"

I took her hand and led her away from the patio and toward one of the large willows I had on my property. I leaned on it and pulled Danica so her back leaned into my front. Everyone seemed to be enjoying themselves, snacks and drinks at their disposal, laughter filling the air. Jordan's friends were throwing around a football and further back, Jordan sat with Jenna on the hammock I had set up for Danica.

As you can guess, Jenna stuck around after the Spring Fling dance. Jordan was smitten with her, and I loved to tease him about it since he loved to poke fun at me and his mother.

My son and I have never been closer. There's not much that he won't tell me and since Mike moved back, the teenager has had his uncle to confide in as well. I love my boy to death, and there hasn't been a day where I haven't heard or seen him reciprocate his feelings toward me since him and his mother moving in.

Heeding to his mother's and my warnings, Jordan has never tried anything with Jenna. Danica watched the two like a hawk at first. At the most, we saw the two hold hands, and they seem to have become great friends.

The girl popped by to do homework throughout the week. She'd stay over for dinner on a few of those days, since her parents worked late and Danica wasn't fond of the girl eating alone.

Jordan denied the fact that the girl had stars in her eyes for him, but to his mother and me, we knew what that look of hers was all about. For a perceptive teenager, he sure was oblivious when it came to Jenna.

Lost in my reverie, I felt my wife squeeze my arm. "Baby, look." I looked in the direction my wife's finger was pointing in. Jenna had pulled out a small box and handed it to Jordan. He opened it and stared, surprised at whatever it was. "I wonder what she got him," Danica whispered.

"I'm thinking that she made him something. You used to do that too." I kissed her temple.

We kept watching as he brushed a loose strand from her face behind her ear and kissed her on the cheek. She blushed, making me chuckle. *That's my boy.* "The kid's got moves."

Danica turned to face me and I wrapped my arms around her. "Much like his father did back in the day." She pecked my lips. "He still does."

"I just hope it works out better for him," I said. "We lost fifteen years. No two people deserve that."

"But look at what we have now," she whispered. Leaning back, she reached for my hands and covered her belly with them.

Her eyes were filled with so much amazement and adoration that I leaned in and pressed my lips to hers. "And I couldn't ask for more."

I kissed her sweet and thorough, her arms wrapping around my neck, pulling me in, as her growing baby bump kept us apart. And I have to add that I was right. I did love her more growing round with a little piece of both of us inside her, but something unexpected happened along with that. The mere sight of her made me hornier than fuck.

"Like father, like son," we heard, breaking us apart. It was Paxton, and he nodded toward Jordan and Jenna from his perch up on the patio.

Danica and I turned to check things out. The teenage pair still sat on the hammock, but my son held her face in his hands, and her hands were on his chest as they shared a sweet kiss. I felt Danica melt into my side.

Hoots and hollers broke the two apart, and the crimson that climbed up both of their faces made everyone laugh. The smirk on his face couldn't be hidden, even if he tried, as his gaze met mine.

"Can you guys come back here for a second—your mother and I have something important to let everyone know," I told him.

Making our way onto the large patio, I stood behind my wife, our hands clasped over her expanding belly and smiled at one another. It was time to deliver the news from our latest doctor's appointment.

"Guys," I began and Danica giggled her excitement. "I hope you're ready for double trouble."

I watched as a few sets of brows furrowed as Danica piggy-backed my words with, "We're having twins!"

"Twins!" Was the collective word all around.

My parents got up with a shriek and a hoot, and everyone else started laughing at their hysterics.

"Well, that's one way to make up for lost time." Mike got up and offered me a pat on the back. "Congratulations, bro."

"Thanks," I said and pulled away from my wife to give him a big, old man-hug.

Danica's best friend, Nicole, was next in the line of hugs and kisses. She and I still had a love-hate relationship, but it had warmed up to being more or less like that of a sibling-type thing.

Of all people, it took Mike to convince her that I wasn't the bad guy that she had been convinced I was. I thought it hilarious that it took a playboy to prove the character of a former one, but I was glad that it worked out—for Danica and me anyway.

For Mike, Nicole's hostile attitude gravitated from me to him. She nagged him about his preference to, "slut around", as she wasn't so eloquent to put it. Regardless of the tension, something seemed to be brewing between the two. Not being the meddlesome type, I figured that they could make peace on their own.

As the sun set on our day, I looked around at the people surrounding us, and knew that I had everything I could have ever wanted in life—and more than I could ever ask for. 'Blessed' was a great description, but I felt like it didn't justify how fortunate I had become over the last thirteen months.

I have a wife that I love more than life itself.

I have a son that I didn't ask for, but got the cream of the crop anyway, and would never want to trade.

I have two beautiful babies on the way that I will grow old to watch thrive and shape their futures from their very first day on this earth, providing me with a chance to redeem myself for the lost years with Jordan.

Above all else, I feel whole.

I am home.

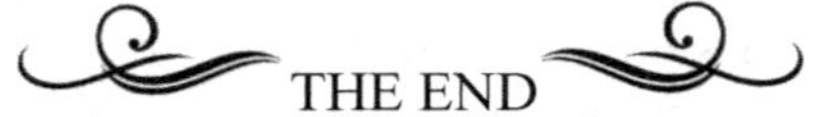

THE END

ABOUT THE AUTHOR

Born and raised in small town Northern Ontario, Canada, Carey Decevito has always had a penchant for reading and writing.

More than a decade later, with weeks of sleepless nights, where exhaustion settled into her everyday existence, she finally gave in and put pen to paper (more like fingers to keyboard!) She submitted to the dreams that plagued her. And the rest, as they say, is history!

A member of the RWA, Carey Decevito enjoys spending time with family and friends, the outdoors, traveling, and playing tourist in Canada's National Capital region. When life gets crazy, she seeks respite through her writing and reading. If all else fails, she knows there's never a dull moment with her prolific storyteller of a daughter, her goofy husband, cat and dog who she swears are out to get her.

Almost Forgotten is the second book in *The Broken Men Chronicles* series.

FIND CAREY AT:

www.careydecevito.com
carey.decevito@gmail.com

<u>ALSO BY CAREY DECEVITO</u>

The Broken Men Chronicles series:

Once Written, Twice Shy
Almost Forgotten

play me to *infinity*

THE BROKEN MEN CHRONICLES

book three

excerpt

carey decevito

I sat at Fairfax, checking out the flavors of the evening while unwinding from a grueling day at the office. It was slim pickings in the crowd, but the night was still young.

Sitting in the back corner at a table by herself, I spotted her. Nicole. I might have turned her unsavory attitude around where my brother-in-law, Jake, was concerned, but the woman now had a gun out for me.

Okay, so you've surmised that I'm single, perhaps even a player, and I'll admit that you're somewhat right.

I enjoy my bachelorhood… well, sort of. I wouldn't say that it's the lifestyle I'd have chosen for myself, more like one chosen for me, thanks to my ex-fiancée.

Loving Tracey with everything I had hadn't been good enough. Despite the numerous warnings from friends, I had been living by the 'denial is bliss' adage until one day, the flip of her hair, the wiggle of her tight ass, and the batting of her lashes no longer clouded my perception.

After six months of dealing with her deceit, I shredded my devoted fiancé card and moved on. I've been playing the field for a year and a half since.

Truth be told, I don't have time for a relationship, as much as I'd prefer one. I'm the CEO of Withers International, a multi-million-dollar company that specializes in public and government relations. Need I say more?

Ben knocked me back into the present as he dropped himself into the seat across from me. "Rough day?"

"Rough few months is more like it." I huffed out a breath. "I need a new assistant."

The man's brows furrowed. "You still haven't gotten rid of Karen?"

A dry laugh escaped. "You mean Tania." I didn't have the gall to look at my friend, knowing I'd be met with his disapproving look, and rightly so. As of late, there was quite the revolving door where my PA's were concerned.

"Why do you do this to yourself?"

Okay, so I may have overstepped the boundaries on employer-employee relations. In my defense, they were the ones who approached me, not the other way around.

Ben shook his head at me. "Tracey really did fuck you up. This is ridiculous."

I took a swig from my beer and let out a loud tension-filled sigh while leaning my bottle in my best friend's direction. "You don't know the half of it."

It was late, and despite the fact that I'd made it out tonight, my interest in entertaining a possible suitor to cap off my day was lost once Ben returned to his bartending duties.

What about Nikki? As soon as the thought occurred, I almost choked on my last sip of beer. I would have to be desperate—no, insane—to even approach that man-eater.

Despite my intent on ignoring the woman who had eyed daggers at me all night, I turned my gaze toward the table she had been occupying to find that she was no longer there.

Nicole was a beautiful woman, and I'd be lying if I said I didn't remember much about her from our childhood. Hell, she'd practically been a sister; and harassing her and my sister had been one of mine and Ben's favorite pastimes. In our later years however, she became skittish, always quick to leave the room as soon as I entered it. The teenager I'd been had always wondered about the possibility of her having a schoolgirl crush. I have to say that I enjoyed cornering her to see that blush, especially that last summer before Mom and Dad picked up and moved us all to Austin.

Shaking the memories from my mind, I left my empty bottle on the table. As I turned to leave, I plowed into a tiny body. Bracing my hands on the soft skin of slim shoulders to prevent the person from toppling over, I found myself staring down into bright green pools laced with flames that were Nicole's eyes.

What color do they turn when…? I groaned at the imagery that flashed through my mind. Forget it, bud, there's no way in hell that you want to go there.

"Watch where you're going."

"Sorry," I mumbled, my voice a few octaves lower than normal.

"D-do you mind moving?"

Her unsettled demeanor had me smirking. "Do I make you nervous, Little Nikki?"

As I let go of her shoulders, she stepped back.

"No." She gave me a saccharine smile, but her eyes showed mischievousness. "You make me nauseous. Now, get out of my way."

As she made to pass me, I grasped her elbow. "You know," I leaned toward her ear, the subtlety of her scent clouding my thoughts momentarily, "if you're ever looking for someone to help you get that stick out of your ass, I'd be more than–"

The claws came out. "Bite me!"

"I'd love to, sugar." I grinned, pulling away just in time to see her face turn a delightful shade of pink. Yes, that blush was still as much fun to bring about now as it was back in the day.

As quick as our interaction occurred, it ended when she turned and trotted off.

My gaze turned to follow her exiting the bar. I let out a low whistle as I watched those hips sway in that skirt of hers. Her rounded ass filled the material to perfection and images of that luscious derrière, bent over as I took her from behind began playing in my head.

Damn! It's too bad she's as cold as ice.

And that was my cue to head home.

I came to a stop in front of my large four-bedroom house and sighed. Purchased to avoid the cramped lofts and high-rise condos, it was a constant reminder of the dream I once had of a home filled with children and a woman to worship. Nowadays, all I had to look forward to was the cold beer in my fridge, my comfortable furniture, and a house filled with silence.

Silence. It was always there when you didn't want it, and never there when you needed it.

Over the last eighteen months, I kept my new façade intact, my machismo held close to the vest in an effort to mask that I was a family man to the core. Being honest, I was miserable. Lonely.

Maybe it's time to take a chance? It had been two years since I'd left Tracey, a year and a half since I chose to have absolutely nothing to do with my ex.

Danica, Jake, and so many others disagree with the casualness with which I treated my suitors, but they understood why I did it. Well, most of them, with the exception of my sister's judgmental best friend, Nicole that is.

So why wasn't I going for it after two years?

The answer was simple: I was scared.

As I settled into bed, I came to realize that maybe it was time I let go of my pessimism where relationships were concerned.

CHAPTER 2

At six the following morning, I was in my office. It was my favorite time of the workday. It gave me time to think. It gave me time to analyze where I was taking this company that my father built from the ground up and then, before he could run it into the ground, left it to me and Danica.

After bumping into Nicole last night, I had a replay of her ass swaying from side to side, her bare shoulders, and those legs of hers capped in four-inch heels, playing on a continuous loop in my mind.

And this morning, the thought of those…

Snap out of it, man!

The sudden twitch below the belt had me groaning. These reactions of mine had come way out of left field, and I'd be damned if I paid them any heed simply because Nicole now appealed to a certain member of my anatomy.

With that said, I could only deal with craziness one person at a time.

And that brings me to another woman that plagued my thoughts as of late: my personal assistant.

I needed to do something about my current work predicament—and fast. Burning the candle at both ends, I was putting in longer hours lately while my sister, and Withers International's CFO, was at home by dinnertime, enjoying life with her husband, their son, and her very pregnant belly.

Ben was right. And I quote, the measure of a great personal assistant is how well she tends to your schedule, files, paperwork and the like, and not how she blows you from beneath your desk. Crass, I know, but true all the same. It was time I got rid of Tania. She was incompetent and she gave me more grief than help on the best of days.

Thinking of my sister, I picked up the phone, figuring she could be of help with my current predicament, but thought better and set the receiver back on its cradle. She'd be in the office within the hour anyway.

Danica and I have gotten closer since my move back to Jacksonville became permanent. We had weekly dinners at her place and she always stopped by my office for a chat first thing every morning.

Like me, she found her way into work a tad earlier than most, unless my brother-in-law found a way to hold her back.

Jake and I have bonded more, and I love the man as if he were my own brother. He got me, for the lack of a better description, and with the way I've been living my life lately, that's something Ben and I haven't been able to relate to. Jake was worse than me a short time ago, but when it came down to his relationship with my sister, I never once doubted his intentions. I knew the man loved her. Everyone knew it. Though years had kept them separated, their love had never faded; no matter how stubborn they had been when Danica moved back, or how my father had conspired to keep them apart.

I released a tension-filled sigh, regaining my focus on the present.

A look at my day's itinerary left me with a burning sensation in my gut. After a nearly a month and repetitive requests, the damn thing was still predominantly blank with the exception of those appointments I had entered myself in recent weeks.

I grunted my annoyance and looked toward the pile of files on the edge of my desk that had only grown instead of finding their way into one of the mahogany cabinets in the far corner.

I was more organized doing everything solo before she came along.

Yes, it was official. I was fed up.

Despite the warnings and reminders, Tania had had her opportunity to prove her worth. Her probationary period wasn't over yet, but I'd be dammed if I allowed her to wreak more chaos over my office for another day. Knowing what I had to do next, and probably should have done yesterday if not last week, I picked up the phone and dialed.

I waited for the woman in question to pick up.

"Hello." She sounded half-asleep.

"Tania."

"Mike?" Her voice came out squeaky.

"Yes." I took a deep breath.

"What's wrong?"

"Tania," I cleared my throat, "I'm sorry to do this, but I won't be needing your services any longer."

"But…"

"I need someone who's organized and knows what she's doing; someone with more experience and who does what I need them to do. I'm saying things need to be seamless and they're not. I think you know what I mean by this." I began to guide the mouse over my computer screen. "I'm looking at my calendar right now and the four meetings I asked you to confirm and add to my agenda before you left yesterday aren't in there. Simple things like that, I shouldn't have to clarify at this point in your employment. I'm sorry but I can't keep you any longer."

"But, Mike!" Her voice grated on my nerves.

"Your belongings and relevant paperwork will be waiting for you with HR by this afternoon. I trust that a week's severance is ample enough seeing as you've only been with us for under a month. When you come in, please ask for Emma in Human Resources. She'll handle everything. Again, I'm very sorry and I wish you luck. Take care of yourself."

I hung up before she could say anything else and took a deep breath.

Putting in a call to Emma in HR and leaving a voicemail with what I needed from her later, I hung up the phone.

Getting up, I grabbed a banker's box from the small supply cabinet in my office and walked to Tania's former quarters and cringed. There were photo frames on the desk; I counted five pairs of shoes, three jackets, a couple of pashminas, and that was excluding whatever personal items would most likely be stored in the desk drawers. I didn't envy Emma at all for what she'd have to do when she got in this morning.

On a groan, I leaned forward with my elbows on my desk and massaged my temples. My mood had taken a downward spiral, and I hoped that the rest of my day didn't follow in the same fashion.

"What's got you down, big brother?" I startled, not having heard Danica come in. My sister waddled toward me with a cup of coffee in both hands.

"That better be decaf." I gestured to the drink she kept for herself after she handed me mine.

"Every morning you ask me that question and every morning I give you the same answer." She smirked, then stuck her tongue out at me. "You know it is."

"Just making sure." I smiled, but the gesture wasn't reciprocal. Instead, she assessed me from top to bottom.

"You look tired." She took a seat in front of my desk.

"Because I am."

"You're working too hard. You need to get out and live a little."

I shrugged my shoulders. "I get out."

"Finding a woman to warm your bed on occasion isn't considered 'getting out'." She was right, but would I tell her that? Hell, no! Just like I wouldn't tell her that the only bed-warming there'd been in the last month, aside from the one time with Tania a few weeks ago, had been done by me alone.

"I know you don't agree with it sis, and I don't need this right now." I ran a hand through my dark brown hair. "I had to fire Tania and, to be honest, I have no clue what's on my agenda for today, plus I have to coordinate with HR to get a new posting out there, and deal with interviews, and…" I sighed.

"Calm down, I know someone who'd be great for you."

Well that got my attention. "Who?"

"Just someone." She gave me a wry grin. "I can say that fucking her won't be a problem for you, which means that her attention will be on her work the entire time. She's the best I know, and if she'd been free when I was looking for my PA, I would have snapped her up myself."

She knows?

She snorted. "Yes, I know about your latest tastes in personal assistants, big brother."

"So who is it?"

"I'll have to speak with her first, see if she's interested." She tapped her index finger on her chin. "As for who it is, I'll leave that surprise to her." She winked. "I'm sorry, but I've got to run. You remember not to expect me in the office after this morning, right?"

I laughed, but my excitement of acquiring a new PA without much effort dimmed as worry for my sister kicked in. "I always said you worked too hard. You need to take it easy, you're due any day now. Your husband's right to worry, you know. We all do."

She laughed, but the humor in her eyes faded and her expression softened as she reached out a hand to me. "Come help me out of this chair and give me a hug." I rounded my desk and helped her up. "I need to get some work done before Jake comes back to pick me up in a few hours. I hate that I can't drive thanks to this belly of mine." Her hands clasped her stomach that held two of the most precious of cargos.

"Hey, that's my niece and nephew you're talking about in there." I gave her belly a rub.

I kissed the top of her head and she moved into my arms to hug me. "So, you'll think about the PA I have in mind for you?"

"Go ahead and send her in." I released her. "I need all the help I can get." *The sooner, the better* was left unsaid.

"Okay!"

"Not now, Joe!" If it was the man in question, I swear I would tear him a new one. I had had more than enough of running interference for him in order to rectify his latest fuck-up.

As you can gather, my day had followed the same route it had started on: with a shitload of incompetence.

A softer knock came as a reply to my grumbling acknowledgement of the initial disturbance.

Didn't anyone get what a closed office door meant? With a huff, I got up, wrenched the knob inward and barked a, "What?"

"Oh hell, no! Not you!" she said.

"Nicole?" I smirked as she started to back up, never taking her eyes off of me.

"I need a job, but not this bad."

Her withdrawal from me was quite amusing, so I leaned against the doorway, my arms crossed at my chest. My day could use a little divertissement, and Nicole's presence was sure to make it entertaining. "So you're the PA that Dani's been boasting about?"

She huffed. "Yeah, and you're the arrogant executive prick that's in dire straits. Funny how your sister left out the prick part."

Feisty! I liked my women that way, but then again, I always knew Nicole had the knack to bite back, despite her shyness.

My feet moved me toward her and she kept backing away. "Nicole." I stifled a bout of laughter when her butt hit the desk behind her and her eyes grew panicked with the realization that she was somewhat cornered.

"Jackass!" she spat, maneuvering away from her trap.

Feisty and skittish all at once made for an interesting combination. Now I saw a glimpse of both of the Nicoles I'd enjoyed so much over the years, and that fact only egged me on.

"It would be Jackass Boss to you," I paused for dramatics, "if I give you the position. Why is it that my sister thinks that you'd be perfect for the job?"

"It doesn't matter. I don't need it."

"Yes you do. You said so just now."

She blushed. "Well I- What I mean to say is…" She pinched her lips and a frustrated sigh escaped seconds later. "Yeah, I need a job, so what?"

"I'm currently hiring," I said with nonchalance.

"So I've heard. And?"

"And, do you want the job or not?" Annoyance laced my words.

I gauged her demeanor. She was stuck between a rock and a hard place. She needed money, but I could tell that the last place she wanted to be was anywhere near me.

Nothing new there.

The woman, even as a girl, had always found a way to give me a wide berth, even at family events, which she seemed to always be in attendance.

"I'll think about it." She turned to walk away.

"You either do or you don't, Nicole. I'd like an answer now so I don't feel as if I've wasted my time."

She spun on her heels to face me. "Oh?" She crossed her arms and spoke with so much disdain. "Did I just waste your precious time finding a slut to satisfy you tonight?"

My eyes narrowed on her. "Keep your voice down. And where the hell did that come from?"

"You know where it came from!" She marched toward me and jabbed her index in my chest as she looked up at me. "You're a sleaze! You're all over a woman one minute and onto another the next. I wouldn't be surprised if you screwed your former PA." Her almond-shaped eyes widened when I didn't hurry to defend myself. "Oh my God, you did, didn't you?"

"N-no I didn't!" Yeah, that wasn't as convincing as I'd hoped.

"Did so!" She cupped her forehead with a single hand. "I can't believe I was about to agree."

"You were?" I thought there'd be no shot in hell that she'd agree to work for me unless I got down on my knees and begged. And there's no way that was happening.

"Forget it!" She waved her hand, brushing off the idea of working with me, then made a mad dash for the elevators, grumbling. "I'm going to kill Danica for this."

She summoned the elevator before I could peel my eyes off of her ass and legs.

"Wait!" I rushed to her, but the doors started closing with her inside. My final glimpse of Nicole was one of her wiping at what looked like angry tears from her face.

Well now you've done it!

Later that night, I had a rather pissed-off, about-to-pop sister knocking at my door.

"Sis…" I kissed her on the cheek, then smiled, hoping that the combination of both would help ease the brunt of her wrath.

"Oh cut the sis bit, Mike! What the fuck did you do to her?"

"To who?" I thought twice about playing dumb. "To Nikki?"

"Yes, to Nikki, you idiot! She showed up at the house, pissed off that I hadn't told her who she'd be working for at WI. I know you two have never really gotten along, but I didn't expect it to be like this."

"Like what?" I was losing my patience. "Where she attacked me by accusing me of making a habit of seducing my PA's?" She arched her brow, crossed her arms, and tapped her foot. "Okay… fine, I've done it, but–"

"But what?"

"But there's no way in hell that…" I decided to go with the obvious. "She's your friend and she hates my guts and–"

"And what?"

"It's Little Nikki." I shrugged my shoulders. "She's

gorgeous and all, but like I've said, she hates me, thinks I'm a player. It wouldn't–"

"Right you are!"

My head snapped toward Danica's car. I'd neglected to remember that my sister couldn't drive and needed a chauffeur.

Nicole slammed the driver's side door and stormed toward us still dressed in her business attire.

"Excuse me?" I said.

She came to a stop beside Danica. "You're right, you are a player."

"You don't know a thing about me," I said and she harrumphed.

"And I don't care to either." She looked over at Danica who growled, and I did the same. The woman looked as if she was about to implode.

"Cut it out, you two! Nicole, you need the job, and bro, you need the help. You don't need to like each other, just help each other out. If you dislike it that much, Nikki, leave when you find something else. And as for you, playboy…" She pointed an index in my direction.

"I'm not–" I protested.

"Maybe not, but you have to admit that you've been… um… Anyway, it doesn't matter. You're a good man and you know that you're not cut out for that shit." My sister turned to her best friend. "And you need to cut him some slack. Now, get me home. I'm tired, I'm cranky, and my feet feel like they're about to burst."

With that, Danica marched to the passenger side of her car and got in while the two of us watched on.

A moment later, Nicole's gaze went from the car to me. "Fine, I'll take it, but I'm out of there the minute I find something else."

"I wouldn't expect anything less. Thank you."

She nodded. "Keep your dick in your pants, stay away from me, and we'll be fine."

When she turned heel and made to leave I said, "What makes you think that I can't keep business separate from pleasure?"

She paused by the driver's side door. "Because," she smirked at me after a slow assessing gaze that had warmth pooling in my belly, "once a player, always a player."

Nicole's last words reverberated in my head long after her and Danica had left. It wasn't true, but she refused to see the proverbial light of day. Something about that fact niggled at me.

I've never agreed with men who saw their bachelorhood as a means to debauch as many partners as they could. So I went home with my fair share of women. It didn't mean I'd slept with all of them. Sometimes it was nice to have an intellectual conversation, or simply hang out, cuddling while watching a movie. Regardless of my activities with my suitors, I was always up front with them about what I was looking for.

Despite my trying to impart this knowledge on Nicole, whenever she'd give me two seconds to get a few words in edgewise, she still managed to make me feel like a complete jackass.

Why do you even care what she thinks, when you've never given a damn about what anyone else thought before?

As much as I'd probably like to deny the why, there was something about the tiny spitfire that set me off. To put it simply, I liked her. Always have. The woman was an enigma, a complex puzzle that was wrapped in riddles that held no answer. For the moment.

My head was pounding by the time I gave into exhaustion and went to bed. Having taken inventory of my life, I found myself grossly disgusted with the man I had become.

For the second night running, I surmised that a change could be good. That macho guy I'd allowed myself to become wasn't me, but how the hell could I let down my guard again?

I drifted into sleep, confused and hating part of myself.

The next morning, I arrived at the office and wondered if Nicole would show up like she said she would. Not having discussed a time, salary, benefits… anything, I'd made sure that my schedule for this morning had been cleared of meetings.

I was drafting up a PR pitch to win a large account when a knock came on my open door.

"Yes?"

"I'm here."

Looking up, I hurried to push most of my paperwork to the side.

"Please shut the door behind you, Nicole." She nodded. "I guess you stuck to your decision. Thanks for coming." I took in her attire. Black pin-striped pencil skirt, up to her mid-thigh… *Nice*; crème satin blouse, unbuttoned enough to see the tops of her peaks… *Gorgeous*; natural make-up, but accented with dark red lipstick… *Sexy as fuck*; and her chestnut brown hair was up in a loose chignon, showing off the length of her slender neck, the tresses begging for a man to let them loose and run his fingers through them… *Beautiful*.

The screeching of a record resounded in my head. *Hold on… What?*

"Where do you want me?"

Sexually explicit answers swam through my thoughts, but I shoved them to the side. It wouldn't do well to anger the she-devil on her first day.

I cleared my throat. "We have a few things to discuss first." I gestured to the chair in front of my desk. "Have a seat."

I went through the motions of explaining that Nicole would have full health and dental benefits from the get-go. She was more than happy with the other perks that came with the job, but a little hesitant about the travelling that would be needed on occasion.

Her eyes bulged when I pointed out her salary, which was a bit short of six figures. "Are you sure about this?"

"About what?"

"Don't you think the salary's a bit much?"

"Are you asking me to lower it?" My brow arched. "I would have thought it obvious, with the fact that you're not my biggest fan, that some kind of compensation would be more than appropriate."

She blushed. "Well…"

The zing to my cock was potent, thanks to her reaction. Clearing my throat and trying to control my lustful reflex, I said, "So it's settled then?" *Please agree before I embarrass myself.*

She gave me a small nod and her game face returned.

"Then I'll need your signature on this stuff." I slapped a pen on top of the packet of papers and slid the entirety over to her before leaning back into my chair and crossing my arms over my chest.

She leaned forward, the white lace of her bra peeking through the gap in her blouse.

My throat constricted, my groin stirred further at the sight.

Nicole signed her life away, got up, and stuck her hand out. I took it and held her eyes, which widened. I held on to her delicate fingers, entranced by the feel of softness and warmth a moment longer than necessary, which caused her cheeks to flush, reminding me to release her.

"So… um… my desk is…" She pointed just outside my door into the open-concept office suite with a thumb over her shoulder.

"Yes. Go ahead, make yourself at home and then we can talk about my agenda and your other duties."

"I don't have anything to settle, so why don't I grab a notepad and pen and we can cut to the chase?" she suggested.

"Sounds good to me."

The moment the woman turned around, I was quick to adjust myself.

Before we knew it, lunchtime had arrived and Nicole was at her desk with a rather extensive list of tasks to perform, eating some kind of leftover meal that didn't seem all that appetizing.

She dropped her fork in the dish and pushed it away from her with a scowl and proceeded to be engrossed in her work-station.

"I thought that you'd be out with friends, celebrating your first day. You know you're allowed to leave the building, right?" I sassed.

Her fingers halted on the keyboard. "Funny." She kept her eyes to her computer screen instead of looking at me. "I thought you said you had a lunch meeting?" She typed a few more strokes and paused.

"They cancelled," I announced. She still didn't turn to look at me, instead, typed a few more additional notes. "Listen, it doesn't seem like you're enjoying the lunch you brought with you. I'm heading out to the deli across the street if you'd like to join me—my treat."

"Thanks, but I think I'll pass."

This time, when her fingers hit the keyboard again, it felt like I'd been dismissed.

"Fine."

During the hour I was out, my phone's alert system was getting some serious mileage. As I checked the source of the chime, appointment after appointment filled my calendar and I smiled.

Quick and efficient, the woman was turning out to be. I made a mental note to thank Danica for her recommendation. Nicole sure knew how to handle an office she was unfamiliar with. I wondered how smooth things would run once she felt comfortable.

When I got back, stacks of paper that had seen far too much of the light of day had been removed and I could only assume that Nicole had filed them away during my absence, seeing as they were nowhere to be found.

I walked into my office and noticed that even my desk looked tidier. The pile of files on the edge of it had disappeared, as well as those others that had been littering the small work table in the far corner.

I turned to say something to Nicole, but found her on the phone.

"I'll be sure to let him know," she said and giggled into the phone. "Sure. Will do, sir." She hung up, closed a file folder and got up in a rush, almost crashing into me. "Uh… here." She pushed the file at me. "Mr. Winthrow called and he's on for Monday at noon. I guess you're flying out to Austin. Did you need me to coordinate your travel arrangements?"

"That would be wonderful, thank you."

"You're welcome." She dropped to her seat, pulled up my agenda and started tapping away at the keyboard again.

Damn! The woman was like my last three assistants combined and on steroids!

The rest of the afternoon flew by, with Nicole walking in and out of my office with various files, removing those I was done with, and everything kind of flowed. Before I knew it, I heard a knock on my door.

"I'm heading out. Is there anything you need before I go?" Nicole asked.

I glanced at the clock on the bottom right of my computer screen. "No." I gave her a warm smile. She gave me an awkward look. "Thanks for today. You were great."

"It's what I do." She shrugged her shoulders. "See you tomorrow."

"Yeah."

When she took her leave, I took inventory of my workload and realized that for the first time in months I was able to leave work at a decent time. Before dinner.

I locked my office, pocketed my keys, and headed out, waving to the few of my employees that remained. The look of surprise at my early departure on their faces was comical.

I drove toward my house and then decided to take a detour. I wasn't in the mood to eat alone.

Circling the block a few times before deciding to stop and park, I walked up the front steps and rang.

Jordan answered. "Uncle Mike, what are you doing here?"

"Hello to you too." I fist-bumped my nephew and walked in. "Any room for an extra person at the dinner table?" I walked into the kitchen and watched Jake in action.

"You're not at work!"

Danica's shock had me laughing. "Thanks for that. Nicole might not be my biggest fan, but the woman looks good and knows how to work."

"Sounds like someone's got a crush," Jordan singsonged.

"Pipe down kid!" I told him.

"I think he might be right," Jake said with a smile.

"Guys!" Danica's warning tone came out. "There's nothing going on with those two, they're all kinds of wrong for each other."

"Some people would have said the same thing about us." Jake wrapped himself around her back and rubbed her humongous belly. "Look at us now." She turned her head sideways to meet her husband's lips.

"Damn you guys make it look easy." I took a seat at the table, pouring myself a glass of iced water and downing half of it in two gulps.

"Do I sense a change of heart?" Danica asked with a smirk, her arms folded over her husband's.

My thoughts about needing a change from the last two nights came to mind. "Maybe."

"Told you, man, it gets old quick… and lonely."

I nodded. Oh, how right Jake was.

CHAPTER 6

It was early—only ten—but I found myself at home, in front of the TV, hearing my phone buzzing incessantly on the table next to me. My phone never buzzed at night.

Picking the device up to check things out, I saw more updates to my itinerary. Why the hell was Nicole working at ten o'clock at night?

I opened up my email and began to type away.

> *Nicole,*
> *Just because you're the CEO's assistant and getting paid the big bucks doesn't mean you need to be working around the clock.*
> *Relax.*
> *See you in the morning,*
> *Jackass Boss*

Despite my message, the buzzing of my phone continued and was now keeping me awake regardless of my dedication to an early bedtime. I turned the thing off, left it on my bedside table, and resolved to have a chat with my overproductive personal assistant come morning.

When my eyes closed for the final time, Nicole was all I saw. And it wasn't the bitchy, turn-her-nose-up-at-me woman, but the sweet, demure, and shy one I knew while growing up.

Friday had finally arrived and I got to the office, expecting to be alone as always, but to my surprise, Nicole was already sitting at her desk.

"Morning!" I said. "You're early, did you sleep at all last night?"

"Of course!" she snapped.

"Nicole?" I waited until she looked up at me. "Can we have a chat in my office for a moment?"

She averted her gaze to her desk, the worried look she wore was nothing less than adorable.

Don't kid yourself… she'll claw your eyes out if given the chance. I snorted at the thought as I headed toward my desk.

She shut the door behind her before taking a seat across from me. "Is something wrong? I'm sorry for snapping. It's been… a rough night, I guess."

"Don't worry about it," I said. "I couldn't help but notice that you seem to be… uh… a little overly productive."

"What do you mean? You said to keep you up to date and that's what I've been doing. I don't have my work phone yet, so I got your appointments to call my personal cell, so we could get them all in the books, and the rest I tackled from my remote connection."

"Yeah… during work hours. Your time off is your time off, didn't you get my email?"

"I did. I'm sorry." She looked away for a moment and then back at me. "I just thought that since you're so far behind that I'd put a dent into things. Plus–"

"It's fine. Really." She released the breath she was holding. "You look tired. Is everything all right?"

"Of course!" She avoided my gaze. "I just couldn't sleep so I figured I'd work."

"Hmm." I eyed her.

The room filled with awkward silence.

"Is that all?"

"Oh… uh… yeah." She got up and left my office as if her hair was on fire.

That night, there were no notifications. Funny how after months of not hearing my phone go off that I suddenly missed the disturbance that only last night had brought.